"Maybe this is a p... ...g, at last, who killed my father."

"Maybe, but it would be a good thing if you stayed alive long enough to find out."

"Yeah, there is that little angle, isn't there?" Now she seemed to be calming a bit, appearing more speculative—which worried Evan.

What if she put herself into more danger?

Damn, but this gorgeous—and foolish—woman exasperated him.

And that wasn't all she did to him...

"Look, Amber. I don't know what you're thinking, but you need to be especially careful now. I don't want anything to happen to you."

She turned and looked him straight in the eye.

Not long ago, he'd have been highly uncomfortable with that.

Not now, though.

He started to reach over to pull her into his arms, but she beat him to it. They were suddenly both standing. Amber pressed herself against him—and raised her mouth to his.

Linda O. Johnston loves to write. While honing her writing skills, she worked in advertising and public relations, then became a lawyer...and enjoyed writing contracts. Linda's first published fiction appeared in *Ellery Queen's Mystery Magazine* and won a Robert L. Fish Memorial Award for Best First Mystery Short Story of the Year. Linda now spends most of her time creating memorable tales of romance, romantic suspense and mystery. Visit her on the web at www.lindaojohnston.com.

Books by Linda O. Johnston

Harlequin Romantic Suspense

The Coltons of Colorado

Shielding Colton's Witness

Shelter of Secrets

Her Undercover Refuge
Guardian K-9 on Call
Undercover Cowboy Defender

The Coltons of Grave Gulch

Uncovering Colton's Family Secret

The Coltons of Mustang Valley

Colton First Responder

Visit the Author Profile page
at Harlequin.com for more titles.

THE SOLDIER'S K-9 MISSION

LINDA O. JOHNSTON

Previously published as *Second Chance Soldier*

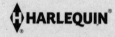 HARLEQUIN®

ISBN-13: 978-1-335-50841-6

The Soldier's K-9 Mission

First published as Second Chance Soldier in 2018.
This edition published in 2023.

Recycling programs
for this product may
not exist in your area.

For questions and comments about the quality of this book, please contact us
at CustomerService@Harlequin.com.

Harlequin Enterprises ULC
22 Adelaide St. West, 41st Floor
Toronto, Ontario M5H 4E3, Canada
www.Harlequin.com

Printed in U.S.A.

THE SOLDIER'S K-9 MISSION

The Soldier's K-9 Mission is dedicated to all dogs and those who train them, including police and military K-9s.

And, as I always do, I dedicate this book to my wonderful husband, Fred. Good thing he likes dogs, too.

Acknowledgments

Since I have been well-trained by my dogs so far, and not so much vice versa, I want to thank everyone who advised me about dog training. That includes the Hollywood Dog Obedience Club and its wonderful officers, trainers and members I've met. They have shown me what pet dog training is all about.

I have also watched several demonstrations of police K-9s in the Los Angeles area, which have proved to be fascinating and useful, and I have additionally been privileged enough to have had discussions with some K-9 officers. I particularly want to thank the Glendale Police Department and its K-9 unit, most especially Officer Shawn Sholtis and his K-9, Idol.

Thank you all!

Of course, *The Soldier's K-9 Mission* is a work of fiction, so if anything seems incorrect that's because I've modified reality to fit the story.

Many thanks also to my wonderful editor, Allison Lyons, and my fantastic agent, Paige Wheeler.

Chapter 1

Was this demonstration going to be as unimpressive as all the others had been so far?

Amber Belott could only wait and watch—and hope that, finally, she and her mom, Sonya, had found their answer at last, a skilled person who could take over training potential police K-9s and other dogs, as well as additional trainers, now that her father was gone.

Evan Colluro was the eighth person who'd come to the Chance K-9 Ranch, just outside Chance, California, to perform a demonstration. A tryout. An audition of sorts.

Evan had just arrived. At least he was right on time, unlike most of the others, whose excuses tended to be how remote this place was. At the top of the driveway near their house, he exited his black sedan along with his dog, who was, unsurprisingly, a German shepherd.

His résumé had described his extensive work with dogs, particularly in the military, but nothing had prepared her for how good-looking he was. He was tall and slender with broad shoulders, and the fit of his charcoal knit shirt implied strong muscles beneath. He wore black slacks and new-looking athletic shoes, somewhat informal attire, yet he looked ready for both a job interview and a critical dog-training test session.

Again unlike some of his either more formal, or more sloppily dressed, predecessors...

Amber, on the other hand, wasn't dressed particularly to impress. Neither was her mother. Both wore casual blue work shirts tucked into jeans. Amber didn't care what Evan thought of her, except as a potential employer.

She approached the man with short black hair who now stood beside his car, his dog at his side. "Evan?"

"That's right. And you're Amber?" Though he stood facing her, he didn't quite look at her. He had a hint of dark beard stubble on his long, angular face, a cool expression in his deep blue eyes that gave no indication at all as to what he was thinking or feeling. Maybe he was watching her mother. Or looking at their black Labrador retriever, Lola, who stood beside Sonya.

"Yes. Welcome. And who's this?" Amber gestured toward his dog, wanting to approach to pet him but recognizing that was a bad idea with a trained K-9 without asking permission.

"This is Bear." There was a note of pride in Evan's voice. "He's been with me for a while."

Which suggested he might be a former military K-9.

"May I pet him?" Amber asked.

"Sure."

While she stroked the apparently pleased dog's head behind his ears, she next asked, "Would you like to come inside for a cup of coffee?" That would mean a chat about Evan's background, which Amber already somewhat knew from their online conversations, or the job, which he'd learned about the same way. "Or just start with the dogs?"

"The dogs," he said with no hesitation.

"Fine." In fact, that was good. Talking with the guy now wouldn't tell her what she needed to know.

Watching him in action would.

"First," she said, turning away from Bear, "I'd like you to meet my mother, Sonya, and our dog, Lola."

Lola, though restrained by a leash held by Sonya, had leaped forward and now traded nose sniffs with Bear. No animosity that Amber could perceive—a good start. Whatever his background, Bear also appeared well behaved.

"Hi." Her mom stepped forward. She held her hand outstretched and Evan grasped it but didn't look straight into her eyes, either. Amber wondered once more what was on this guy's mind.

"Hi," he responded, letting go right away.

Amber exchanged a brief glance with her mother, then turned back to Evan. "The first puppies who need training are over there." She pointed toward the location just beyond the wide driveway that he had probably noticed before.

Three German shepherds about six months old stood watching them from a small area surrounded by a chain-link fence, just beyond the main wood-plank fence at the edge of the rolling lawn. The pups had been selected by Amber's dad when they were even younger as having the temperament to potentially have a future as skilled police K-9s.

By Amber's now-deceased father...

Now wasn't the time to think about that.

For the first time since he arrived, Evan smiled. "I noticed them," he said, not taking his eyes off the canines. "Okay if I join them and check out where they are in their training?"

"Sure," Amber said, but almost before the word was out of her mouth he began striding in that direction.

Trading glances once again, Amber and Sonya followed, not far behind. Her mother still held Lola's leash, restraining their dog from getting too far ahead—and in Evan's way. Bear stayed at his side, though, without a leash.

It was May, and the air was warm, the sky a brilliant blue. A lovely day—if there could be such a thing in this family any longer. A good day, at least, for this kind of test.

As Evan reached the fenced area, the ranch's

barely trained K-9 German shepherd puppies—Rex, Hal and Lucy—all stood as they saw him, clearly excited. Rex started barking, the sound shrill and loud, inciting the others to do the same.

Evan looked down into the face of the initially guilty dog, gestured and said, "Sit!" softly yet firmly.

Amber was both amazed and pleased to see Rex immediately both sit and quiet down, and the others followed suit.

"Wow," whispered her mom at her side, obviously equally impressed.

Was it this man's body language, his clear intent to take control? Amber had no idea, but it felt different, very different, from the others who'd been here before him. Some had yelled orders above the barks, some had shoved the pups into place, and some had done both. Others had bribed them with treats.

Evan's approach was different. So was his attitude. He seemed strong yet caring.

And that was just the beginning. Without looking toward Amber or Sonya for consent, Evan opened the nearby gate to the lawn, and he, Bear and Lola—whose leash he'd removed—then entered the smaller fenced area.

"Hi," he said to the pups, who all squirmed on the ground beside him. He appeared to study them for a while, then Rex dashed around and the other two rolled on the grass as if wanting to be petted. He didn't touch them but asked Amber for their names. He repeated the names, watching each dog to see their reactions. "Okay," he finally said. "Let's do it."

The three young shepherds plus Lola were then subjected to a whirlwind of instructions, including commands they might not have heard before. Bear, too, participated, clearly knowing and obeying each order.

Evan's large, strong hands moved in an assortment of gestures that were each tied to one of those verbal commands. He sometimes repositioned his large, lithe body while getting the dogs to move, too. His hand movements were gentle as, looking straight into their faces, he guided them into the positions he wanted them to achieve. Each time they obeyed a command, a touch or both, he rewarded them with praise.

His tone was encouraging, as if the dogs understood every word, and maybe they did thanks to his accompanying gestures or their limited prior training.

Evan seldom scolded them, but he did distract one or another when they didn't obey by walking in front and grabbing the dog's attention by movement and a strong tone of voice.

He also rewarded them now and then by extracting a toy that resembled a small fabric suitcase handle that Amber knew was called a tug from one pocket, and at other times a ball out of another pocket, each time tossing it for an obedient dog to chase and bring back.

Meanwhile, Bear followed all of Evan's commands, as if he provided an example each time.

The pups that Amber found so adorable, so

sweet—and so disobedient—now acted as if they couldn't wait to receive and obey the next command.

After about twenty minutes, when Evan had worked with all the shepherds—plus Lola—several times, he turned and looked toward Amber and her mother, who both watched him over the fence. It was the first time he'd glanced at them since starting.

"I gather that these pups have had a small amount of training," he said, "but they've a lot to learn. I'll want to hear more about their background. I assume the intention is for one or all of them to wind up as police K-9s, so I could start their initial training for single-purpose use—just finding and attacking bad guys. But most police departments prefer dual-purpose dogs, those that can also do drug or explosive sniffing, cadaver location, search and rescue or more, and I can help prepare them for that, too, though what they're taught will depend on their individual skills and what their ultimate handlers will want from them."

"And you can provide all that training?" Amber asked. She was definitely impressed. None of the others she'd invited here had come even close to what Evan had already accomplished.

"Well, sure," he said, as if that was a foregone conclusion. He briefly looked her straight in the face, as if trying to read her mind, but only for an instant before he glanced away and turned back toward the dogs.

Amber started walking away and gestured for her mother to follow. They didn't go far before she stopped, looked at her mother and asked in a low voice, "What do you think?"

"Grab him while you can," Sonya said equally softly, but with a large smile.

Amber nodded, then called to Evan, "We'd like to discuss a possible job offer with you." She walked toward him and added, "Please shut the pups into their enclosure, then let's go into the house and discuss it, okay?"

"Okay," he agreed—and Amber knew her responding smile was even larger than her mother's.

Unsurprisingly, after more commands, followed by petting, verbal rewards and a few more tosses of toys, Evan got the three young pups to sit and stay while he locked the chain-link fence gate behind him, as if the dogs lived to obey him. Amber could only grin about that.

But surprisingly, rather than join them directly, Evan held back as they walked toward the house. Amber turned often to look at him, admiring the wide smile on his angular face that was leveled only on the two canines still with him, Lola and Bear.

Maybe it was a good thing he was so wrapped up in communicating with the dogs...for now. Once they reached the house, only the humans would be speaking.

"I'm really surprised," Sonya whispered from beside her. "I'd figured we'd find the right choice thanks to one of your dad's cop contacts."

All the others who'd come to try out for this job had either been sent by nearby police departments after Amber had contacted them, or were recommended as skilled trainers by the law-enforcement associations her father had joined because they had K-9 handler members.

But none had worked out. And this guy, from what Amber had seen online, had appeared potentially perfect.

She knew from his résumé and the references he'd provided that Evan Colluro was in his early thirties, a couple of years older than her. His credentials were impressive: seven years in the military, the last three working in a K-9 unit. He had earned several commendations and had left the military just over a year ago after an injury.

"Hey, I know you're not an internet fan," Amber replied softly, smiling as she looked down at her mom. "But sometimes people even meet their true loves thanks to websites. It's worth a shot at trying to find the right employee there."

Amber winced at her own words. She had badly misstated her thought. A shot? How stupid of her to use that term.

But, of course, she thought about gunshots constantly since the morning two months earlier when her mother had called to tell her that her dad had been killed.

She hazarded another glance at her mom, who was shorter than Amber and somewhat heavier. Her wavy auburn hair—which, unlike Amber's, was not its natural color—blew in the breeze.

Amber had worried about her mother, too, before

she'd returned home, since her dad had been killed for no apparent reason on the ranch's grounds. She still worried about her but had seen nothing threatening since she'd gotten back. And the local cops seemed to think the killer could have been a former student, since her dad wasn't always as nice to the people he taught as he was to the dogs, or maybe it was a robbery gone wrong.

"So how are you going to handle this offer?" Sonya asked, fortunately not latching onto how Amber had misspoken.

"We've discussed some terms in emails," she told her mother, focusing again on what she needed to. "He must be okay with that part, at least, since he's here." But however she phrased the actual offer, she wanted to make sure the guy liked it. They needed him to accept it.

Of course, despite that impressive demonstration, no one could ever be as good at training as her father had been. No one could ever fill his shoes. He had worked alone, with no assistants, and had been wonderful at it. But Dad was gone. Dead.

Murdered.

By...who?

The K-9 Ranch was still here. And thanks to her dad's loner attitude, there was no one skilled enough to take over where he had so abruptly, and terribly, left off.

Amber had no intention of closing the ranch and ceasing the dog training that had been so important to the whole family. Unfortunately, she'd never been taught the necessary skills. She could only hope that Evan Colluro was the right person to take over as their first new trainer, to make sure that the Chance K-9 Ranch survived. "We'll see."

They reached the base of the porch and she turned to face the potential employee, who was only a few steps behind them. She tried to look him in the eye, but though he seemed at first to mirror her smile, he quickly lowered his gaze back down to the dogs.

Interesting.

Was this really going to be a wise decision?

Evan knew he should be more outgoing, talk about all his experience and what he could do here, rather than walking behind the two women as if he only wanted to be in contact with the dogs. Which, in some ways, he did.

But he ought to make small talk, thank this gorgeous and sexy woman who'd communicated with him online and invited him here to possibly teach dogs and other trainers and, most important, to also train police K-9s and their handlers, and perhaps eventually service or therapy dogs, too. He'd have some learning to do himself to accomplish it all, but it was still his ideal situation.

He at least thought his audition had gone well.

Even so, was this a bad idea?

He'd been wondering that before, particularly as he'd driven here from Los Angeles. That was where he'd hung out over the last months, to be near its veterans' facilities, as well as police K-9 units and instructive handlers. He'd taken some classes himself, and eventually landed jobs teaching others how to train dogs.

But he hadn't felt comfortable there.

Well, here he was. This sounded like the perfect long-term job for him—working with dogs and some human trainees, way off the usual grid of stress and having too many people around.

And Bear was with him. Dear Bear. They'd saved each other's lives in more ways than one…

The two women reached the front porch of the main house on this vast piece of property. They stopped, turning to look at him.

"Come on in," Amber said. Before, when he first introduced himself, he had looked her straight in the face only long enough to see how pretty she was, with smooth skin and full lips, and wavy hair that was a pretty reddish color. He'd also noted how intense her deep brown eyes were as they regarded him. That was why he'd quickly looked away.

He'd observed the rest of her then: Amber was curvaceous in her casual clothes.

Her mother, Sonya, who resembled her, was an older, shorter version. Again without looking her straight in the face, Evan had observed her. He knew she had recently lost her husband, had suffered pain.

He identified with that, though the circumstances were very different.

Now Amber had invited him into their house so they could chat for a while. Discuss a possible job offer.

And maybe interrogate him.

Well, she would be his boss if all went well. He had to deal with it. Once, he would have considered how to lure someone as gorgeous as her off to bed. Now, he had to decide only if he could put up with her giving him orders.

"Fine," he said. "Is it okay if Bear joins us?"

The amazing shepherd, at his side, heard his name and snuggled against Evan's leg. Evan couldn't help smiling down at the wonderful dog.

"Sure. I'll bring Lola in, too."

Evan stopped briefly behind the women as they walked up the tiled stairs to the wide porch at the front of the ranch house. It was a two-story home, its facade made of long slats that looked like redwood, with decorative lighter wood arching over the door and around the windows at either side and on the second floor, as well as framing the entrance. The sloping roof was covered with contrasting black shingles. In all, it was a nice place and fit the rural, sparsely populated surroundings Evan was seeking.

Once they were inside, Amber led them into the moderate-sized kitchen, where Sonya started bustling around, brewing coffee. Amber gestured for him to sit at the round wooden table, and put a plate of cheese and crackers in front of him. She seemed like a nice person. An attractive woman…a *very* attractive woman. A welcoming woman. He started to relax, at least a little.

"Okay if I leave Bear loose?" he asked. It was.

Soon all three humans sat at the table with coffee in front of them. Bear lay down on the tile floor beside Evan, and Lola settled near Amber.

Then the fun began… Not.

Amber started with easy questions. How long had he liked dogs? How long had he worked with them? Where had he worked with them? He could answer those without much angst.

But then she began asking about the military experiences he'd had while working in the K-9 unit in Afghanistan.

It was all he could do to remain sitting there, answering, not looking at her…while the pain throbbed inside him.

Even so, he remained honest. Yes, he'd enjoyed what he'd done…but, yes, he had been wounded overseas. Bear had been there for him. Had saved him, bringing help when he had been injured by an improvised explosive device. And then…

Evan cringed. He saw again the IED's explosion. Heard the concussive blast. Felt the pain. Watched Bear bring the other human member of his team who saved him…and saw Bear as he was shot by an unseen sniper.

Never mind Evan's own injury, his agony. He'd stood and found a way to lift his dog and get him into the armored vehicle his comrade had driven there.

"Evan, are you all right?"

He hadn't noticed Amber rise and rush over to him. Now she stood at his side. Bear, too, was standing.

He glanced toward the area around Bear's hip

where he had been shot, where his coat had grown back over the scar. Then Evan closed his eyes for a moment, taking a deep, calming breath. For the first time, he looked up and stared deeply into Amber's brilliant brown eyes and managed a smile.

"I'm fine," he said. "Just a touch of PTSD. But working with dogs? That's what I do. Did you say you wanted to discuss a possible job offer?"

"Yes," she said, her voice cracking. "I do."

Was this a mistake? This man she'd considered handsome and sexy and more, apparently had a messed-up mind.

PTSD. She was aware of it, of course, without really knowing how it worked.

It wouldn't make a difference if this guy truly could train dogs and handlers the way he'd claimed.

He'd certainly looked good at it. And hopefully, with his experience, he'd do much better than the others.

"Okay, I'll tell you what I've been thinking." She knew her smile wavered a bit. But before she pulled her glance away she felt gratified that, for the first time, Evan Colluro had actually looked her straight in the face for more than a nanosecond.

His PTSD might be why he hadn't before, but his stare at her now, his wry grin, made him appear different: vulnerable, sad, damaged, yes, but also even sexier.

He listened as Amber told him that the first classes he would teach would be to a core group of

her father's students from this area who'd been helping each other with their pet dogs to keep the skills
they'd already learned here fresh. They would be at
the ranch tomorrow afternoon, and Evan could start
right away by working with them.

"But we'll want you to go into it deeper, teach
them more—just general training skills, though, not
K-9. You'll work with our three shepherd pups for
that, and we'll hopefully place them with police departments when they're ready. Plus, you can provide new and refresher classes to other police K-9
handlers soon. But tomorrow's students? We'll use
them as our basis for bringing in even more students
who have their own dogs. Some can become therapy
dogs, and we may also acquire younger puppies to
start training as service dogs. If classes increase the
way we hope they will, we'll hire additional trainers to assist you, and you'll get some say in who we
bring on. Does all that work for you?"

"Definitely," he responded. "We'll need to figure
out the scheduling, of course, and we'll also need to
talk about a hiring protocol once bringing in other
trainers becomes more likely, but it's a good way
to start."

Their earlier correspondence had included what
Evan's base compensation would be if he was offered
the job, and how it would be increased depending on
expansion of their classes. Plus, he would get a home
to live in here on the ranch, rent free. So, though they
were talking terms, it was more about how he'd teach
rather than his salary and benefits.

To be fair, she had also mentioned why they were looking: her father's death. Detailed news reports were online, so Evan was likely aware that the situation remained unsolved, although the cops didn't think there was any residual danger. Amber hoped not, of course…but couldn't be certain. And she'd be willing to discuss the difficult situation with Evan if he happened to bring it up sometime.

"If all that is okay," Amber finally told him, pushing some paperwork and a pen toward him from across the kitchen table, "I've had this agreement drawn up. I'd like us both to sign it."

"Sure." But Evan took his time reading it, probably a smart thing to do. Soon, though, he picked up the pen off the wooden table and signed and dated two copies of the contract as indicated, then pushed them back to Amber. She was the one to sign them, not her mother. They had previously agreed that Amber would take charge of the ranch.

"Great," she said after placing her signature on both copies and passing one back to Evan. "Now, let's go show you your new home."

Chapter 2

Okay, it was done.

Rather, it was just beginning. Amber continued to hope she hadn't been too impetuous, too impressed by a tryout that appeared wonderful...but might not mean Evan could produce the many elements of dog training they needed him to do. Still, he'd been great with the puppies. That was what was important. The other stuff—his quiet demeanor, his admitted PTSD, his seldom looking straight at her—was just peripheral to what he needed to do around here to start fixing Chance K-9 Ranch until it was as successful as it had been under her popular, skilled and versatile father.

They were all back outside now, including the two older dogs, who now cavorted as if showing off to one another and to the humans around them. If Amber tried to motion to them or give them a command she doubted they'd change their ways. But if Evan did… Well, not now, though.

"There." Pointing, she drew closer to the end of the paved path away from the house. It traversed the middle of the rolling green hills within the ranch's enclosing wooden fence, and along it were some of the other homes on the ranch property. Those were for staff, and some located in the other direction could be rented out to students as they came to learn training methods, although there were also hotels nearby, including the one next door.

Four houses stood in a row here, all compact, single-story structures also constructed with redwood-resembling exteriors. Her mother and she led Evan past the first three to the one at the far end, then Amber turned to look at him. He stared at the house with an expression that appeared both assessing and pleased. Good. That was another plus on his chart.

"This one will be yours." She walked up to the front entry, a plain wooden door with a window at the top. Having already dug the key out of her pocket, she unlocked the door, pushing it open to let him enter first.

Instead, he gestured politely for her to go in, then her mother. They both did so along with the dogs, though Amber had hoped to see more of Evan's reaction to the place. Not that the house was anything fancy, but she'd checked its condition when she'd started looking for a trainer and thought it was adequate. The house had been built for ranch hands and their families by a prior owner, but had been rarely used recently, since her dad had had few live-in assistants. He'd kept it up, though, and always believed in treating any employee well.

The door opened into the compact living room, where a fluffy brown sofa and matching chairs faced a small wall-mounted television. A hallway led from it to the kitchen, bedroom and bathroom.

"Bear, come." Evan headed first to the kitchen doorway. That was sweet, Amber thought. He appeared to want his dog's opinion. Evan peered in as Bear ran inside, then back out again, followed by Lola. By then, Evan had moved to look through the bedroom door. The furnishings in both rooms were as utilitarian as those in the living room—adequate, but not particularly decorative.

Well, if he didn't like anything, he could always replace it for as long as he was here.

Which, Amber realized, she hoped would be a long time. Provided, of course, that his teaching skills were as good as she believed they were thanks to his demonstration.

"Very nice," he said. The compliment added to Amber's estimation of him. He was polite to the point of exaggeration.

He'd turned toward her mother, his craggy facial features lifting into a smile. Amber realized she liked his smiles, despite their rarity and how short-lived they were. She liked it even more when he aimed them at her, but she had the impression he felt more comfortable with Sonya.

That was okay. Amber also liked the idea of her mom getting more involved with the ranch and dog training. It might help her move on with her life a little faster.

"Do you think Bear likes it, too?" Amber asked.

"Oh, yeah. It's compact enough that he should feel pretty comfortable sleeping near me." He bent to pat his dog's head as Bear looked up at him.

Lola, meanwhile, was now beside Amber, sitting on the hardwood floor of the living room as if given a command to do so. Amber couldn't help bending down to pat the black Lab's furry head, too, and followed with a quick, warm hug. Similarly, Lola slept in Amber's bedroom of the main house and had done so since her return to the ranch, though Amber had tried encouraging the dog to sleep in her mother's room.

But Lola's staying out of that room appeared to be a sign of her grieving, since Sonya remained in the master bedroom of the house even now that her husband was dead.

Amber didn't mention that, despite a wave of her own grief pulsating through her as it did so often.

When she looked up from Lola's back, she noticed Evan watching her.

"Well," she said cheerily, handing him the house key, "were you optimistic enough about this job to bring any belongings with you?"

"Yes," he said, "I knew you'd hire me. How could

you resist?" That must have been partly a joke, since Amber saw the slightest of grins appear on his face as he continued looking down toward Bear. "My stuff's in my car. I'll get it in a bit. But—"

He seemed to hesitate, then turned toward Sonya.

Her mother smiled, though her smiles these days were a lot more serious than when Amber's dad was alive. "Anything we can do to help you get settled in here, Evan?"

"Not really, thanks. Although—"

What was causing his hesitation? Amber got right to the point. "What else would you like us to do?"

His gaze moved this time to land on her. He didn't look away immediately, and in fact appeared to center his attention right on Amber.

A strange current of confusion and interest swept through her. Not good. A new employee was supposed to be just that: someone to perform the job he was hired for, and that was all.

But Amber found herself highly curious about Evan Colluro. Highly interested in him.

In more ways than one.

"I'd like some additional information about the Chance K-9 Ranch and how training has been conducted in the past. I looked it up on the internet but I'd like to know more before I start conducting classes. Could we all go out to dinner tonight to discuss it?"

A frisson of some kind of emotion tickled Amber, but she sloughed it off. It wasn't like he was asking her on a date—even chaperoned by her mother.

But what was it about this man that strummed at her sensations so much?

In a completely businesslike tone she said, "Of course. Sounds like a good idea."

Only then did she glance at her mom—and couldn't read her expression. Sonya remained an attractive woman at her age, yet since her husband's death her facial features had seemed to go slack a bit, and there were more lines—definitely not laugh lines—at the corners of eyes, which were brown, like Amber's. Right now, her pink lips were drawn up on one side as if in wryness, or pain.

"Sorry, dear," she said in a low voice. "I think it's a good idea that the two of you get together and talk more before the class tomorrow, but I won't be able to join you."

"Really? Why not?" Amber prepared herself to convince her mom that this was simply a business get-together. She needed to ensure she wouldn't be alone with Evan on this outing. Not that she'd ever consider it a date, but she also didn't want her mother, or anyone in town who happened to see them together, to think it was.

She was floored a bit by her mother's response. "I've agreed to join Nathan for dinner tonight." She glanced toward Evan. "That's our neighbor, who owns the resort next door." She returned her attention to Amber. "He's been so—so kind since we lost your father. It's just a nice gesture on his part, not a date or anything like that. You know I'd never do such a thing. But, well, he invited me, and—"

"I understand, Mom," Amber interrupted, lying somewhat but not wanting her mother to suffer any further because of anything she did or said. "It's probably a good thing for us to go out with friends right now." But was this, unlike her prospective dinner with Evan, actually a date with their next-door neighbor, Nathan Treggory? Unlikely, especially since her mom recognized how it could look and rejected the idea.

But Amber still would want to hear more about it after the fact.

"Thanks for understanding, dear. And, Evan, I'd be glad to talk to you nearly anytime, answer questions and all. Just not tonight."

"I get it," Evan said. "Let's talk some other time."

So, date or not, Amber found herself committed to going out for dinner with Evan tonight to discuss the ranch and business and whatever else came up in the conversation.

About him, though. She had no intention of talking about herself.

And yet… The idea made Amber's insides churn even more. What was it about this man that made her get all mushy and weird? The fact that he appeared to be sad and needy?

The fact that he clearly was a damn good dog trainer?

She'd have to keep in mind that she'd just broken up with the guy she'd thought was the love of her life and had no interest in getting involved with another man.

"All right," she said brusquely, heading for the front door. Her mother was at her side with Lola. Evan and Bear were behind them. She turned. "It's four o'clock now. Come over to the main house at six and we'll decide where to go downtown—somewhere without our dogs?"

Why did Evan's look seem as uncomfortable as she felt? And then he glanced up, briefly met her gaze and nodded. "Fine with me."

And Amber, despite feeling trapped, felt herself smile.

Evan followed the women outside along with the dogs. Dinner with just Amber? Should he call it off? Tell her he'd forgotten other plans? Tell them he'd wait for a time when Sonya could join them?

But heck, some of what he wanted to discuss would be helpful at that first class he would apparently teach tomorrow.

Besides, being with Amber—lovely, in-charge Amber—might be one more step toward his forcing himself to leave old issues behind, plant himself firmly in this new life with all its promise.

"See you at six," he said to her, then noticed a man walking up to the small house next to his along this row. He nodded toward him. "Who's that?" he asked.

Both Sonya and Amber turned. "Oh, that's our ranch hand, Orrin Daker," Sonya said. "Come on. We'll introduce you to him."

Another new acquaintance? The idea felt unsettling to Evan, yet meeting someone else he should know as long as he lived here would be another step into his new existence.

"Thanks." With Bear at his side, he followed the two women and their dog past the nearest houses to where Orrin, who'd apparently seen them, waited.

"Hi, Orrin," Sonya said. "I'd like you to meet our new dog trainer, Evan Colluro. Evan, this is Orrin."

"Hi, man," Orrin said. Probably in his early twenties, the guy had a tall head of light brown hair and a matching beard and mustache. He wore a red Chance, California, T-shirt over scruffy-looking jeans. He stared—no, glared—at Evan as if he was an interloper out to steal his job and his home.

Which made Evan highly uncomfortable, yet he stared right back at the guy despite the effort it took—at least for a few seconds.

"Hi. Good to meet you. Make sure you let me know what you're up to if you think it'll affect my training here, and I'll do the same with you."

"Yeah. Right." Orrin then slipped into his house.

"He's really a nice guy," Amber said unconvincingly. "He does a good job for us, and my dad even used him sometimes when he was all dressed up in a protective outfit as the guy the K-9s he was training attacked. His family has lived in Chance forever but his being right here on the ranch makes it easier for us to let him know what we need to have done."

"Makes sense," Evan said. It also made sense, judging only by this first, uncomfortable meeting, that they might want to fire the guy and get someone more personable and accommodating.

Did Orrin really like being an agitator during training sessions, or did he feel forced into it?

Well, Evan would find out. He was the newcomer. He was the one with the most to learn—and, hopefully, would have the most to give—in his new position.

Amber was standing beside her mother, and appeared impatient as she looked at him.

"Like I said, see you at six at your house," Evan told her, hoping this entire situation wasn't a big mistake.

Bear sidled up to him as if feeling his unease and wanting to make it go away. He hadn't been trained as a service or therapy dog, but his effect on Evan these days was similar.

"Come, boy," Evan said as the women and Lola walked off in the direction of their home. He began to follow at a discreet distance. He needed to move his car along the driveway extension they'd shown him behind the houses and park behind his new place. Then he could unload the clothing and few other items he had brought along.

He was about to start his new life—and that night, while he was with Amber, he would find a way to ensure he get along with her—and also turn off any totally inappropriate attraction he felt toward her.

His job here was to work with trainers…and dogs.

It was nearly six o'clock. Amber waited outside in the cool, brisk air beside her silver SUV, which she'd retrieved from the garage at the rear. It was now parked at the front of the driveway, near her house, right beside the main dog-training area, as she watched for Evan to appear. He had apparently moved his car since it had previously been parked right here. She assumed it was behind his new quarters. Good. For now, it should stay there.

This would be an interesting evening. For one thing, her new employee had invited her to join him for dinner. Her mother, too, of course, although that wasn't now the situation.

Earlier, after returning from showing Evan his house, she had left her mother watching her favorite afternoon talk show on TV, and, in her own bedroom, used her laptop to do some online research about PTSD to see what she might learn about Evan.

From what she read, PTSD could involve quite a few different symptoms, from ongoing nightmares and depression and even suicide wishes, to just wanting to avoid people, including family members—and strangers.

But he'd invited his new employers to join him in a strange environment for dinner. Though Amber didn't know what went on in Evan's mind, his avoiding eye contact a lot indicated he wasn't much for socializing.

That suggested he really wanted to work here. Maybe it was because he'd be dealing with dogs even more than people. That was fine with her.

Her mother had driven her own car to go meet Nathan a short while ago. That was good. He hadn't come to the house to pick her up—which would have appeared more like a date, highly inappropriate considering how recently they'd lost her dad.

Just before Amber got ready to leave, she'd brought the pups in training inside the home, along with Lola. She enclosed the pups in the family room that her dad had outfitted to accommodate young dogs, since her mother would be gone, too. It contained crates and dog beds, and a washable linoleum floor. Fortunately, the dogs were all trained well enough already to be loose and not closed into crates for now.

She spotted Evan striding up the walkway in front of the employees' houses. He cleaned up well, she thought as he drew closer. His interview and demo outfit had been nice but fairly casual. Now he had on a beige button-down shirt tucked into brown slacks, though he still wore athletic shoes.

She, in turn, had donned a blouse and midlength skirt, both in pale green. Her shoes were casual pumps with low heels.

They were both dressed as if this was, in fact, a date. Well, she'd make sure he remembered, as the evening progressed, that she was his employer.

"Hi," she said as he approached. As they'd decided earlier, he hadn't brought Bear, and she had left Lola in the house with the pups. That would give them more leeway about the restaurant they chose. She had a pretty good idea where to suggest. First, though, she asked in jest, in an attempt to ease any tension Evan might feel about spending this evening alone with his new boss, "What? A dog trainer without his dog?"

She liked his quick smile and shrug. "And a dog-ranch owner without her dog?"

She laughed. "Come on. I'll drive us to town." She motioned toward the passenger side of her car. An expression she couldn't quite read passed over his face but he said nothing. Surely he wasn't some male chauvinist who expected to drive, even under these circumstances, when she knew the town a lot better than he did?

Or...was that somehow related to his PTSD? Had he somehow been injured in a car?

She wasn't about to ask.

"I intended to meet you here first to make sure we were still on for tonight, then go get my car," he said.

"No need." She motioned for him to get into the passenger's side, and with only another second's hesitation, he complied.

Chapter 3

Amber started the engine and headed down the country road toward town, only a ten-minute journey. They soon passed the resort owned by Nathan, and Amber wondered how things were going with her mother's non-date with him.

Evan remained silent. "How's Bear doing?" Amber finally asked, determined to cast aside thoughts of her mom.

"Fine. I left him in the kitchen, though he's a good boy and should do fine with the run of the house in the future."

"I'll bet." She searched her mind for another topic he might be interested in discussing. "How was your drive from Los Angeles?" That was where he had been living when they first began communicating about the job.

"Some traffic, but not bad." He looked straight ahead, not at her. She, though, glanced toward him. He appeared relaxed—and was as good-looking as she'd considered him before.

"Good." She again watched the road in front of them. "I hope you don't mind, but we're making a couple of stops before dinner."

"Really? Where?" He did look toward her now. Was he concerned about the location, or how many people he'd see, or...well, she had no idea.

"The local Pets and Products first. I need to pick up some dog food." She'd also see one of her closest friends around here at the shop, the local franchise's owner Mirrisa Jenkins.

Mirri would be happy for Amber, that she'd finally found someone to restart classes at the K-9 Ranch.

"I'd like to visit there, too," Evan said. "I need some supplies for Bear." He paused. "Where else?"

"You'll like this one." She hoped. "I need to see a guy at our local tech store. He maintains the ranch's website, and I want him to let the world know that we'll be starting more classes again." When Evan said nothing, Amber wondered if he felt uncomfortable about the concept of "letting the world know."

"Of course, if you don't want your name mentioned, just tell me."

He seemed to hesitate, but only for a second. "No, that'll be fine—although, don't you want to wait until you see how the classes work out before you start promoting again?"

"Are you saying you may mess up?"

Again a hesitation, but then Evan said, "Absolutely not. You've hired the right guy."

"That's what I figured." Amber couldn't cross her fingers easily since she was driving. But considering the other candidates, she believed what he'd said was true.

They were finally at the restaurant called The Joint.

Evan allowed his prior tension to ease up, relaxing his shoulders and breathing evenly. He would now get to start the conversation he had planned.

Not that he'd minded being at that Pets and Products shop. It was like every other one he had gone into over the years, and it sold the wholesome food that he always fed Bear, as well as the healthy treats he gave his dog, though not part of any training.

That friend of Amber's—Mirri—kept looking from him to Amber and back again, as if assessing whether there was more than a new employer-employee association. He fought down the urge to tell her that what she was looking for was simply not there.

So far he liked Amber…sure. But if he finally got to the point, ever, when he was ready to start some kind of relationship with a woman again, it wouldn't be one in a position to tell him what to do.

He'd had enough people doing that while he was in the military. Although his connections with his senior officers had been as expected and appropriate, he'd not been close friends with any of them. And now that he was fighting with his own psyche to regain internal balance, he wasn't about to make things more difficult by getting involved with yet another person who was able to give him orders.

When they'd completed their purchases, they had gone around the corner from the pet store, which was on Chance Avenue, to the Cords and Clouds shop on Mercer Street. It was a small tech store run by a guy named Percy Relgin, who looked like the stereotype of geekiness: he was young and thin, with puffy hair and glasses. Amber had introduced them, then told Percy she wanted him to update the ranch's website again, as he had recently. But this time he was to focus on Evan and add a description of his excellent lessons for pet dogs and potential trainers, which were about to begin, and to say that more classes, including police K-9 training and instruction for therapy dogs and possibly service dogs, too, would be scheduled eventually.

Evan sloughed off his concern about being able to meet her standards. He could do it. He would do it. And he forced himself to give Percy all the information about his background and skills that he asked.

Amber and Percy then talked briefly about the ranch's email. Apparently the guy had figured out her father's password, which now meant Amber could access what was there. Then they left.

The Joint was between the two shops, on the joined corner of their respective streets. He had noticed it when he had first driven through Chance on his way to the ranch. The restaurant owner knew Amber and greeted her right away. "I've got just the right table for you now," he said, which was good since the place was crowded.

"Thanks, Gus," Amber said. "By the way, this is Evan, my new dog trainer."

"Hi, Evan." Gus reached out to shake hands. He wore a black T-shirt and jeans, less dressy than the servers, who had on gray knit shirts and dark trousers. "Glad to meet you." He preceded them between the tables, and Evan watched as Amber said hi and waved to several seated patrons.

At an empty table in the middle of the room, Gus handed them menus, then walked away.

The restaurant appeared to cater to everyone. Evan noted the assortment of families and couples and groups of men and women seated around tables similar to theirs: plastic with a wood-grain finish. The acoustics were what he'd anticipate in a place like this, with a hum of conversations that was loud but didn't drown out the server's voice when she asked what they wanted to drink.

Since they were here to discuss his questions he didn't want any alcohol, not that he feared he wouldn't stay sober, but because he wanted to appear professional. He ordered a cola.

"So," Amber said once the server had gone. "What did you want to discuss tonight?"

He first asked about the ranch: how Amber's father had started it, why it was at such a remote location and how he'd nevertheless lured in people from all over to learn how to train not only pets, but also police K-9s and therapy dogs. She responded that her dad believed in himself and wanted students to come to him and learn, with dogs, in a comfortable environment. And it had worked well, she told Evan, which he knew from Corbin Belott's reputation on the internet rating sites and the numbers of classes he'd apparently taught. But Evan recognized her worry about the future and was both grateful and concerned she would be relying on him.

In answer to further questions, Amber said her dad had loved working with dogs and even training other people to work with them, but had enjoyed doing it all himself, so he'd had no backup employees. She said he'd made a good living at it.

Evan also wanted to know what the family believed had happened to Corbin Belott, though he wouldn't mention that now. Corbin had been murdered, Evan knew from his research. Shot, and his body was found on the grounds of his ranch by a ranch hand, whom Evan now believed was Orrin.

According to news reports, the case remained unsolved. Did his family have any idea about his enemies? Might his wife and daughter be in danger, too?

And Evan wondered how Amber and her mother handled such a horror. Sure, he had seen and dealt with death in many tragic ways, had nearly died himself—and would have, had it not been for Bear. But he had been at war, in a dangerous situation that he had chosen, somewhat, to face.

That was very different from what had happened here.

But this wasn't the time or place to ask Amber

about what had happened to her dad. It might never be appropriate, despite his curiosity.

Evan instead went to another item on his mental list that was more critical to him and his new job. "I know I'll be working with some of your long-standing students tomorrow, which is great. I'll get a taste of the classes your father taught both to potential pet trainers and to their dogs that need training, and that should help a lot. But I gather there aren't other classes of any kind scheduled right now."

He looked across the table directly into the brown eyes that studied him so intently. "Not yet," she said. "I hope we can get other kinds started fast, which was why I wanted to update our website right away. You'll need to work with our shepherd pups, too, but I know enough to understand it'll be a while before they're ready to be sold to police handlers and become actual K-9s, although I want word to get out that it'll be coming. It would also be good if we get some interest now from officers who bring working K-9s in for additional training."

"I agree," Evan said. "And as for these pups, you're right that it's usually best not to turn them over to handlers until they're a bit older and well trained, but if they progress well things could go faster."

"Really?"

He liked the way Amber smiled at him, although he glanced over her shoulder after meeting her eyes.

"Really," he said.

Their server returned with rolls and butter, so the conversation stalled just when Evan had thought it

most interesting. But when they were alone once
more—as alone as they could get in this crowded restaurant—he continued. "You've talked about therapy
and service dog training, too."

"That's right," Amber said, looking down toward
the menu, then back at Evan's face. "Assuming I find
the right trainers to assist you. I recognize they're not
your specialty. I'd eventually love to do even more
than my dad did. But I want to do things right and not
rush into anything." Those eyes narrowed a bit, as if
she was trying to look into his mind, determine how
quickly he could settle in and get down to work—and
what he thought about service dog training.

Uncomfortable, he glanced away but made himself look back at her. "I understand. I'll want to know
more of your expectations about those other classes,
including K-9s, though we did touch on the possibilities when we communicated by email. But for now,
tell me about the people you expect will be here tomorrow. What's their background in being trained
so far, with just pets, right? Did they all start their
classes with your father at the same time? And—"

He stopped abruptly as Amber's eyes looked away
from his and widened hugely. She looked troubled,
and he ignored his sudden urge to stand and take her
into his arms for comfort.

He wouldn't—couldn't—have done that even if
she hadn't been his employer. Instead, he turned to
see where she was looking.

A woman was making her way between the people seated at the crowded tables, heading toward
them—a woman in a cop uniform.

And Evan hoped that he was about to learn at least something about Corbin Belott's murder.

It wasn't surprising to see anyone in town here at The Joint, Amber told herself. Although, this evening, no one here that she knew had done more than toss a few friendly greetings toward her and return to their meals and conversations.

But Assistant Police Chief Kara Province was clearly heading in her direction.

Amber had met Kara after a local parade, then chatted with her at various town functions when she had come home to visit her parents. She was glad now that she had, since even though Kara wasn't the primary cop assigned to investigate her father's murder, she was at least somewhat forthcoming and kind, and kept Amber as apprised as she could about anything the police found.

Which so far hadn't been much.

She reached their table at the same time their server did. "I'll come back in a minute to take your order," the server said, looking with irritation toward the cop as if she didn't like the delay. Then she hurried away.

Kara was a tall, slender woman who looked completely at home in her black police uniform. She was only in her thirties, yet she had already risen through the ranks to become assistant chief of police, which Amber had admired even before she had any need to know a cop.

"Hi, Amber." Kara's soft voice was surprisingly audible over the louder voices around them. She glanced briefly down toward Evan, then back at Amber.

"This is my new dog trainer, Evan Colluro. Evan, meet Assistant Police Chief Kara Province."

Amber watched them shake hands as Evan stood politely and glanced toward Kara's face, but only briefly. Kara's eyes rolled down him as if assessing him with interest. Amber didn't like the pang of irritation that shot through her. Kara was most likely looking him over as a potential suspect in something, maybe even the murder of her father, but nothing personal. And even if she was flirting, well, so what?

"We haven't ordered dinner yet," Amber said. "Would you like to join us?" She glanced toward Evan to see his reaction to the idea, and assumed he wouldn't appreciate it. She was surprised, therefore, to see a positive expression on his face as he nodded his approval.

"Not for dinner, but I will join you for a minute, if that's okay."

"Of course." But Amber felt her body go slack. Was Kara about to tell them something new in the case regarding her dad?

If so, something helpful—or not?

Not, as it turned out. "I just wanted to let you know that we haven't forgotten about you or your father, Amber," Kara said, taking a seat at the side of the table between Evan and her. "But so far we have no new leads. We're still—"

"I'm sorry," Evan interrupted, "but I hope you don't mind if I ask a few questions. I'm not in law enforcement, but I have a military background, and have also been taught to work with police K-9s and other dogs."

"Yes, I figured at least part of that from Amber's introduction of you as a new trainer at her ranch," Kara said.

The server returned and placed glasses of water in front of all three of them. She must have assumed Kara was joining them—which was true, if only for a short while.

"I don't know much about the case," Evan continued, "but I checked out the ranch before applying for the job. I understand Mr. Belott was found on his ranch's grounds, and he had been shot."

Amber closed her eyes and shuddered. She knew that, yet every time she was reminded of it, she wanted to break down and cry. She made herself open her eyes again and looked toward Evan, only to find he was watching her, maybe more directly than he had done since they had met.

His sympathetic expression only made her want to cry even more.

"That's correct," Kara responded.

"Does your department have a K-9 unit?"

Of course he would ask that. The question almost made Amber want to smile. Almost.

"Yes, although it's a small one, only two officers. Both they and their dogs were partially trained by Mr. Belott, in fact. And before you ask, yes, we did have them examine the crime scene. That didn't lead to any results."

"I see," Evan said. "Well…do you have any suspects?"

Amber noted Kara's glare, as if Evan had told her she wasn't doing her job, but she answered anyway. "There are several persons of interest, partly because we were told by a few of Mr. Belott's students that he'd been arguing with some of their classmates. We're more inclined to believe, though, that it was a robbery gone wrong, since his wallet and cell phone were missing, and someone attempted to use his credit card shortly after the murder—in Nevada. We've looked at visitors to this area then, including guests at nearby hotels, but haven't yet zeroed in on anyone, including whoever attempted to use the card. Anyway, I'd better go back to my own table." Kara stood as Amber swept the room with her gaze and saw other uniformed officers at a table at the far wall. "But please feel assured, Amber, that we're still on the case."

"Thanks, Kara," Amber responded, even as she wanted to shout that they hadn't gotten anywhere so far, so why try? As Kara left, their server returned to take their order.

Amber wasn't surprised when Evan ordered a hamburger dinner with several sides, a substantial meal.

She, on the other hand, ordered a relatively small salad.

She had lost her appetite.

Evan had continued to watch Amber's face when the cop was present at their table and afterward.

His new employer's attitude had gone from "I'm

in charge so listen to me" to "I'm lost." He might not be thrilled that she could ultimately give him orders about dog training—his specialty, not hers—even though she was, in fact, his boss. But he hated to see her appear so sad.

Well, as he'd said, he wasn't in law enforcement, but he did train K-9s and their handlers. He was also well aware that any help well-trained K-9s might have been able to offer before was probably impossible this long after the crime.

But he would be on that ranch with dogs he was training. Were any of the students he'd be working with tomorrow considered potential suspects? Would he wind up working with additional former students who were? Did any of them present a potential danger to Amber or her mother?

He'd try to check about who the primary suspects were. And it certainly wouldn't hurt for him to learn exactly where the crime had occurred, in the remote chance that there still might be clues that a dog could sniff out.

Then, maybe, he might be able to get his gorgeous, sexy employer to smile at him…at a time he could smile back.

Chapter 4

But this evening came first. He wanted to get through it in a manner that could only help his future career here. In a way that would hopefully impress Amber.

That resulted in Evan surprising himself. Tonight, he was the one to start conversations.

It almost appeared as if Amber and he had traded personalities. She wouldn't look at him as she ate her salad. She didn't seem interested in talking to him.

Not at first. Not until he stopped attempting banalities, like how good his food was and how nice the crowded restaurant was with its homey decor, its tables filled with talkative patrons…and that police presence in the far corner.

Not until he jumped into a subject he knew would be difficult, but would at least grab her interest.

"So tell me." To keep himself going, he picked up another wheat roll from the basket in the center of the table and started to butter it. "How did your father get into dog training? Knowing that will help me figure out the best way to follow in his footsteps—or paw prints, so to speak."

She actually looked up from watching the fork she twisted in her salad greens and shot him a brief smile. "So to speak," she repeated, "or so to bark?" Her tone was lighter now, and he felt damn good about it as her expression grew pensive. "Interesting enough, there are a lot of similarities, I think, between your background and my dad's. He was career military, though. He stayed in the army for twenty years, so that defined my early life, too. I'm not sure how or when he became a K-9 handler, but he did."

A look he couldn't interpret passed over her face, but it seemed awfully sad. He wanted to reach out and hold her hand but didn't. "Hey, he had to have been one smart, amazing, wonderful soldier, like all K-9 handlers," he said instead, hoping his joke would cheer her a bit.

"Of course." She shot him a look that suggested she was irritated, yet somehow appreciative of his attempted humor.

"Okay, continue," he said. "Tell me more."

"Well, when he got out, he decided to come to this area, near where he grew up in San Luis Obispo, but that's a larger town than Chance. With my mother's okay, he bought this ranch, which was vacant then, to train dogs here. Away from most people, except for us and minimal contact with others. I wonder now that I've met you…well, maybe he had some form of PTSD, too. His decisions after his military retirement may have been before PTSD was as recognized as it is now. Or maybe I'm wrong. But he seemed to have decided he'd spent enough time surrounded by people."

"Yeah, I can identify with that." He looked her straight in the face for a few seconds. Then he decided he needed some water and glanced toward his glass as he grabbed it. "So you lived with them at the ranch for…well, how long?"

"I was in my late teens when we moved here. I went off to college at San Diego State after about a year, though I always came back for holidays and the summer. But when I graduated with my business degree I stayed in San Diego and got a job with the home office of a big retail manufacturer—Ever Fitting."

Evan had definitely heard of Ever Fitting. In fact, everyone who ever wore jeans and casual clothes probably had.

"Impressive. Do you think you'll go back there?" He didn't want to ask if she had quit or been fired or anything like that.

"I have a K-9 ranch to run now." He couldn't tell from her tone if she was unhappy or thrilled with the idea. He hoped it was the latter, but in any event how happy she was with this area might wind up depending on him.

That kind of pressure wasn't what he was after.

But working well with dogs and their training was. He could handle it. He *would* handle it.

For now, he needed to keep this conversation going. "So how did your dad start his training classes here?"

For the next few minutes, he listened as Amber, a pensive smile on her face, described their move here from her father's last military assignment, which had been in Fort Leonard Wood, in Missouri, not far from St. Louis.

"I'm not sure how he found the ranch property, but my dad was always very goal-directed. He knew what he wanted to do and the general area where he wanted to do it."

When they moved to the ranch, Corbin had apparently also found ways of getting word out about his K-9 training background and the kinds of classes he intended to begin, such as teaching others, in small classes or one-on-one, and how to train dogs, including their own pets. Plus, he'd contacted breeders of German shepherds and Belgian Malinois to acquire his first puppies to teach as potential police K-9s.

"For them, he went to a bunch of breeders who already had pups available and chose three at a time that he thought would have the best potential of being wonderful K-9s. All three were eventually acquired by smaller police units when they were older and trained. Their new handlers would come to the ranch for training, too, and to decide which to choose. My dad always acknowledged this was a small ranch in a remote location, but said it was definitely worth visiting by anyone with, or wanting, a dog."

"Your father sounds like one smart and determined man," Evan responded, then wished he hadn't. His comment apparently reminded her of what had happened, not that it was likely to be far from her consciousness.

"Yes," she said simply, "he was." Her voice was gravelly and when he glanced at her he saw tears in her eyes.

Damn whoever had killed the man! Evan had already imagined trying to solve the crime while working for this lovely woman who was his boss. Now he was determined to dedicate himself to investigating in his spare time.

When he wasn't busy training the dogs and handlers Amber had hired him to teach.

She hadn't intended to do anything at this dinner besides answer Evan's questions about how his new position should start and evolve. But after their conversation with Kara, Amber had let her emotions run away with her.

Especially now.

"Okay," she said, gathering all shreds of bravery within her that she could find, "enough of this. Here's what I want to do tomorrow. The first class you'll teach will be in the afternoon. In the morning, I want us to go out on the lawn with Bear so you can run him through what he knows as a demonstration and a lesson to me on how you'll be instructing those and other students. Does that work for you?"

She was amused that Evan not only glanced toward her, but also met her gaze, appearing surprised she'd gotten her guts back, or at least that's what she figured.

"It sure does," he responded.

They didn't discuss her dad for the rest of the meal, a good thing. She missed him. She loved him. And she couldn't replace him, but she had to get the K-9 ranch up and running again, return it to its former state, minus him.

Would they ever figure out what had happened to him? Who'd killed him and why?

She hoped so, but whether or not that occurred she still had her life to live, her mother to help and the Chance K-9 Ranch to run to benefit a lot of people, and dogs, too.

At least for the moment she believed she had found the right person to take over the training now that her dad couldn't do it.

She'd find out for sure soon.

It was a business dinner, Amber had tried to convince Evan. And it was, but it had been his idea.

He didn't have a lot of money as a partially disabled veteran, but he had been working in LA at random jobs at dog-training schools and even sometimes with police K-9 units.

He certainly had enough to spring for this dinner—but his new boss had made it clear she was in charge and she was going to pay. Period.

Which both annoyed and amused him, especially now that they were back in her car, with her driving back to the ranch she owned and ran.

Good thing he had no romantic interest in her, or her asserting her position like this, no matter how appropriate, would have destroyed it.

Yet now, as he sat beside her in her car, he found himself glancing at her often, admiring how pretty she was, how sexy despite her insistence about being top person around here.

Or maybe there was something about her being in charge that he oddly found sexy...

"What time do you want to start working with me in the morning?" she asked while driving along the narrow road up the mountain leading to her ranch.

He had no food at his place for breakfast and needed to factor that in. But before he suggested a time, she added, "Of course, you'll eat with us first. I haven't given you time to buy groceries. I know you have food for Bear, though, in the back of my SUV."

"Of course. I know who's important in my household."

She laughed. "Dogs always come first. Anyway, why don't you join my mom and me at about eight o'clock? We can decide then if we'll start working together right after that or if you'll want a break first."

"Sounds good, as long as Sonya doesn't mind."

"My mom's a lot easier to get along with than I am," Amber said. "She'll be fine with it."

They soon pulled up the same driveway that had taken Evan to what was about to become a new chapter in his life. Another car was parked there, and Amber drew in her breath.

"Looks like my mom still has company." She didn't sound thrilled about it.

"Her dinner date?"

"It wasn't a date," she retorted quickly. "That's our neighbor Nathan's car. He's been kind to her since—since we lost my dad. He must have followed her back here after they ate dinner together, like we did."

Which Evan knew had been far from a date...yet he now, in a way, wished otherwise. Except for the fact she was his new boss. Amber parked, got out and popped open the back door of her SUV to extract the stuff she had bought at the pet store. She then hurried toward the house, leaving Evan behind as if she'd forgotten he was there. No matter. He was a mere employee, and, again, this hadn't been a date.

Still, to be a polite employee he wanted to say goodnight, at least to Amber and perhaps to Sonya, too. Plus, it wouldn't hurt to meet a neighbor, since he hoped to live here for a long time. He took out Bear's food and closed the rear door. Leaving the food on the porch, he followed Amber and pushed open the front door that she had left slightly ajar. Good. She apparently expected he'd follow.

He didn't see her right away as he entered the front hall but heard voices that he believed came from the kitchen. He headed that way.

Sure enough, Amber stood there near the doorway, and Sonya sat at the wooden table where Evan had signed the paperwork to join the ranch as an employee. A man sat opposite her. He looked to be in his fifties, with a full head of silvery hair and a concerned frown on his long and lined face.

"So glad you two had a good time this evening," Amber said. "We did, too—we discussed a lot about Evan's dog training."

"How fun," Sonya said. "And appropriate. I'll want to hear about it."

"Sure, Mom. I'll fill you in on everything soon."

The guy, meantime, glanced toward Evan and nodded a greeting. Evan did what he figured was expected and approached, hand out, though he avoided looking the guy in the face. He didn't feel entirely comfortable with this nice, kind neighbor who apparently wanted to help Sonya. What would he think of a former soldier with PTSD being their new employee?

It doesn't matter what he thinks, Evan told himself. Amber was clearly in charge and she made her own decision. He simply had to make sure she continued to believe it was the right one.

"Hi, I'm Evan Colluro," he said. "Nice to meet you."

The guy stood, his hand now out, too. He was dressed nicely in a white shirt and black trousers. His clasp was firm but blessedly brief. "Nathan Treggory. Sonya told me they just hired a dog trainer." Although his tone remained neutral, an expression of dubiousness passed across his face.

"That's right. I've got a lot of military and other

kinds of experience," Evan said, then wanted to kick himself. He didn't need to justify his being here to this neighbor.

"I'm sure you're a fine trainer," Nathan said, though he sounded as if he wouldn't be particularly impressed even if Evan was the premier dog trainer in the world.

Which suggested he wasn't really a dog person. So did the fact that Lola had been lying on the floor at Sonya's feet, but now rose and came toward Evan, as if the sweet Lab was taking his side in the discussion.

He kneeled briefly to give her a quick pat, then rose again to see Amber smiling at him. He grinned back and looked away, to see that Sonya, too, looked pleased.

Good. He was on the right side of the people in this room who really mattered, and the dog, too.

Everything would be fine. He hoped.

Evan said good-night and left nearly as soon as he'd greeted her mom and Nathan. That was appropriate, Amber thought, although she wished he'd stayed a little longer—at least as long as Nathan was there.

Fortunately, Nathan soon followed Evan without her even having to hint about it. "Call me anytime," he said to Sonya at the doorway where Amber also stood to see the men off. "Thanks for joining me for dinner tonight."

"Oh, thank *you*." Sonya's smile was soft and almost sad. Amber wanted to hug her, especially as they closed the door and faced each other in the entryway.

"You okay, Mom?" Amber realized that was a stupid question. Of course her mother wasn't okay and might not be for a long time.

But she was a sweet and caring lady. "I'm fine," she insisted. "It helps to have friends like Nathan and others here in town. They're just being kind, but their company does help me move forward. And your company, well—" Sonya reached out and the two women hugged tightly.

Amber felt tears in her eyes and held on for a moment before releasing her mother and stepping back. "Your company helps me, too, Mom," she said. Then, as Lola, who'd followed the crowd from the kitchen, nosed her side she bent and petted the dog's head. "And yours."

As her mother laughed, Amber's mind inappropriately imagined Evan with them, too. *And yours*, she thought, picturing his handsome face. But instead, she asserted, "Almost time to go out, Lola. I'll start with you soon."

"Are you sure you don't want me to accompany you with one of the pups?" her mother asked. Amber had gotten into a routine of taking each outside individually, or two at a time every night, though they all were pretty much housebroken. The personalized walks would help with their ongoing training.

"No, I'll be fine."

Amber knew that the short walks outside with these canines were good for her as well as the dogs.

But all the dogs had previously belonged to her dad and kept reminding her of him.

Well, the new regimen of Evan's training sessions would start tomorrow. That should help Amber move on.

First, though, she went outside to pull her car into the garage. Then she returned to the kitchen, and her mom and she each had a small good-night glass of wine. Sonya briefly described her evening with Nathan—just a nice dinner where they talked about how things were going with Chance Resort, Nathan's luxury hotel with corporate conference facilities on his nearby property. All sounded fine and success-ful, and he made it clear he'd be delighted to accom-modate people who came to the ranch for their dog training—including their dogs, as long as they were well behaved.

Depending on who they were and how long they'd be hanging around, that was Amber's idea, too, much as things were when her dad was around. Not every-one would stay in the small, nonluxury accommoda-tions they had for visitors, or downtown.

They'd also talked about how Sonya was doing, and she'd said she was fine, especially now that the lessons her husband had started here were about to recommence.

"Sweet man that he is, Nathan wished us luck and said he hoped we'd hired the perfect person to back up what your dad did." Sonya took her last sip of wine and looked into Amber's face with her sad brown eyes. "I hope so, too."

"I'm sure he'll do great." Amber wasn't lying, though that might be an exaggeration. She definitely hoped Evan was the perfect choice. But tomorrow would hopefully do a lot more to convince her. "Anyway, we'll find out soon. Now it's time for me to walk the dogs—and for you to head to bed. 'Night, Mom." She gave Sonya a kiss and told Lola to come as she headed toward the family room to grab her leash first.

She walked all four of the dogs one by one. Each outing took only five to ten minutes. Amber tried to prevent herself from looking toward Evan's house. Even if he was outside walking Bear, so what? What did she want from him? A good-night kiss?

She grinned wryly at her silliness. She must be more tired than she realized. Evan was her employee. They had said good-night already. And she certainly didn't miss the kisses she had gotten from her unreliable ex. No, she wanted no man in her life, for now at least, except as an employee or a friend.

She didn't see Evan anyway, a good thing. Soon, Amber closed the three pups back in their room and got Lola to come upstairs with her. Her mom had apparently already gone to bed.

Amber showered quickly in the hallway bathroom, then closed the bedroom door behind her with Lola inside. And wondered…

She shut off the light behind her and, after glancing down to ensure her floral cotton pajamas were buttoned and nonsuggestive in the off chance she was spotted by anyone in the vicinity—Orrin or Evan—she opened the blinds at her window.

And saw in the distance, where the fourth house stood at the end of the row, an outside light, just as she had hoped.

As she had hoped even more, there were forms moving within the glow: Evan, tossing a ball or something else that Bear fetched and brought back. She simply hadn't been outside late enough to see them...

They stopped, almost as if Evan sensed he was being watched and from where. He was far enough away that Amber couldn't tell for certain, but he seemed to look toward her.

With no lights on near her, she doubted he could see her, but that didn't prevent her from waving to him as she rested her other hand on Lola's soft furry head beside her.

"Good night," she whispered toward Evan. "And may we have a wonderful day tomorrow as an omen of even better ones to come."

Chapter 5

Evan woke early the next morning, lying on the comfortable bed in the house that for now was his. It was the home he hoped to occupy for a long time because he intended to keep this dog-training position—but that would depend a lot on what he did or didn't do today.

He'd slept well but now leaped out of bed, ready to start his new job. He moved so quickly that Bear, on an area rug on the hardwood floor beside him, nearly leaped up, too, and growled before setting his gaze on his handler, who just grinned at him.

"Good morning," he said to the dog. "Ready to run?"

As if he understood—and maybe the smart canine did—Bear stood and stared toward Evan, his shepherd ears at attention and his tail wagging.

"Good boy." Evan reached out and scratched the dog's head, then turned toward the door of the closet, where he'd stowed the clothes he'd brought, mostly casual stuff he could easily wear while engaged in training exercises with dogs and their handlers, but also a few dressier items like what he had worn last night. He'd slept in his briefs and a T-shirt, though he had brought pajamas.

He shaved, showered and dressed quickly, fed Bear some of the kibble he had just bought, then headed outside with the dog. Surely Bear was welcome to visit the others at the house at breakfast, too.

He jogged along the narrow front walkway to the main house, carrying Bear's official working vest but leaving his dog unleashed at his side. Evan recalled how he'd stared at that house late the previous night when he'd brought Bear out for his last short outing. Though he was too far away to see anything but the exterior, he nevertheless imagined where Amber was at the moment. Last night he'd attempted to figure out where her bedroom was and glanced now and then toward the window at the end on the top floor, where he'd noticed a light on.

And let his imagination go wild, wondering if Amber, too, went to bed last night wearing only her underwear…

A door opened beside him and Evan slowed as Orrin exited his house. "Good morning," he said to the young guy whose blue T-shirt had a Los Angeles Dodgers logo on it.

"Yeah, good morning," the man replied. "You working with any dogs today?"

"My own this morning—" he nodded toward Bear "—and some students this afternoon."

"In the field?" He gestured toward the portion of the large rolling lawn near them.

"Not sure where Amber will want to do it yet."

"Okay. I need to mow some of the lawn but can wait until later just in case. I'll check with her."

So despite seeming grumpy, Orrin, who hurried around the other side of his house, apparently had a sense of responsibility, a good thing. Eventually, Evan would chat with him about how he'd helped Corbin with his K-9 training exercises, including acting as an agitator as Amber had mentioned.

Amber. He felt as if he'd silently called to her since suddenly there she was outside her house, directing the leashed shepherd puppies into the smaller fenced area of the lawn where he had first worked with them. "Good morning," she called.

"Good morning," he returned. He and Bear caught up with her while she closed the chain-link gate behind the pups, their leashes now loose in her hand.

The smile she directed at him made him feel more than he should, considering she was his boss. To drive his thoughts in a different direction, he mentioned how he'd seen Orrin and that the handyman intended to mow the lawn when he received her okay.

"He's a good guy," she said. "I'll talk to him later. For now, my mom's got our bacon and eggs nearly ready."

"Sounds great. You're going to spoil me here." He managed to look straight into her gorgeous brown eyes a little longer than was comfortable, but it helped that she was still smiling.

"Oh, don't count on that. We just want to make you feel good on your first day working here. After this you'll be pretty much on your own for breakfast. Besides, we usually stick with toast or cereal and coffee, nothing fancy."

"Of course." He'd need to make that run downtown later to stock up on supplies besides Bear's.

Amber started to turn away. He approached the fence and motioned for the pups to come to him, which they did. Good. Corbin had chosen young dogs with good training potential. Plus, they'd already been socialized, at least somewhat. Evan would enjoy continuing to work with them.

"Good morning, Rex, Lucy and Hal." He scratched each behind the ears.

"I'm sure they say 'good morning' back," Amber said, humor in her tone. "Now let's go inside before my mother gets upset that we're not at the table yet."

Once they got through the door Lola and Bear traded sniffs once more.

Speaking of sniffs, Evan immediately caught the aroma of their breakfast, including bacon and, he believed, some pretty special coffee. "Hey," he said, "maybe I should make my working here conditional on getting the kind of breakfast I think I'm about to eat."

"Too late," Amber said. "You've already signed the contract."

Evan laughed and followed her down the hall, Lola at her side, to the kitchen. There, he saw Sonya at the stove working with a full frying pan of eggs, another pan of bacon behind it.

"Good morning, Sonya," he greeted, glad she was too busy to glance at him even though he'd managed to look Amber in the eye briefly.

"Morning. Hope you like eggs and bacon but I didn't have time to ask before I started to cook." She hesitated, then said, "This was my husband's favorite breakfast."

Even if he'd hated it, Evan wouldn't have said so after a statement like that. Fortunately, he could tell the truth. "It's about my favorite breakfast, too, although, one morning soon, I'll have to get some pancake mix and invite you both to my place."

His place. He realized he was taking a lot for granted—though Amber had been the one who'd just mentioned the contract they'd both signed. But there was a provision that allowed her to fire him, and another that permitted him to quit. The terms were mostly about what he'd do and how he'd be paid as long as he worked here.

"Sounds like a good payback," Amber said. "Meantime, for today, have a seat. It's our turn to feed you."

Which they did, fairly quickly. The food was as good as it smelled. And though Evan had given Bear a quick breakfast before leaving their house, his dog also got another morning snack.

As they finished up around that round wooden table, Evan expressed again to Sonya how much he enjoyed his breakfast. Then he glanced briefly toward Amber.

She seemed to be staring at him, which made him uncomfortable. He mostly studied his plate and the cup of coffee beside it on the table. He'd been feeling somewhat at ease in her presence before, especially after she'd demonstrated sorrow and other emotions yesterday that he could identify with.

But this was an important day. He would be in the spotlight—and working, later, with people he didn't know. She would be watching him, questioning him, evaluating his skills further.

Would he measure up to the standards she was setting?

He had to. In fact—

"So you about ready for our demonstration with Bear and our discussion this morning?" He looked her straight in the face and made sure he didn't turn away.

She looked surprised and maybe a bit amused as she continued to look at him. Smiling, she said, "I'm definitely ready. Are you?"

Amber answered a quick call from Mirri first, promising to let her friend know how the day went, then exited out the front door. Evan put a dog vest he'd been carrying on Bear and they followed Amber down the steps toward the fenced-in lawn. She would have remained completely aware of Evan's tall presence behind her even if she hadn't heard his footsteps on the porch.

Not that he wasn't welcome to walk beside her. Was he worried about his upcoming performance?

She doubted it.

At least she was glad he'd said he was ready to begin around the same time she was about to ask him. She wanted to get things started.

The outside air was chilly and humid, but even if she became uncomfortable, that was just a risk of working outside. Now she crossed toward the left, just short of the houses where students could stay during their lessons. Here, the paved driveway was large and square, a suitable area for some kinds of dog training.

"Hey, let's go somewhere closer to the pups," Evan called.

She turned to face Bear and him. "Is it a good thing for them to see training sessions they're not involved in? I thought it might confuse them." She looked toward Bear as if she expected him to answer, but the lanky shepherd just sat on the pavement and looked at her.

"I don't mean right next to them," Evan said, catching up with her, "and there is a difference of opinions at times between professional trainers, but my belief is that it's good for pups to see that they're not the only ones humans are working with."

"You're the boss," Amber retorted, keeping her expression wry to ensure he knew she was kidding.

Although, for the moment, he actually would be in charge.

Did it help that he looked a bit military? His T-shirt today was a camouflage print, which he wore over jeans. Maybe he was attempting to impart a silent message, or a reminder of his background, or— Well, she'd just have to see how things went.

She had donned an outfit that morning she felt was appropriate for her both being a student yet being in charge…sort of. It was a loose black T-shirt with white letters that said Chance K-9 Ranch, something her dad had gotten made when he'd bought this place and had given shirts as rewards to students in his classes.

He hadn't given Amber an opportunity to take part, but she had at least received a shirt. Today, she wore it over athletic pants.

She held back a little to follow Evan and Bear through the gate and beyond the area where the pups were again enclosed. They continued for a short distance, yet when Amber caught up and turned, she saw the young dogs jumping in their enclosure, all three seeming to watch what was going on.

A good thing or not? Well, Evan would be the one to work with the pups so he'd better know what he was doing.

"Okay," he said. "First, I want to reiterate that Bear is retired from the military and doesn't do any official active-duty police K-9 work, either. But he's great to demonstrate training skills. I gather that you want me both to give a demo today of what Bear can do, and also to explain how he learned it, maybe give you an initial lesson in training K-9s, or other dogs, too."

"That's right." She stared into his face. His expression was solemn, but he didn't look away. "I'll want you to give me further private lessons, but today's will just be a start."

Private lessons? Why did the term make her insides turn suddenly warm? Sure, the guy was hot, but no way could she follow up with anything between them that was truly private.

Besides, with his PTSD, he probably had no interest in getting close to any woman, especially not his employer.

"Fine. Okay, first I'd like you to stand there and watch while I put Bear through his paces."

For the next ten minutes, Amber was in awe. Evan had done a good job working during his interview mostly with the minimally trained shepherd pups, but Bear? He was wonderful!

The regular stuff at first, like *sit*, *stay*, *down*, *heel*, both with verbal commands and motions, all appeared completely natural to Bear. Evan's tone working with him was soft yet sure, and each time the dog obeyed, it was followed up by praise. The humid air seemed almost to reverberate with "good dog." And once he was through with that, Evan pulled a tug toy from his pocket. This time, instead of throwing it, he grasped the rope tied to one side and engaged in a short tug-of-war with the dog, who made amazingly happy growling noises in return.

One of the most impressive things was how, at heel, Bear stayed right at Evan's side even as he turned and twisted, no matter how fast he did it.

"This is an important ability for military and police K-9s," he told her. "Bear's also skilled in sniffing out things, particularly explosives. I'll have him demonstrate that someday, too."

Eventually, he stopped and Bear sat down immediately at his feet. Evan looked at Amber. "Your turn now."

Her heart rate quickened. She told herself that it was okay if she didn't do great. Bear was Evan's dog. She had purposely left Lola inside with her mom, since their Lab wasn't to be part of this training episode, even though she had been taught well by Amber's dad.

"Fine." She hoped her tone sounded professional enough. "Tell me what I should do."

"Okay, here's how I'll start teaching future trainers, whether or not they'll eventually get special K-9 handler lessons." Standing facing her, with Bear lying on the ground beside him, Evan described a scenario where the trainer was to choose a particular command. "You know the drill as far as what's standard. I always use regular short and precise words, always the same to get the same result. I'll walk away now and you can go through the same commands I used before, but do them in a different order."

Before he stepped back, he edged up to Amber and pulled a ball from his pocket so that it was hidden from Bear's gaze.

"Can't he smell it?" she asked.

"Of course, but he's a good boy. And though he

gets games as rewards, he's trained to respond just as much to praise."

"From me?" Amber figured Bear would be much happier if his master praised him.

"You'll see."

Amber felt Evan's hand at her side near her own hand and had an urge to grab his warm fingers and hold on. Instead, she gripped the ball and stuffed it into her pocket—not easy to do with her snug pants—as Evan moved away.

"Ready?" he asked.

She took a deep breath and looked him straight in the eye, needing some kind of nonverbal reassurance that she could do it, but figuring he'd just look away.

He didn't, though. His deep blue eyes looked back into hers, and he smiled and gave an encouraging nod.

Heck, it wasn't as if Bear would attack her, or even ignore her, if she did things wrong...

She nodded back, then looked down toward the reclining dog on the ground. She walked away a few steps, then said, "Bear, come."

She wasn't surprised when Bear rose and approached.

"Good dog," she said, feeling mushy inside. Sure, she got Lola to come on command, but Lola was her dog. Or at least her mother's.

"Good," Evan said. "Now the next one."

For the next ten minutes, Amber put the smart, obedient shepherd through his paces, listening as Evan praised her at times, and also gave her suggestions of what to do next, and when to throw the ball as a reward.

His voice, his praise… Amber felt proud of herself, as if she was the dog obeying commands. She also had an urge, when the exercise was over, to dash in Evan's direction and give him a big hug. Though actually, he was the one who should hug her as part of his praise…

"Good start, Amber," he finally said, coming over to her and gesturing to Bear. "Sit, boy." Of course the dog obeyed.

Amber would probably have sat at his command, too, just then—she was that happy, that revved up by her success.

And was that the first time he had called her by name? Probably. On top of everything else, it made her feel all warm inside.

Still… "I've made an internal note about what you told me, but I was still only working with Bear."

"So far," Evan agreed. "That's the first part. Before you can teach anyone else, you need to know how to do it yourself. You'll be able to observe it when I work with your students this afternoon, assuming they've really learned lessons about training dogs. Otherwise, I'll start fresh with them, too." He paused for a moment. "You're okay with how we're doing so far?"

He hadn't appeared to lack confidence. He still didn't.

But Amber appreciated that he did recognize that

she was in charge—or at least that he wanted it to look that way.

"Sure," she said. They began walking back toward the gate, Bear at Evan's side. Did she want this exercise to be over?

She'd see Evan again this afternoon, watch him training the others—but they wouldn't be alone.

And she still had a lot of curiosity...

She moved slightly ahead of him, then stopped. "Can I ask you some questions, like why you use the methods you do? When I was interviewing others for this job, I saw a lot of different ways to train."

"And there are a lot of methods that work well, but mine's best." His smile appeared cocky and, despite his looking away quickly, sent a shiver of interest through her. "I'll tell you why I chose it, but let's go get a cup of coffee, okay? It could take a while."

"Good idea," Amber said.

Spending more time in Evan's presence sounded like a good idea—especially since the reason was to teach her something more. Or so she tried to tell herself.

Chapter 6

Rather than choosing to sit inside as they had for breakfast, Amber invited her mom to join Evan, Bear and her on the front porch for coffee…and conversation. She had a couple of reasons for doing that: to ensure her mom didn't remain by herself, and because she knew her mother would refill their coffee cups often if they needed it.

Plus, the idea of being alone in Evan's company, in essence, some more…well, she liked that but at the same time didn't. At least they'd be talking about dog training, and she'd appreciate her mother's company.

She was happy but unsurprised when Evan offered to bring the folding garden chairs onto the porch from the garage behind the house. She was equally happy but unsurprised when her mother accepted her invitation, made a fresh pot of coffee and joined them. Lola came outside, too, and laid down near her, as if reminding Amber of her presence since she'd worked with another dog that morning.

"So," Sonya said after filling their mugs with hot coffee, "tell me about your demonstration."

They'd mentioned it at breakfast, and in a way Amber was surprised her mom hadn't been more insistent about coming to watch. But Amber had wanted this to be one-on-one since she figured she would learn more that way, so had gently turned down her mother's suggestion but promised she could do it another time.

Besides, she knew her mother had often observed her dad's training sessions and it might be painful for her to watch.

"Well, it's no surprise, but your daughter did a good job of telling Bear what to do." Evan, who'd been sitting tall on the tightly woven green webbing on his chair, bent to pat the dog beside him on the head. Amber grinned in pride as Evan described in detail her short but fun episode working with Bear.

"So you train dogs mostly with verbal commands?" Sonya asked when he was done.

"And hand signals, too, with praise and toys as a reward. And gentle pushes or pulls when needed." He paused, and Amber saw him look straight into her mother's face for a moment. "I know there are a lot of training methods, some that aren't as kind but can still get results. I was in the military and had to get used to taking orders from superior officers, but there were some I liked better than others, so that helped in my dog-training choices."

"Really?" Amber threw wryness into her question. "I'd have thought someone like you, who gives dogs lots of orders, wouldn't have minded taking them himself."

His gaze moved to her, and this time he didn't immediately look away. "The officers whose orders I liked best seemed to care, to empathize with those reporting to them, even if they gave those orders as curtly as everyone else. That's what I did when I started working with dogs—and I found some instructors for K-9 officers did the same. So that's what I do—without the curtness unless absolutely necessary."

"Maybe for the same reasons…it's the kind of training my husband preferred, too." Sonya seemed to find something highly interesting in her coffee cup as she stared into it, and Amber couldn't help herself. She put down her cup and hugged her mother. The tears in her eyes mirrored her mom's, and even Lola sensed their sorrow and came closer to snuggle with them.

"From all I've heard about him," Evan said softly from behind her, "Corbin sounds like he was one really good, caring trainer."

Giving her mother another squeeze, Amber turned and looked at Evan. "Yes, he was." But she couldn't help wondering what her dad had said, what he'd done, to apparently upset one of his human students enough to get him killed—if that was what had happened. Or why he'd been targeted by a robber. They weren't particularly wealthy.

Or—

Maybe one of these days Amber would try again to confront Kara Province and demand more information.

She'd met the students before who were coming this afternoon. They were local, and she had encouraged them to continue meeting here to practice their training exercises as a group without a teacher. They all seemed nice. She doubted they were among the cops' suspects, but she couldn't just assume they all were innocent.

She wouldn't let her mom go out alone with any of them, in case someone held a hidden grudge…

She felt, rather than saw, her mother move behind her and turned. Sonya was standing now, holding her coffee cup firmly.

"Corbin was an amazing man," she said. "I just wish he had written a book on his life. Or at least on his methods of dog training. That would have helped us a lot right now."

"I wish he had, too, Mom." Amber touched her arm once more, then turned to Evan. "Maybe you and I can interview some of his returning students this afternoon. We can ask how your methods are like his, and how they're different."

And maybe she could look over the contents of her dad's computer again. She'd done so before, almost as soon as she had come home. She had hoped that somehow there would be information on it, maybe an accusation, to help her figure out who'd killed her father.

Not if it had been a random robbery, of course. And she hadn't found anything helpful. Her moist eyes now were nothing like the tears she had shed then.

"Sounds like a good idea." Evan watched her with a sympathetic look, not quite into her face, but he had to see the sorrow she projected from inside. "I've never considered writing a book about dog training, but I like the concept, particularly comparing and contrasting how Corbin did it with my methods, if we can figure that out."

"Let's give it a try soon," Amber said. She liked that this man, this dog trainer who was taking over her father's position, was willing to give Corbin Belott credit for being a good teacher, whether or not his way of doing it was the same.

Her dad had built up a wonderful reputation. Amber felt sure that Evan, too, was good at what he did, and she hoped this afternoon's exercise would help to start getting word out about the new, upcoming classes.

Chance K-9 Ranch should have a wonderful future. And she'd work hard to achieve that.

Whatever the reason for her dad's death, he deserved that kind of legacy.

Okay, it was nearly time. Evan knew he needed to get his act together.

He would do it.

At the moment, he remained inside his house with

Bear, but the students were due to arrive in ten minutes and he wanted to be outside waiting.

Even though they would be a group of four, not just the one-on-one students he preferred, he could, and would, handle it. He had to, both to keep his job… and to impress his boss.

He had eaten a quick pastrami sandwich for lunch. Once he'd left Amber and Sonya that morning, using his necessary shopping expedition as an excuse, he had closed Bear in the house and driven downtown to the grocery store he'd noticed and stocked up on easy-to-prepare foods, like sandwich fixings and pre-cut salad as well as breakfast items. He also remembered to buy hotcake mix and syrup. He'd promised to make breakfast sometime for the two women who had been so kind to him so far.

He had managed to act friendly to the store clerks, even answering the cashier's question about why he happened to be in town. He didn't get the woman's name or look at her much, but she clearly knew the Belotts and understood they had been seeking someone to take up where Corbin had left off.

"That's me," he'd said cheerily as he'd picked up his bags and hurried out of there.

Corbin had definitely been well-known around here, even though he hadn't lived in the area very long. Evan recognized that he had major shoes to fill—and, hopefully, surpass.

He wondered what kind of reaction he'd have gotten if he had asked the cashier her idea of how Corbin had died…but he knew better than being that pushy.

Any questions probably wouldn't yield answers, and, if the wrong person heard, it could even result in danger to him and, worse, to Amber and Sonya.

He'd do all he could to figure it out, but subtly.

But for now... "Bear, come." He opened the front door and, standing on the front stoop, snapped an ordinary woven leash onto Bear's ordinary woven collar. Bear would therefore know he could just act like a regular dog around the others, without his special K-9 vest or other training equipment.

He would still be well behaved, of course. That was Bear.

Walking briskly along the narrow walkway, Evan headed toward the main house with Bear at his side. This time Orrin didn't pop out to say hello. But as Evan reached the home where Amber and Sonya lived, their door opened and both came outside.

Sonya held a leash similar to Bear's, with Lola at its end.

"Hi, Evan. Is it okay for me to stand outside the fence with Lola to watch you?" she called. "I won't get too close." She hadn't changed from her casual clothes, but her reddish hair looked more formal in the upswept bun on top of her head.

Though she hadn't watched him work with her daughter—because it could be more emotional?—this was fine. "Sure," he said.

"Great!" Amber smiled down from the porch. She'd changed into a long blue shirt over beige cargo pants, apparently wanting to dress up a little more for the class.

She looked good. More than good, probably no matter what she wore.

Or didn't wear.

"Let's go wait for them," he said hurriedly, forcing his thoughts back to reality. He glanced toward the fenced lawn area. The shepherd pups weren't enclosed there. "Glad you left the young guys inside. Watching this might only confuse them."

"But though I liked your demonstration with them yesterday, I do want to see you give them more of an official pre-K-9 class soon"

Okay, so Amber was again making it clear she was in charge, and knew it—like a commanding officer. Somehow, that didn't change his inappropriate attraction to her this day.

Maybe the way she acted around his upcoming regular class now would handle that. He hoped.

"Of course," he responded. "Soon, but not today."

The students began to arrive. Two cars headed up the sloped driveway toward them, a boxy SUV and a nicer sedan. Two students in each with their dogs?

The SUV stopped first. A woman had been driving, and her passenger was a guy. Both got out and opened the rear doors to let out two dogs.

The sedan's situation was similar, although the people inside were both men.

Evan took a deep breath and approached, Bear still at his side. At the same time, Amber skipped down the porch steps, followed by her mother and Lola.

"Hi, everyone," Amber called. All four people

shouted greetings back, each scrambling to leash their dogs.

Evan's first impression was that training classes appeared necessary. Good.

"Follow me," Amber said, then, instead of the paved area she'd said was mostly used for K-9 classes, she entered the large fenced lawn area through the gate. Sonya held back with Lola, watching for now, from near where the cars were parked.

When they were all inside the gate, Evan half expected them to let their dogs loose, but they didn't. Each had metal correction collars on their dogs, a good thing for training—as long as they used them correctly, without choking the canines.

"Okay," Amber called but didn't have to. All four people, dogs at their sides, formed a straight line on a relatively flat area of the lawn and smiled toward her.

"We're ready," called one of the men, twentyish with a goatee as dark a brown as his Doberman's coat. "You want us to go through our paces?"

"Not yet." Amber faced them. "First, I want to introduce you to our excellent new instructor." She motioned for Evan to join her. It was too early for the surge of pride he felt as he reached her, but she had already complimented him even before he showed these dog owners his merit. "Everyone, this is Evan Colluro. Evan, I want you to meet Grady Jermann, and that's his Dobie, Mambo." She gestured toward the guy who'd been talking with her. Then she introduced the others: the woman, Julie Young, and her golden retriever mix, Squeegie; Aaron Perkins and his Belgian Malinois, Baxter; and Stewart Saule and his sheltie mix, George.

"And this is Bear," Evan said when he was done shaking the humans' hands. He was amused when Julie got Squeegie to sit and give her his paw.

"Hi, Bear," they all called, and the wonderful dog at his side stood in acknowledgment but didn't otherwise move.

Amber then said, "Everyone, I want Evan to watch your initial training exercises today first, but, Evan, feel free to jump in and do some teaching. Okay?"

Of course it was.

For the next fifteen minutes, the group, mostly led by Grady but also sometimes by Julie, put their dogs through their paces. "This is the way Corbin taught us," Grady said solemnly when he was in charge. His knit beige shirt looked tight, though he didn't appear to have much in the way of muscles beneath. "He was a good guy."

"That's for sure," Julie said. She looked a little older than the others and wore a long-sleeved blue dress that reached just below her knees. At least her white tennis shoes looked comfortable. Her golden retriever, Squeegie, seemed fairly relaxed as Julie ran him through his paces. So relaxed, in fact, that he sometimes needed several repetitions of the commands before listening.

That would provide fodder for the short class Evan intended to give at the end of their demonstration.

"I'm sorry I didn't get to meet Corbin," Evan responded, then glanced down at Bear as the two students both began to look him in the face. Damn it. If he was going to be effective here, he needed to cast aside his discomfort with having eyes on him, even with four strangers.

He glanced toward Amber. Unsurprisingly, she was watching him. Scorning him? But, no, she actually appeared supportive. And emotional. "I think my dad would have liked to meet you, too," she said huskily.

Evan made himself turn back to the students to stop himself from approaching Amber and giving her a hug.

Standing inside the fence in the soft sunlight of afternoon, arms crossed, Amber was happy to watch the class members go through their exercises with their dogs.

She had grown fond of all of them. These same people had shown up at the ranch with their pets in support of her mom even before Amber had been able to speed home after her dad's death. She had stayed for only a week then before returning briefly to her San Diego apartment, arranging for all her belongings to be shipped here, quitting her job and hurrying back to Chance permanently.

And this group had reappeared a day or so after her return to resume their classes—on their own, helping each other and their dogs without an actual instructor.

She observed their paces now, how they all demonstrated some of the simplest of the exercises Evan had shown her earlier with Bear, as they had done weekly since she'd moved back here. Each took a turn at being in charge, sometimes leading the others into a more tricky exercise just for fun.

Did they know enough of her father's training methods to be interviewed if Evan and she actually did try to write a book? She'd have to see and ask questions, though not today.

But she loved the idea of that kind of tribute to her dad.

When she'd told these students a few weeks ago that she was seriously looking for someone to take over teaching the classes, she'd half expected them to criticize her for even considering attempting to replace her dad—but they'd all been supportive and said they would give her new instructor a try.

So now, how would they do with that new trainer?

At the moment, Evan stood not far from her and her mom, who was also observing. He'd indicated he wanted to check out these students first, see where they were in their training, then determine how he could best help them.

But she really wanted him to do more than just watch, even now. When would he take over?

She found herself watching him from the corner of her eye even more than she looked at the students and dogs. His expression was serious and he seemed to concentrate on what he was seeing, even if he was conscious of her presence.

Sometimes he smiled. Sometimes he frowned. He seldom looked straight at any of the students, but occasionally moved slightly as if he wanted to jump over the fence and tell them what to do.

Which, to Amber, was a good thing. But for now she would just wait and watch both the class and Evan's reaction to it.

She'd give them all a bit more time. Soon, though, as the end of an hour approached, she would step in and tell Evan to show them a command or two.

And show them all, if necessary, that she remained in charge.

Chapter 7

Evan enjoyed watching the group, though some of the things they did made him cringe.

At least Bear, at his side, helped to keep him cool despite his internal irritation. His dog was well trained and simply watched.

Still... Evan made himself stand casually near the fence no matter what. There were times Aaron was too rough with the prong collar if his smart but energetic Malinois, Baxter, was too distracted to obey right away. Sometimes trainers taught that method, but it wasn't Evan's way, and he'd gathered from how the other students worked that it hadn't been Corbin's, either.

But he stayed still, at least at first. This class was to be a demonstration to him before he took it over.

In addition to Bear helping to keep him steady, he was very much aware of Amber standing nearby watching him, as well as the dogs. He was interested in the class—but he was also interested in her. The impression he made on her. It had to be good, and he realized he didn't feel that way entirely because of the job.

Did she want him to jump in faster? She glanced at him often as if that was her intent. In any case, he might decide to just take over, especially to encourage this group—one member, at least—to be kinder with their dogs as they engaged in lessons.

"Everyone heel," shouted Julie. "Then let's run!" Her dog, Squeegie, leaped forward beside her with apparent glee.

Even Bear moved a little but calmed when Evan said softly, "Stay." Bear looked up at him, and Evan praised him with a "Good boy."

The entire class group followed Julie, dogs at their sides, and fortunately all moved at a good pace that didn't require correction.

But then she called, "Stop!" The three others gave the same command to their dogs but, unsurprisingly, Baxter didn't immediately slow. Aaron pulled on his leash, tightening the collar, and Baxter's head seemed to turn toward his master before the rest of his body.

That had to hurt. And it angered Evan.

He kept his temper in check, though, as he tied Bear to a wooden slat of the main fence, then climbed over without looking at Amber.

"Hey, everyone," he called as he hurried toward them. "You're all doing great." A little lie didn't hurt if it got their attention, even the most aggressive student's. He reached the group and looked straight at Aaron, then looked away. "I'm enjoying watching all of you, but you know I'm here not only to observe. I have some suggestions, especially for you." This time, he addressed Aaron directly, knowing his tone was stern. Then he looked at the others. "Are you all ready?"

"Sure," Julie said. Grady and Stewart also responded affirmatively.

Was Aaron? Evan asked, "And you?"

"Yeah, sure," Aaron grunted.

Great. Evan let his breath out a bit. He could be as assertive as necessary to achieve an important goal like this one, no matter how much it bothered him inside. But he much preferred that things remain noncombative in all respects.

In all respects. The other thing he'd been doing during his observation was to key in on the pet owners' personalities and how they interacted with each other. This wasn't the most likely situation for him to determine if any of them was aggressive enough to kill their instructor because of a disagreement or something else, but it was at least an introduction.

So far, the only one he found potentially too aggressive or unkind was Aaron, but a few inappropriate tugs on his dog's leash didn't make him a killer.

Or a threat to Amber or her mother, and that was Evan's even larger concern.

At the moment, the other three kneeled and hugged their dogs, praising them. That didn't mean any of them couldn't have killed Corbin, either. If any had harbored a grudge, possibly because of how he treated, or had them treat, their dogs...

That still seemed a stretch. He had no idea why the dog trainer had been killed.

Not yet.

"So what will your first lesson here be?"

Hearing Amber's voice behind him, he turned. "Bear and I will give our own demonstration of this kind of heel-and-stop lesson—with no tugging on a corrective collar."

Her expression seemed irritated. With him? With these students?

With the world?

It wasn't his job to make her feel better, no matter how much he wanted to. But it was his job to provide a lesson.

"Great idea." Her face softened, and she smiled at him, then turned to look toward Bear at the fence. Her voice was low as she added, "I think you two can teach these students some really good lessons."

Amber felt sure that what she'd said was true. Despite not having seen him work before with any group of people, she trusted Evan.

After all, she had seen him in action—with the pups, and with Bear and her.

Nevertheless, she saw Aaron's questioning look toward her. He had been criticized, after all, though in a benign way. But his first impression of Evan probably hadn't been great, despite it being his own fault.

She watched as Evan had them line up, dogs all leashed loosely at their sides as Bear was beside him, also leashed.

Amber glanced outside the fence toward the gate. She was glad her mom felt comfortable enough to be there with Lola, watching but staying back.

"Now," Evan called, "here's a demo of some of the elementals of what military and police K-9s are taught that you can use with your pets. You used some of it before and, like I said, you mostly did a good job. But take a look at this." The exercises he ran Bear through now were similar to what he'd shown her that morning and had turned into a class for her.

Some were also similar to what these students had demonstrated earlier, although the heels and turns and sits were much crisper without any tugging on Bear's leash. He ran with Bear beside him, too, like what Julie had had the other class members do, but Evan was smoother and Bear seemed to watch his every move as he ran at his handler's side.

There were a couple of additional exercises, as well, like a brisk walk broken up by several quick "sits," and a "down," where Bear had to remain on the ground without moving while Evan hustled around him.

After Evan was through with this display, he took his tug toy from his pocket and, after releasing Bear from his leash, tossed it for the dog to fetch. Bear worried it in his mouth before bringing it back to Evan, who accepted it with a "good boy."

Evan then told the students some commands to try.

"Great!" That was Grady, who went first. His Doberman, Mambo, seemed highly attuned to what his master wanted. Then came Julie with Squeegie, and Aaron with Baxter. Stewart went last with sheltie George.

They all did fine, except that Amber believed Aaron was still too rough with Baxter. It wasn't up to her to correct him. At least he'd eased up a bit on his yanks on Baxter's leash.

Amber watched the nonverbal interplay between Evan and Aaron, too. She had no idea if it was hard on Evan, but he observed every move Aaron made, a critical scowl on his face. He even looked Aaron in the eye for part of it, impressing her since she realized that might be difficult for their new trainer.

Finally, they were done. "You're such a wonderful dog," Julie said, kneeling to hug Squeegie. "Right, Evan?"

Evan laughed. "That's not exactly the praise I'd give, but if it works, it's fine for a pet, though not for a K-9. At least not while they're being trained on duty. Now, you've all gotten your dogs to obey, at least somewhat. How about a special 'good dog' to each of them and we'll end this for today."

"But what about a new trick?" Julie asked. "Corbin always taught us one new trick at the end of a session." She looked straight into Evan's face, and he turned his head, appearing uncomfortable.

"Er...this is an initial get-together," he responded. "For us to meet each other. Maybe next time I'll come up with a new command to teach, but I don't fully know those you've already been taught."

"We'll tell you. Right, guys?"

"Sure," Grady said.

Amber liked that idea. But for now, Evan looked as if he needed this class to end.

"Great," he said. "But that's for next time."

Julie didn't look completely pleased, but she, Grady and Stewart followed through with their praise.

Aaron placed himself in front of them and their dogs, allowing Baxter to hang back without tugging on his leash. "But you see how my dog doesn't obey like yours even with commands he's been taught," he said to Evan, sounding so plaintive that Amber almost wanted to hug him in sympathy. Almost. He might well have trained poor Baxter to respond only when he was harsh. "I don't want to tell him 'good dog' now. How do I get him to listen to me without tugging hard on his leash?"

Evan didn't hesitate. "Well, let me give it a try, okay?"

"Sure." Aaron handed the end of the leash to Evan, who told Baxter to heel, holding the leash loosely. Baxter followed but didn't exactly remain at his side despite his clear heel command.

Not at first.

But once they were a short distance from the rest of the crowd, Evan told Baxter to sit, which he did. Evan bent to lavish praise on him while looking him straight in the face—which Amber realized must be easier for Evan while staring at a dog.

Baxter's tail wagged, and from then on he followed all of Evan's commands.

"Now you try it," Evan eventually said, handing Baxter's leash back to Aaron. Baxter clearly knew he was back with his original trainer, and he sat and began panting.

Would Aaron get frustrated again and hurt him? Amber was ready to pounce if he did.

Instead, though, with a sheepish look on his face Aaron looked down at Baxter, then stood beside him. "Baxter, heel," he said. When the dog instead laid down as if expecting to be choked, Aaron again said, "Heel." This time, he pulled on the leash until the prong collar tightened but didn't yank on it. Baxter looked up at him…and stood. When Aaron started walking slowly, the dog stayed at his side, looking up, then straight ahead. And as he'd done with Evan, Baxter obeyed Aaron's commands.

Aaron soon stopped and said, "Sit," then kneeled and hugged Baxter. "Good dog," he said, and everyone—his fellow owners and Evan and Amber—clapped their hands and congratulated Aaron and Baxter, too.

Amber knew for sure she'd done the right thing in hiring Evan.

She glanced toward where she had last seen her

mother with Lola, wondering if she'd observed what had just transpired. Sonya was, in fact, where Amber had last seen her, but she and Lola weren't alone. Their neighbor Nathan was with them.

Well, fine. It was a good thing for Nathan to know that things here were going well, that classes might ramp up and the possibility of his getting more hotel guests who were students here had also possibly gone up.

But Sonya and Nathan were talking, not looking toward the handlers and dogs, at least not then.

Which made Amber cringe. She could still be misinterpreting it, but was her mother actually heading into a relationship with their neighbor?

Too soon, she thought again. As she turned, she caught Evan's eye briefly…and believed she saw in his look a hint of concern, or maybe sympathy, which suggested she wasn't imagining things.

If only she could be more like Evan and cultivate more of a relationship with dogs than with people.

It had gone well. Or so Evan believed. It was all he could do to keep himself from grinning and patting himself on the back.

As the students and their dogs got ready to depart, he said goodbye and arranged for the next class with this group for the following week. It would be early evening then, since they'd all chosen this time to meet their new instructor as soon as they could, but it wasn't the most convenient for them. They each had jobs of their own.

Then they all got their dogs to heel and moved forward on the rolling lawn toward the gate—and every one of them, Aaron included, did it well. Even the dogs appeared happy, tails wagging and heads turning as they walked to look up at their owners.

Evan began looking for Amber. Maybe she would be the one to pat him on the back, and the idea sounded good, especially if it consisted of a real pat on his back with her hands. He quickly spotted her just down the lawn from him. She was also watching the class leave…or was she? As he followed her gaze he noticed that she was looking at Sonya. Amber's mom stood there, not alone with Lola, but also with the neighbor, Nathan.

His initial reaction was to smile toward the ground as he and Bear walked toward Amber, up the hill. Sonya might have plans for dinner that night. Maybe he could eat with Amber again. It could become a habit, their sharing many meals to discuss dog training and more…

Before he reached Amber, though, she began walking toward the gate. He couldn't quite read her expression but she didn't look thrilled.

He shut the gate behind them and watched the class members leave in their cars. Another car, Nathan's, soon followed, after the neighbor said a brief hello and goodbye to Amber and him as Evan joined them on the driveway.

As it turned out, Nathan and Sonya weren't having dinner together, but Sonya and Amber were. They didn't invite him, so he didn't ask.

No reason for him to feel so disappointed. They were his employers. Eating together wasn't part of his job.

Plus, he had brought more than lunch meat home with him from the grocery store. He wouldn't starve that night, nor for breakfast the next morning since they weren't getting together again then, either.

But what Amber and he did discuss briefly was that they'd meet again tomorrow fairly early in the lawn's smaller fenced-in area.

It was time for him not just to demonstrate with them, but to dig in and begin training the three shepherd puppies with the preliminaries they needed to know to eventually become K-9s.

Which was a good thing. He'd feel even more comfortable doing that than training owners how to work with their pets. It was what he knew best. And it didn't involve other people.

Although…well, he remembered his idea about patting himself on the back.

He'd done well, after all. But he should do even better tomorrow.

Chapter 8

They were in the living room with the TV tuned to the national news. Lola was lying on an area rug that covered the hardwood floor between where Amber sat on the sofa and Sonya occupied the nearby gray upholstered chair. The dog, black nose in the air, clearly hoped that one of them, or maybe both, would drop some tuna casserole or salad on the floor so she could eat it.

Amber couldn't pay attention to the news. She felt too frustrated. Her mother clearly had something on her mind. She'd cooked a meal that included one of Amber's favorite dishes from childhood but hadn't allowed her daughter to help prepare it. Nor would she talk while cooking. "We'll chat later," she said when Amber attempted to start a conversation.

It was later now. But Sonya seemed glued to the news commentator's rundown of a store robbery in the Bay Area, where the owner's ten-year-old son helped to stop the bad guys. Kind of sweet, but it wasn't what was occupying Amber's mind.

That afternoon was. And—

Her mother suddenly reached out with the TV control and turned the sound off, then stared at Amber. "You wanted to talk," her mom said.

"Well…yes." But Amber wasn't quite sure how to start this conversation, how to ask about the amount of time her mom suddenly seemed to be spending with their neighbor. It probably meant nothing more than that Nathan was a nice man. He'd lived around Chance longer than her family, and his hotel and resort facilities seemed to be doing well. Maybe he was an advocate for the area and its residents, someone who tried to ensure his friends and acquaintances were as happy as possible.

As far as Amber knew, he wasn't married. He might be taking advantage of this situation, the idea of propinquity bringing him next door more than he should. "I noticed that Nathan came by again today," she began, taking a bite of casserole to appear casual.

"Yes…and, well, I wanted to talk to you about that, too."

Uh-oh. Was her mother going to admit she was attracted to the man? How could she be, so soon after her husband's death? Amber knew her parents had had a wonderful relationship, loving and caring and…well, enviable.

And why did Evan's face superimpose itself on the TV screen as Amber's imagination went into over-drive? She had just recently met the guy, and though she needed to get to know him better, the only emotions that should be involved had to do with saving her family's reputation and ranch—nothing at all resembling what her parents had had.

"He does seem nice," Amber ventured, to keep the conversation going. "But we really don't know him very well. I'd be careful about getting too friendly with him." Although her mom knew him better than she did. Perhaps they'd become friends after Amber moved away, while her father was still alive. Maybe her dad and Nathan had been buddies.

Or not. Amber couldn't help considering everyone she met around here as possible suspects in her dad's murder, though she'd no reason to think it was Nathan.

And even if the former was the case, Amber hoped her mother wasn't putting herself in a situation where she'd be hurt in another way. The death of her husband was surely more than enough for now.

"Maybe, but the thing is, he does appear to be a wonderful businessman," Sonya said. "He's mentioned to me how he approves employees for his hotel, and supervises his staff in charge of hiring. He checks into applicants' backgrounds and skills and, well, while he watched your training class with me this afternoon he pointed out possible problems with Evan and how he does his new job."

Oh. That was none of Nathan's concern, or it

shouldn't be. Still…well, Amber had been in merchandise distribution before with the Ever Fitting clothing company, not human resources. She believed Evan was the person they needed to keep the K-9 Ranch going, but— "What problems?"

"Evan's dog skills seem fine," her mother said hurriedly, "but his people skills… We already talked a little about his PTSD but I guess it's obvious to more than just us."

"I thought he did fine with our students. Aaron needed a little disapproval, or at least some instruction in how best to get poor Baxter to obey commands without hurting him. Evan demonstrated how to do that."

"Right, but— Well, I just hope it got Aaron to change his ways without hurting his dog any more. Evan might have been too nice to the guy."

"But he singled him out, showed him how to do it right," Amber protested.

"Was that enough? And there was something going on also when Julie seemed to ask a question and Evan got all…well, uncomfortable. She looked concerned for a while. We didn't know what was going on, but you were right there." She looked expectantly toward Amber.

She'd been a little concerned about that, too. Julie had asked Evan to do something out of the routine he'd anticipated, like coming up right away with a new command to teach them. He had definitely seemed uncomfortable.

But he also promised to do that kind of thing in

future classes. It wasn't enough reason, not even combined with his way of quietly criticizing Aaron, to think he wasn't the right guy for the job.

Although she realized she might be biased. After all, she had chosen him from among other candidates.

And the fact she had started feeling a little attracted to him— Well, that was irrelevant.

She looked Sonya in her concerned brown eyes— something Evan was unlikely to do—and said, "I understand what you're saying and will keep it in mind while I supervise Evan. And learn what I can from him, too. Maybe even work with him on that book idea, about how Dad trained dogs and taught other potential trainers. If things don't work out, I may wind up being the head instructor, or I can hire someone else—though I really think Evan will be fine." She made herself smile at her mother.

Sonya's expression still looked troubled. "Maybe. Well…let me know if I can help. I think it'll be better if I don't let Nathan come around while classes are going on. He's not particularly into dogs and their training, so he may not be the best of judges. But—" She seemed to hesitate as she took a final bite of her tuna.

"But what?" Amber prompted in as lighthearted a tone as she could.

"But Nathan is so nice, and kind… And successful. He told me earlier how well things are going at his resort, that his property is the perfect size for him to keep expanding his hotel and related facilities.

But he also said that if things don't go well here he doesn't want us to suffer any more than necessary. He told me to let him know if we need help, and if so he would even try to work things out to buy our property for a good price so we wouldn't have to keep an unsuccessful business going."

Yeah, and offer her mother a job there? Her, too? Otherwise, they would probably leave town, Amber thought. Then what would happen to the apparent relationship with Sonya that guy seemed to be after?

Maybe it would be a good thing after all…

But what he described simply wasn't going to happen. They would be successful. She would make it happen. And she genuinely believed Evan would be an essential part.

"That's nice of him," she said, forcing herself not to show any emotion. "But if the subject comes up again, please let him know I'm sure we'll be here for a long time to come."

It was getting late. Evan had enjoyed his dinner alone with Bear, or so he'd told himself. That was how he'd spent most evenings for a long time before moving here. He was used to it. He had all the company he needed.

Never mind that he avoided glancing out the window toward the main house.

"We're better off on our own," he told Bear now as he washed his dinner dish and other things he had used in the metal kitchen sink. "Less stress." But as much as that phrase had helped him in the recent past, he felt less concerned about such things now. Sure there was a bit of stress in what he was doing, but the results would definitely be worth it. His most recent goal in the military—as opposed to when he was just concerned with surviving and healing—and in the work he had done afterward had been training dogs. He'd been schooled in it. Loved it.

And that was what he was doing here…thanks to Amber.

Too bad he couldn't just turn to her at the dinner table now and thank her again…

For dinner this evening he'd thawed a frozen meal that he'd bought. Bear's healthy canned dog food had looked more appealing. Yet he refused to use the idea of not liking what he'd had available for dinner as an excuse to go see Amber.

He had instead used the opportunity to go over in his mind what he'd accomplished that afternoon with the four students and their dogs. It had worked well. Some minor glitches, sure. But he would be prepared for Aaron's unnecessary forcefulness, and Julie's extra training ideas, next time. And he could incorporate what he'd learned as he took on additional students, since Amber clearly wanted him to start other classes.

Best of all, tomorrow he would work with those future K-9 puppies of Amber's again, and demonstrate to her how that kind of training was done.

He finished, putting his dish, flatware and a glass in the drying rack. Now, he could stay here, get on his laptop, or watch TV, or…

"It's time for a walk," he told Bear, who sat near him on the kitchen floor. His shepherd perked up immediately. Bear recognized a lot of words, and "walk" was among his favorites. He stood and began slowly circling Evan, who laughed. "Okay, let's do it."

Because he didn't know the kinds of creatures who might also be out after dark on this ranch, or other kinds of distractions that could cause Bear to react, he decided to leash him despite what a well-behaved dog he was.

Besides, one of Evan's excuses to himself was that he wanted to approach the main house and check to see if his young canine students of tomorrow might be outside, possibly being walked by Amber or even just fenced in for their final nighttime outing.

He had no intention of knocking on the door if they didn't happen to be out, though. He had no reason to believe that Amber or her mother were in any kind of trouble that night or in dire need of talking with him.

No—no genuine excuses other than that Bear and he needed an outing. Although if he happened to see Amber outside with any of the dogs, he would be happy to say good-night to her.

Evan pulled on a gray sweatshirt though the May night wasn't too chilly. "Let's go, boy." Bear bounded toward him and Evan fastened the leash onto his collar. After he'd flicked on the outside light above the front door, they exited onto the front stoop. He looked around. A pole light he had noticed before was lit at the top of the main house's driveway, strong enough to provide a little illumination even this far away.

Tugging slightly on Bear's leash, he headed in that direction along the narrow walkway. He heard nothing except his footsteps on the paving and Bear's on dried leaves beside it, the distant motor of a plane and…was that an owl?

But he didn't hear Amber's voice talking to any of her dogs. His idea of possibly running into her seemed unlikely. It still wouldn't hurt for Bear and him to circle the house as part of their outing. He didn't have to mention it to Amber as his concerned way of ensuring their safety.

They passed the other houses along this row. There were no lights on inside or outside of Orrin's place, so the ranch hand must have gone to bed. They neared the main house, and Bear stopped walking and assumed the position he took while on duty as a K-9 when alerting because there was a potential bad guy ahead.

Evan stopped, too. He bent and whispered, "Good boy," without knowing what was on Bear's mind, but he trusted his dog. He rose and stood perfectly still, listening.

But he heard nothing more than he had before.

Bear's attention appeared riveted toward the back of the main house. Evan gave the hand signal to move, then slowly, quietly, he walked with his dog in that direction.

He saw a dim light, as if from a flashlight, behind the house. It was moving.

Damn. He wasn't armed—nor had he been since his return to the States. He needed to remain as stealthy as possible, sneak around to see who it was.

It might just be Amber walking around her backyard, with or without a dog. But if it was her, or her mother, why use a flashlight rather than turning on the house lighting? Or why not stay in the front, which was already illuminated from a light on a pole?

If it was Orrin, still awake, he'd surely have had his lights on.

Evan gave the motion to Bear to heel, not saying the word this time. He moved stealthily toward the house, intending to stay close, in its shadow, as much as possible. He just hoped Lola wasn't a good enough watchdog to sense them and start barking. The pups, even if they barked, probably did so enough that they wouldn't alarm the human occupants.

His shoulder nearly against the wall, he listened while continuing to move slowly but with determination. When he reached the corner, he motioned for Bear to stop and sit. Then, as carefully as he could, he peered around toward the back of the house.

He had walked there before with Amber, in daylight, on a brief tour of the property. Along with the driveway to the garage, this area consisted of another lawn not connected with the large, fenced expanse. It contained a garden, where flowers struggled to bloom this spring. Amber had also said she was growing tomatoes and other vegetables, but it was too early in the season for them.

None of that was relevant now. Whoever was there stood right behind the building, the flashlight indicating he—or she—was walking slowly toward Evan.

What should he do? He saw no weapon in the person's hands but that didn't mean he wasn't armed.

Nor did it mean he hadn't armed some kind of explosive nearby, perhaps against the house. But Bear was an explosives-detection dog and he hadn't reacted, so that was highly unlikely—and just Evan's military mind at work.

He motioned for Bear to stay, although he was prepared to give his dog a verbal command to attack. He pulled his phone from his pocket, and as he turned on its light he strode from behind the wall.

"Hi," he said in a normal tone of voice. "So who besides me is sneaking around this house?"

He heard a gasp, and the person stopped. Evan shone his phone light onto his face.

It was the most logical person to be out here: Orrin. But why was he sneaking around, and at this hour?

Chapter 9

"What the hell are you doing here?" Orrin demanded, aiming his flashlight toward Evan.

"I was going to ask you the same thing," he said calmly, stepping from the shadows with Bear at his side. He reached down to unhook his dog's leash, not a threatening gesture but it would hopefully keep this guy from doing anything foolish—unless he wanted a seventy-five-pound German shepherd attacking him. "Do you prowl in the dark around the ranch a lot?"

"Yes, if you really want to know." Orrin, dressed in black, approached Evan, though he kept his gaze down on Bear. "I'm sure you heard that the owner, Corbin, was murdered, right here on the ranch."

"Yes, I heard, although I'm not sure where it was."

"I know where, since I found him. Maybe I'll take you there someday." The young man's grin in the shadows, surrounded by his light beard and mustache, appeared almost threatening. Even Bear must have thought so since he moved slightly, but Evan put his hand in front of the dog's face to stop him— for now.

"Maybe so." Evan pondered whether to ask the question that was on his mind. Heck, why not? "I don't suppose you know who killed him, do you?"

Orrin's expression changed, and so did his tightened grip on the flashlight. Was he planning to attack Evan with it? But he didn't move. "The cops thought for a while that I did," he growled. "But I didn't, in case you're wondering. And even the cops don't think so now—though I don't know who's in their headlights at the moment."

"Glad to know that. So…why are you wandering around here in the dark?" He half expected the ranch hand to get even more defensive, ask him the same thing—anything but tell the truth, whatever it was.

"I do it a lot, just because." His chin lifted. "Two women live here. Maybe they can take care of themselves, and maybe not, but until a couple of days ago I'd been the only man around for a while—since the one in their lives was killed."

So maybe he was a nice guy—and not a murderer. Or was that all a put-on to keep Evan from asking more and suspecting him of the murder?

"That's very good of you," Evan said mildly. After all, if it was the truth then maybe what he did was a good thing. "But I'm sure you can see why I'm concerned about why you're out here in the dark with your flashlight." And hopefully no weapons. "I'm also concerned about those women now that I'm here." A thought struck him. "I assume you were buddies with Corbin, and that he treated you well, but I'd imagine that the women also—"

"What makes you assume that?" Orrin's voice was sharp, scornful. "He was a nasty SOB at times, definitely not generous, but I had to stay here and work because my family... Never mind. I don't want to get into it. But I had issues with him, and that's why the cops— Hell. I'm going to bed." He took a step forward, then stopped, looking down at Bear. "Is that animal going to attack me?"

"This is Bear. He's a well-trained dog." Evan paused, making sure he was in Orrin's path. "Do you like dogs? If not, this is a strange place for you to be working."

"Like I said, I don't want to get into why I work here. I like dogs okay but I sure as heck don't want to spend my life working with them like Corbin did— and you do. Now, let me by. Good night."

He sidestepped Evan and Bear, circling to the paved path that led to the nearby houses without another word.

Interesting, Evan thought. He decided that Bear and he would take their time on their outing tonight to make sure Orrin didn't return.

Plus, if Orrin did this a lot, maybe Evan and Bear would prowl around some nights, too.

Somehow, Orrin didn't strike him as the protective type, out here just to ensure his female employers weren't being attacked by whoever killed Corbin.

But he hadn't attempted to break into the house, nor had he attacked Amber or Sonya before Evan had been hired, when there was likely no one else around to protect them.

Did that mean he wasn't guilty? No, but it didn't make him the obvious murderer, either.

For now, Evan waited until he saw lights go on inside Orrin's house. That didn't mean he was inside for the night, but since the man knew Evan and Bear were out here he'd at least consider his options before coming out again.

Evan decided to complete his walk around the house, check to make sure that the doors were locked and no windows were open that would allow anyone to enter. He didn't expect to find other prowlers around but it wouldn't hurt to look.

He would tell Amber about Orrin tomorrow. She needed to know about her ranch hand, even if it was a completely innocent, or even protective, act.

"Come," he told Bear, snapping his leash on again. There might be no additional human prowlers, but nocturnal creatures could be out and about.

They remained, for now, at the back of the main house. There was a dim glow from somewhere inside but no indication whether anyone was still awake. No need to rouse Amber to tell her anything now, or Sonya, either.

Still… Evan, Bear at his side, walked up the paved

area to the narrow wooden door and reached to check whether it was locked.

And drew in his breath when, as he touched the knob, the door opened.

"Oh, hi, Evan," Amber said in as casual a voice as she could, flicking the inside switch so a light came on in the backyard. "You, too, Bear." She had one of the pups, Lucy, on a leash behind her. She'd intended to use a short walk as an excuse to be outside.

"Er, hi, Amber," Evan returned. "I didn't think anyone inside was still awake. I was just checking to make sure the door was locked."

She looked at him under the light. Despite his apparently being startled when she'd opened the door, he appeared alert but far from anxious now, even looked her briefly in the face. He also looked good, his dark hair somewhat windblown and a trace of beard on his face. His gray sweatshirt hugged his wide shoulders, and he held Bear's leash loosely in his right hand.

"Thanks… I guess. I think Lucy, Lola and I were the only ones awake, but I left Lola in the kitchen." The Lab was waiting for Amber to go to bed, still uneasy with sleeping in Sonya's room. But Amber had been working with the pups when she could, and this had seemed an appropriate outing for one.

Although if she'd needed some kind of defense… well, Lola was trained, but not as a protective K-9. But Amber had heard in advance who was outside so not having a defensive guard dog was okay.

"Everything all right inside?" Evan asked. "I didn't hear anything when I decided to check the lock."

"That's why you jumped when I opened the door. I get it, and I'm sorry."

Not exactly true, though it was polite to say. Maybe it shouldn't amuse her to have startled Evan, but she had been in the kitchen near the door to the rear of the house eavesdropping on his conversation with Orrin. Before they'd begun talking, she had been sitting nearly in the dark at the kitchen table sipping a cup of chamomile tea, hoping it would relax her and let her get to sleep, though it hadn't seemed to be working.

She hadn't known they were there until the two men began talking.

Orrin prowled a lot at night? She'd seen him out late now and then while walking Lola or a pup, but not often. Did he sometimes hide, even from the dogs? If so, why? And why had Evan been out there tonight, his second night at the K-9 Ranch?

Somehow, though she felt a bit uneasy about Orrin's presence there, she felt grateful for Evan's. Even though she had startled him.

"No problem. And now that you and Lucy are here, let's take a quick walk around the house in case either Bear or her have something on their minds before going to bed."

"Good idea." It also felt like a good idea to be in Evan's presence one last time for the night. Not that she expected him to teach her something new about dog training. But she liked to be with him.

Neither said anything to the other at first, but they both watched and praised the dogs with them. Then Evan said, "I'd initially just come outside to walk Bear—and maybe check on the property's security. Bear sensed Orrin outside your house, and I wound up confronting him. I got the impression he did that a lot, maybe to do as I was, ensure that all was okay. Were you aware of that?"

"Not really." She admitted, though, that she had occasionally run into him when she took a dog out late. "He's never said what he was doing, but I had the impression he was just trying to tire himself out before sleeping."

"Or make sure all's well around here. How long has he worked for your family?"

They were now approaching the flat part of the driveway at the side of the house, where her father had conducted a lot of his K-9 lessons. That was where Amber would ask Evan to start working with the pups tomorrow. For now, she just let Lucy's leash grow slack as both dogs continued their sniffing.

"Since we bought this place," Amber finally replied. She had heard him talking briefly with Orrin about her dad. "Orrin's parents were my father's neighbors and good friends, as he grew up in San Luis Obispo. They'd stayed in touch, and when my dad decided to run this ranch he learned that Orrin was looking for a job—apparently something that required more strength than thinking. The timing just worked out, and it was also kind of a favor to Orrin's folks."

"That's good." But Evan's tone sounded dubious. Should she tell him more? Maybe.

"Orrin doesn't get along too well with anyone, but that was okay with my dad. They argued some but everything necessary got done. And though he sometimes delays for a while, Orrin is also doing what we need him to around here now, handyman stuff. Otherwise, I'd find as kind a way as possible to fire him."

Evan grew quiet, then said, "He did mention your dad while we were talking. He also mentioned how they didn't always get along."

"And you're wondering if Orrin killed him." She couldn't help it. She stopped walking and all but confronted Evan.

Not because she resented what he was suggesting, but because she wondered that sometimes herself.

"Yes," he responded softly. "But we don't need to talk about—"

"Yes, we do. If not now, then sometime. I don't know if it was Orrin. I don't want to think so, but it could be. And you know that my dad was found, his body was found…" She had to stop as her throat closed up.

Evan suddenly was right beside her, holding her, hugging her close. "Orrin said he found him, on your property. And, of course, Orrin had access to it."

"So did a lot of other people," she said hesitantly. "Including Dad's students—and some argued with him. Also, anyone who felt like going through our unsecure wood fence around the place could come through, so the robbery idea makes sense, too." She was shaking but at least she wasn't crying...yet.

"I think it's time for us to stop this," Evan said. "If it's all right with you I'd like to come in for a glass of water."

And to make sure she was safe, she figured. She appreciated it.

"That's okay. *I'm* okay." She pulled gently away, though she immediately missed the feel of his strong arms around her, the way she had been able to rest her cheek against his hard chest. "Time for Lucy and me to go to bed."

"Sure, if you think—"

"I'll be fine."

But he didn't move, and neither did she.

Then she asked something that had been on her mind since Evan first arrived with Bear, a trained K-9. "Evan, does Bear have scenting skills?"

"Yes. He's an explosives-sniffing dog, among his other abilities."

"Anything else?"

"He knows how to sniff out bad guys and their scents when they're afraid, and more. But why—"

"Because...well, after all this time there's not going to be anything at the spot where my dad was found, and the local cops brought a K-9 or two to the site. But I've wanted to observe a dog who knows what he's doing sniffing around. Sometime. Not right away. But would you be willing to bring Bear?"

"Of course." He took a step toward Amber as Bear stayed with him, looking up. He'd probably heard his name. "You're right, though. After all this time there's not likely to be anything he can react to. But we'll give it a try when you're ready."

Amber attempted to smile at him as she said, "Thanks." Then, to punctuate the word, she moved toward him, reached up and pulled his head down to plant a grateful kiss on his mouth.

He responded right away, holding her closer, deepening the kiss. This was a guy with PTSD who didn't want to get too near people?

Maybe, but he was also one hot, hard, sexy guy, who made her mind go in another wrong direction in addition to thinking of her poor, deceased dad.

She threw herself into the kiss for a long minute, then pulled away. She gave the leash a gentle tug, then said, "Let's go, Lucy." She looked back toward Evan. "Good night. We'll see you around nine tomorrow morning so you can start the pups' preliminary K-9 training."

He looked at her, straight in the face. His expression seemed bemused—and maybe a little regretful that she'd pulled away. But he just said, "Right. Good night. See you in the morning."

"Great." She turned, then ran to the house's front door. She used the key in her pocket to open it.

After ensuring that Lucy was inside, too, she locked it behind her.

Chapter 10

Around nine o'clock the next morning, Evan prepared to head to the main house to start his dog training—the pre-K-9 kind that he especially enjoyed, though not as much as the actual K-9 training. Still, this day promised to be a good one.

"So, Bear." He looked down at his shepherd, who stood wagging his tail inside the door to their house. "Sorry, but you'll stay here for now." Bear knew what he was doing and he was damn good at it. But dogs, unlike humans, didn't necessarily learn much from watching others who were well trained. Today was about continuing the minimal training the puppies had previously received.

Evan had already walked Bear, fed him and rewarded his good behavior by playing with the tug toy with him.

Evan had eaten, too—some of the cereal and milk he'd picked up in town. He looked forward to inviting Amber, and Sonya, too, over for a hotcakes breakfast, but that would have to wait.

He wouldn't mind having Amber sleep here so he could feed her breakfast after a night of…

Hey, where was his mind going? The charcoal athletic pants he'd pulled on that morning beneath a matching shirt tightened, and he made himself start thinking again about the nonsexy but fun lessons he was about to give.

As he got more into training and the pups grew older, he would wear something resembling a K-9 police officer uniform to get them used to it. But at six months of age, they still had time to mature and learn the basics before more official training kicked in.

"See you soon, boy." He patted his dog and gave him a good-sized treat, then walked out, shutting and locking the door behind him. He'd locked it before, but after last night it felt even more critical.

On his doorstep, he stretched his arms and body, looked up at the overcast sky and grinned at nothing and no one. He had awakened feeling good. Part of it was that he'd confronted Orrin last night, so just in case the ranch hand had something nefarious in mind he would be aware now that he was on Evan's radar. If anything happened around here that shouldn't, Evan would go to him first.

And had Orrin had anything to do with killing

Corbin? Evan certainly hadn't crossed him off the list, particularly since Amber hadn't.

He even pasted a scowl on his face as he passed Orrin's house and looked in that direction. Not that he expected the guy to be looking out, but, just in case, he wanted it clear he was watching him.

As soon as he turned away, that scowl became a smile. He was about to see Amber. His boss. But what a boss…

Revving up his pace, he soon found himself on the porch stairs of the main house. He knocked on the front door.

He couldn't help smiling as he heard the barks, deep ones and shrill ones, of the canines inside. Apparently they considered themselves watchdogs. Sure, he could train that out of them, but sometimes it was a good thing to have the additional security.

His smile vanished as he thought of why that was potentially even more necessary here than other places.

The door opened. Amber appeared with Lola at her side. "Hi," she said. "You're right on time." Her smile and nod changed his mood once more, though not entirely. She might be acknowledging him in a good way, but his mind remained on his concerns for his boss and her mother.

And what had happened somewhere on this ranch to the man whose training position Evan had now taken.

"Good," he said, following Amber into the house,

with Lola now at his side. He patted the dog briefly, and Lola looked up into his face as if thanking him.

Amber wore a blue work shirt today, loose over her jeans, and it was decorated with small yellow flowers. He resisted an urge to stroke them…or her. He hoped she would just lead him to the room housing the young dogs so he could get Hal, the one he'd decided to train first that day.

Instead, she led him into the kitchen, where Sonya was loading things into the dishwasher beside the sink. "Good morning." She stopped to face Evan. "Do we get to watch you today?"

"Of course. My dog students need to learn to obey whether there are people or other dogs around—although, today I want to work with them one at a time."

"Great." Sonya wiped her hands with a dish towel. She was dressed more casually than Evan had seen her previously, in a plain yellow T-shirt over jeans, and both her clothes and her demeanor appeared comfortable. "Which one first?"

"I think it'll be—"

He was interrupted by the ringing of Amber's cell phone, behind him. He turned instinctively. Looking at her mother, Amber mouthed *Percy.*

Evan wondered what the computer geek wanted, though it wasn't any of his business. But that turned out to be partially wrong.

Amber left the room as she said hello, and Evan told Sonya that he intended to begin working with

Hal. "Any of them would be fine, though, since I'll have a session with each of them today."

As he finished, Amber returned to the room. "I'd like you to join our conversation," she said to Evan. Sitting at the kitchen table, she pushed the speaker button before holding out the phone.

"Er," said the voice at the other end. "I—I was telling Amber I thought it would be a great thing for the K-9 Ranch website to have a section containing videos of some dog-training classes. Okay? Evan, are you there? She said she wanted to check with you."

Evan sat down beside Amber, as did Sonya. He gazed into Amber's face. Its usual loveliness was marred a bit by a questioning look. "I rather like the idea," she said. "At least once we're ready to start scheduling more classes. I'll be looking for all kinds of ways to attract potential students. What do you think?"

Him. His classes. The good parts, the not-so-good parts, preserved for posterity on video. And not only preserved, but also available for the whole world to see.

On the other hand, all those viewers wouldn't be right in his presence, in his face, which would be a relief. And for him to do his job right, he would need to do as Amber wanted and find ways to attract new students.

He knew he was a skilled trainer. Even so... "Good idea," he said, hiding his hesitation. "But to get people to come here with their dogs, let's just provide a few teasers, show a bit of what our dogs in training have accomplished without detailed demonstrations of how they got there. Okay?"

He looked toward Amber, who nodded. "Sounds okay to me. We'll let you know when we're ready, Percy."

Silence at first, then he said, "Fine. I was hoping, though, to come there and start filming, maybe even today."

Amber's eyes widened, then she appeared irritated. "As I said, we'll let you know. Thanks for the idea, though. The other ones, too."

There had been other ones? Evan was curious what they were.

Maybe the geek had some kind of crush on Amber and was attempting to come up with ways to see her.

And maybe—

Something occurred to him. "Percy, does the website have any videos of Corbin's classes? If so, I can understand why you'd suggest new ones to encourage students to come now."

"No." The word came hastily. "He didn't want them, but he had a great reputation already so he didn't need to do that."

Evan met Amber's annoyed glance again, and also felt Sonya stir behind him at the table. "Yes, I gather he did," Evan said. "And I hope to attain a great reputation eventually, too." He enjoyed watching Amber's expression morph into a grin, and he grinned back at her. He turned then to look at Sonya. Her smile wasn't huge, but she nodded encouragingly.

"Are you doing okay accessing the ranch's email now, Amber?" That was Percy's next question.

"Yes, and I appreciate your getting me access to it But it's mostly junk mail, though some messages are from former students asking if there will be more classes soon."

"Well, if you need any more help getting into email, or blocking spam or whatever, you know how to reach me."

"I do, Percy. Thanks. 'Bye now." She pressed the button to hang up.

Sonya was the first to speak. "I think he means well, but… I thought you just wanted him to update the website."

"True, but as I've given him input I made it clear that my technological knowledge is minimal and I didn't mind suggestions." She paused. "I may pull the plug on that, though he isn't charging for ideas, just the things I ask him to do."

"I get it," Evan said. "Now, if you ladies will excuse me, it's time for me to take Hal out for his lesson."

Amber stayed in the kitchen with her mother and Lola for a few minutes, attempting to get her thoughts together.

Percy was a nice guy, good at what he did. But he'd been getting in touch with her more often than she felt comfortable with, almost daily, with lots of questions and ideas, and suggestions that they get together to discuss them.

Still, until she felt the website was all she'd wanted it to be, she didn't want to alienate him. Even then, she would need him to update it now and then.

The good thing was that she had wanted to get word out that the K-9 Ranch was up and running again. And having Percy add teaser videos as well as updating the website with the reopening announcement, and hints about when different kinds of classes would be starting, could only help.

So did encouraging the four initial students who'd already been here to let other potential ones know.

As she'd already indicated, Amber even planned to contact her father's former students once Evan was ready to start additional classes—including all those whom she would list as having sent messages to the ranch's email address.

And, of course, she would give a copy of the list to Kara to have those people checked out, too, in addition to the list she'd already given her that contained her dad's computerized list of students.

But for now, it felt good to hurry outside to the training area at the top of the driveway to the side of the house. The flat area there was large enough to allow for larger classes when the time was right. She'd told Evan to work with Hal there.

When she reached it she stayed back, watching. At the moment, Evan was kneeling on the pavement playing with Hal with a tug toy. The pup pulled on it, crouched and growled, his tail wagging. Maybe it was the way he would pull on a bad guy's arm or leg after he was a fully trained K-9. Amber remained quiet, feeling her grin light up her face.

Evan must have been aware of her, since, without looking at her, he said, "Good dog. Now we'll give a demo of what we did that led to this game as the reward."

Evan stood and clipped a leash on the correction collar already around Hal's neck. "Come," he said, and the pup immediately released the tug toy and stood. Then Evan said, "Heel," and began walking slowly away from where Amber stood. Hal remained at his side with the leash loose, no pulls or corrections necessary.

Evan picked up the pace and Hal remained with him. Then, abruptly, Evan gestured and said, "Sit." The pup again obeyed immediately. "Good boy," Evan said warmly, then gave the command to heel again. This time he walked faster and so did Hal, keeping up as they went in a circle, then a figure eight, then Evan stopped and said, "Sit." Hal obeyed, and Evan laughed. "Good boy."

This time, Evan pulled a ball from his pocket and, after unhooking the leash from Hal's collar, he threw it. Of course, Hal went after it. As the pup dashed in that direction, Evan looked at Amber.

"Care to heel?" he said. "Oh, that's not a command. Heel." He nodded almost curtly but didn't look away at all. "Or should I put a collar on you, too?"

Amber laughed as Hal returned with the ball. "I think you already have the right company for that." Evan smiled, too, and tossed the ball once more.

This time when Hal returned with it, Evan told him to sit. The pup again obeyed, and for the next ten minutes Amber stood at the side of the training area watching as the pup who had seemed playful but less than eager to follow commands—though not as naughty as his brother, Rex—obeyed perfectly, again rewarded now and then with a little playtime.

Amber could have watched this forever, but as Evan appeared ready to end the lesson her mother joined her.

"Sorry, I meant to come out before," she called. "Could you give me a little demonstration?"

"Sure." And Evan went through the same exercises again. This time Sonya laughed and clapped and cheered, and Amber felt pleased all over again about having hired this skilled trainer.

Eventually, though, he stopped and joined them. Hal was at his side without a leash on and was sniffing the ground.

Amber grinned. "Looks like your new friend is happy about listening to you, at least today."

"Yep, at least today." He aimed a smile at her, then turned it toward her mother. "But I've got two more students I need to work with. Will you continue watching?" His tone had changed just a little—he seemed somewhat hesitant—and Amber recognized that he must be feeling at least a little uncomfortable.

"For a while," Amber said. "Especially since I liked what I saw. So who's next?"

She met Evan's gaze. He'd relaxed. In fact, he now looked at her with a different expression. It was

warm and… Sexy? No, couldn't be, though everything about this man, when he wasn't looking away
in discomfort, seemed inappropriately hot to her.

Maybe she should stay inside for his next lesson.
Or leave right away to handle the idea percolating
in her mind. But probably not.

"It's Lucy's turn," he said.

As they returned to the house for him to take in
Hal and fetch Lucy, Evan was pleased when Amber
offered to bring both the other pups for a brief visit
outside.

"Sure," Evan answered. They made a good team
when it came to the dogs.

He followed her and her mother inside to wait in
the hall with Hal. Sonya indicated she would stay
there with Lola.

Amber soon joined Evan and Hal in the entry with
the other pups, both leashed. As they walked the pups
slowly, Rex in particular strained at his leash, so Evan
traded, giving Amber Hal's leash and also Lucy's.

"Heel," he told Rex, then stood still until that pup
stopped pulling. Rex stayed at Evan's side as he led
the whole group to the special fenced-in area for
the pups.

Once they were inside, all three were released.
"Go," Evan said, and they ran around energetically.

"I thought you at least wore Hal out," Amber said
with a smile, standing beside him at the gate.

"So did I. Maybe he's communicating to the others what we did, which would be a good thing."

They remained there for about five minutes, Evan glancing often toward Amber and enjoying the pleased look on her face as she watched the playing dogs.

"Hard to believe they'll be obedient K-9s someday," she said. Was there a question in her voice?

"They will," he told her with confidence. Maybe even nearly as good as Bear. So far he believed Corbin had done a good job in selecting these three, even as young puppies, as potential skilled working dogs.

Corbin. The more Evan learned about the man, the more he wished he'd met him, maybe even worked for him—although he knew as much as anyone that Corbin Belott had been a solitary trainer of dogs and people, and hadn't even allowed videos of his training on his website. Evan understood that.

So what person had turned on him?

Almost as if she sensed his thoughts, Amber looked toward him. Her pretty, reddish hair blew in the breeze, a sexy cap that caressed her cheeks and taunted him to do the same. But, of course, he didn't. "So," she said, her voice soft in the outside air, "would you like me to take Rex and Hal inside so you can get started again?"

"How about the other way—I'll take them in, and you wait here with Lucy." He wanted to ensure that the two males settled into their quarters quietly, not that Amber was unqualified to handle them. But this way she would still be outside on his return.

"Sure," she said, and Evan got the three pups to the gate to be leashed.

"Be right back." He handed Lucy's leash to Amber.

He had no problem enclosing the males in their room. Evan saw Sonya and invited her again to watch, but she thanked him and said no.

When he returned outside, Evan watched, amused, as Amber accompanied Lucy on her wide walk around the lawn and part of the driveway. Lucy was a member of the pack with the other two, but now that she was on her own, she demonstrated special interests—and useful skills—even before they reached the training area.

She seemed fascinated by smells along the ground, including the driveway, and even stood up with her paws on Evan's leg as she sniffed his slacks as if checking his pockets for treats.

The toys were there, undoubtedly smelling like happy dogs to the pup. He had included a few dog treats, too, but that wasn't his training method so he hadn't given them out yet.

Even so, her clear fascination with scents was a great thing to know about for her training.

She might even have demonstrated an early version of it when Corbin picked her and the others out from whatever litter he'd found them in. He'd have known that well-trained K-9s usually had to have additional skills besides finding and restraining bad guys, and an exceptional sense of smell was among them.

Bear, for example, was a great scent dog, both for finding bad guys and explosives. He'd found the one that had detonated… No. This was certainly not a good time to recall that.

"I wish I knew what she was smelling." Amber's call brought his thoughts back to the present.

"Probably nothing we'd enjoy." He attempted to sound cheerful despite what was going on inside him. "But it's great that she appears to. Okay, come to the training area and let's get started. If you have questions about my methods, be sure to save them and we'll talk about them later."

For the next half hour, Evan put Lucy through the same kinds of exercises that he'd used with Hal. She did well, clearly wanting, once she had gotten used to the idea, to obey him and even excel.

Of course, Evan knew he was attributing human thoughts to the dogs. He did that often—particularly because the idea seemed to fit the smart canines he worked with.

When he finished with Lucy, Amber was still watching. Smiling. That made him happy, too.

He went to get Rex. That lesson was a bit more challenging but he believed he made progress with that energetic young dog. Despite Rex's occasional disobedience, Evan believed the pup would eventually make a skilled K-9, one who'd excel at cornering and bringing down bad guys.

Evan felt proud of his progress, even with Rex, and the apparent approval he saw on Amber's face. Sonya seemed to approve, too, when the older woman came outside a couple of times to watch.

When he'd finished with Rex and rewarded him

with an energetic ball game, Evan approached the two women by the fence. "We're done for today. Want to ask any questions now? We could go inside and talk."

"It looked wonderful," Amber said, boosting his ego even more, and he looked forward to talking with her. But that anticipation vanished when she continued, "I definitely want to talk to you later. And, Mom, I'd appreciate it if you'd save any comments you have until later, too. I need to go downtown for a little while now."

To see that Percy geek? Buy something? Whatever her reason, Evan felt a bit deflated.

Still, he just said, "Okay. We'll talk later."

Chapter 11

Amber hurried into the house, leaving her mother with Evan, Rex and Lola. Her mom would be able to help Evan get inside to put Rex back in the den with his brother and sister.

Their earlier discussion with Percy had planted a seed in her mind that had escalated into a strong desire: to go hand Kara the list of addresses from emails sent to her father by former students as soon as possible, and then talk to her about the current status of the investigation. Amber loved watching Evan's wonderful training exercises, but she could no longer ignore that urge. She was going downtown.

She hurried into her bedroom, an adequate-sized hangout for her, with a queen-size bed with a neutral peach-colored coverlet on top, a tall dresser and a small table with a chair in front of it that she used for a desk when she wasn't at the dining room table.

She grabbed the list of emails she'd previously made on the computer, printed and brought in here so her mom wouldn't see it and get upset. She had stuck it in a small pile of magazines and snail mail she'd left on the table, figuring her mother would have no interest in rummaging through that. She picked up her purse, checked to make sure her phone and car keys were in it and left.

She was glad to see that Evan appeared to be working with her mom and Lola, maybe giving an obedience lesson, as Rex dashed around the fenced-in area around them. Unsure if they noticed her, she waved goodbye anyway as she went around to the garage.

She sat down in the driver's seat, but before starting to back out she called the Chance Police Department and asked for Assistant Police Chief Province. Though Kara sounded a bit surprised, her tone seemed almost sympathetic as she said she could spare a few minutes to talk.

Ending the call, Amber headed down the driveway and toward downtown Chance. She met no cars going in either direction until she reached the town's outskirts. She continued to think of what she would say—and why she was going there.

Kara undoubtedly guessed the topic of their upcoming conversation, but not the entire reason for it. Amber had mentioned the emails to her, her excuse for coming. They needed to be turned over to make sure the authorities had that information in addition to the computerized list of her dad's students that Amber provided before.

The only urgency about getting the email info to them this quickly was inside Amber.

Ridiculous, yes, but as she'd watched Evan give those three young potential K-9s their classes, she had recalled watching her dad do something similar now and then when she'd been visiting and he'd brought other young dogs in for initial training.

Their methods were far from identical. The verbal commands were similar, and some moves for sitting and heeling were, too. But despite probably having been trained similarly in the military for working with K-9s, the two men had their own methods of turning and repositioning and ensuring the pups' attention.

That concerned Amber. What if her dad had been murdered because he'd been so good at giving those lessons?

Stupid? Yes. But no good motive had yet been found for his death. Her mind had just come up with another scary idea. And in the remote—very remote—chance that it had been some kind of jealous dog trainer or someone whose reason was equally odd, she was now concerned that she had brought Evan into a potentially dangerous situation.

She'd be concerned about anyone she might have endangered. But Evan— Well, she liked the guy…perhaps too much. Admired him, even with his PTSD. Maybe partly because of it, since he appeared to be dealing with it relatively well.

She wanted him to do a good job, especially since she hoped he would be working with her for a long time.

She reached the first traffic light as she entered the small yet busy town and made the turns to the police station. She wouldn't tell anyone, especially not Evan, what was on her mind.

Probably not Kara, either, in their upcoming conversation.

She only hoped she would be able to get initial answers from the assistant police chief.

Evan enjoyed the small lesson he was imparting to Sonya, here on the sloping, fenced-in grassy area.

For one thing, Lola was a smart dog, and Sonya clearly enjoyed working with her—and with him.

For another, it kept his mind off Amber's abrupt departure—sort of—and his curiosity about what she was up to.

The air was warm this late May morning. The dew on the lawn when he'd first started his lessons was dry now. He was glad, since he would have hated to see Sonya slip while working with the dogs and him.

He wondered why he was the one to be teaching Sonya some of the elementals, why her husband hadn't done it while he was alive.

But Evan had already gotten the impression that Corbin had been happy to teach other people how to become trainers only if they'd take on that mission elsewhere. Corbin had no assistants to help him with any teaching here on his K-9 ranch. He'd been somewhat solitary, as Evan tended to be—though Evan recognized that as part of his PTSD and was working hard to get past it.

"Okay, Lola, sit," called Sonya, off to Evan's right. She made the motion he had shown her. Lola just looked at her.

"Keep it simple," Evan told her. "Just say 'sit.'"

She nodded, and her reddish hair, like her daughter's, bobbed a little despite being fastened up on her head. "Okay." She walked closer to her Lab. "Sit." She made the same motion. This time, Lola obeyed. That got a cheer from Sonya, and she kneeled to hug her dog.

Evan just laughed. "We need to work some more on this if you really want to learn training techniques."

As her daughter clearly did. Evan wished Amber was here, too, learning the lesson with her mom.

"I'm enjoying it anyway," Sonya said with a smile that quickly faded. "I just wish I'd learned… My husband preferred doing this on his own."

Evan simply nodded. "Well, I'm here to help now. Just tell me how much you want to learn and I'll try to work it out."

He continued to wish he had met Corbin. Maybe he would have a better understanding about the guy's teaching methods. Corbin must have been a good guy in many ways, not only because he worked well with dogs, but this very nice woman had also been married to him.

And Amber was his daughter...

Amber. What was she up to? It wasn't his business, yet he remained concerned about her, a feeling that would continue for as long as he worked here. Maybe longer.

Especially if her father's killer wasn't found.

He'd make no promises, of course. But if he accomplished little else while he was here, he hoped to help remedy that situation.

While he did a damn good job training dogs.

The Chance Police Department was located in the small civic center on Chance Avenue. Amber had given her name to the policewoman at the reception desk and was shown into Kara Province's office right away.

Kara, in her black uniform, was behind her large, neat desk, looking as slim and tall while seated as she did while standing. "Please sit down, Amber." She motioned to one of the chairs on wheels facing her. Her dark hair formed a feathery frame around her face, and her deep brown eyes looked concerned. "Everything okay at the ranch?"

Amber took a seat. The chair was stiff and uncomfortable but she hadn't come here to relax. "Things are going pretty well," Amber said. That was true. Evan had certainly made a difference—in multiple ways. "But I'd feel even better if we had some answers about...well, you know."

It wasn't really in her nature to dissemble that way, but she felt uncomfortable asking a cop about how the investigation into her father's murder was going. Even though that was why she was here.

"I wish I had answers for you." The look on Kara's face seemed compassionate and understanding—but it didn't provide Amber with what she wanted. "You can be sure that once we solve that crime, you'll be the first civilian we let know about any apprehension of a suspect."

Which meant they not only had to figure out who'd done it, but would probably also find and arrest that person before telling Amber anything more. She could understand that but didn't have to like it. "Thank you," she said anyway. "The reason I came was to give you this."

She handed Kara the printed list she had made that contained the names and email addresses of those who'd sent emails to the ranch's account.

As Kara looked at it, Amber said, "I know I already gave you the list of students who'd attended my dad's classes for the last year or so, but I only got access to this email account recently and thought this information might be helpful, too." At least as long as the authorities considered the possibility of any student being disgruntled enough to have hurt her father.

She still preferred thinking it was some kind of random trespasser who'd decided to rob her father instead of someone her mother, or even she, had met, or perhaps even a jealous fellow trainer…but if that was so, the person might never get caught.

Kara looked toward her. "Can I see the emails, too?"

"Sure. I can forward them to you, if you'd like. There's nothing particularly personal about them. Or threatening, either. I just wanted to make sure you had whatever information I could pass along."

"That would be fine."

"Oh, and another thought I had," Amber said, "is that my father had such a wonderful reputation as a trainer... Well, are you looking into the possibility that any competitor wanted to eliminate him?"

"That's one potential motive we've been looking into."

"Great." But Amber almost regretted that they'd thought of it, too. She wasn't suggesting anything new, anything they could jump on now and quickly solve the crime. "I can give you the list of trainers we interviewed before we hired Evan, but I doubt it would be any of them."

"Fine. It wouldn't hurt to check." Kara's smile was sympathetic. "As I've told you, we're doing all we can to solve this. There are very few homicides in Chance, and the department wants to bring in whoever did it as soon as possible."

"I understand," Amber said. She also understood what Kara wasn't saying. Their police force wasn't large. Their resources were few. With hardly any homicides to investigate, their skills might be limited.

In other words, there might never be a resolution to what happened to her father.

Amber considered that unacceptable—but she also considered it probable reality.

She asked, "I don't suppose you've found anything to indicate that continuing to give dog-training classes at the ranch will somehow cause whoever killed my father to strike again, have you?"

"We have no reason to think you or your mother are in any danger," Kara said, "but please be careful and let us know if you get any sense of someone intending you any harm."

"And our new trainer? Does he— I mean, does the fact that we have someone now giving lessons as my dad did mean our new guy could be in trouble?"

"Once again, we don't have reason to think so, but you should inform him of what we've been talking about, too. He should also remain alert."

"Like the dogs he trains," Amber said, unable to help herself.

"Yes," Kara agreed. "Like the dogs he trains. Look, I understand how scared you might be and how hard this situation is, Amber. It's not in my job description to be too friendly with anyone affected by a crime, but I'd like to stay in contact with you, and not just for gathering evidence. Maybe we could meet for lunch or dinner someday and just talk. I like dogs, you know. I thought about becoming one of our K-9 handlers but wound up getting into administration instead. But maybe I could take a class anyway to learn that kind of skill, too."

"Maybe so." Amber smiled.

"Great," Kara said. "Now, I hate to kick you out,

but I've got another meeting coming up. But if you happen to get any additional ideas about who killed your dad, feel free to call me anytime."

"Of course," Amber said. And she hoped she would get some new amazing insight immediately that she could pass along so they could learn the truth.

Amber's mind remained on their inconclusive conversation as she walked to her car in the civic-center parking lot. Nothing new yet.

She purposely drove past Percy's Cords and Clouds shop as she started back to the ranch, wondering if that was a mistake. But she didn't see him through the shop's relatively small windows, and he probably didn't see her.

Even if they'd seen each other, so what? She felt sure the tech guy would stay in touch, wanting whatever business he could get from the ranch and the upkeep of its website. And maybe to flirt despite her not encouraging it.

But other than giving her access to the ranch's emails, he had done nothing to help her figure out what had happened to her father.

What else could she do to find answers? Even if she wanted to, she had no idea how to goad the killer into revealing himself—or herself—without having any idea about motive, let alone identity. Unless it had been a robbery, and if so, that person was unlikely to return to do it again, assuming it was a visitor to town.

And why would a resident do such a terrible thing?

She turned onto the narrow road toward the ranch, still feeling frustrated. She wanted to do something.

She had to do something.

And then it hit her, what she could actually do this afternoon.

Would it result in the answers she wanted? Highly unlikely, especially after all this time.

But it would at least be doing something positive.

Something Evan could help with—better than anyone else around here.

And he'd expressed an interest in doing it.

All Amber had to do was to finally schedule the time to lead Evan, and his well-trained K-9 specializing in scenting skills, to the area where she believed her dad had been murdered.

All she had to do…could she do it?

She had to.

Chapter 12

Evan was in the puppy room of the main house when he heard Amber return from her outing and start conversing with Sonya in the kitchen.

He didn't suppose that was what she or her mother called this room—a den, maybe, or family room. But it had been fitted out and organized to house the pups in training. He supposed family room fit best, since he considered canines he trained to be relatives of sorts, even those who wound up being acquired for their trained skills by other people or police departments. He gathered that Amber and her mother considered these young dogs, and Lola, their family, too.

His own family—parents and older sister—lived in Chicago. They kept in touch, cared about him, but no one had been pleased when he'd joined the military. Nor did they particularly like dogs. They'd made it clear they expected him to return home once he was discharged after his disastrous deployment in Afghanistan, but he had too much to deal with to try to become the son and brother they'd hoped for. At least not yet. And Bear was even closer to him, and more understanding, than they were.

Now he was down on the linoleum floor, socializing with the dogs. Well, playing with them, a good form of socialization.

He was nearly ready to head back to Bear and put his smart dog through his paces to help his own state of mind. But he'd hung out here hoping to see Amber again.

He needed to learn what she had planned for him tomorrow, Saturday. He wouldn't usually have weekends off, but Amber hadn't confirmed yet whether she had scheduled any classes on this one. As time went on, he would do most of his scheduling himself.

He held rambunctious Rex against his chest and patted tail-wagging Lucy. Hal just sat watching them. "See you guys later." Evan put down Rex and rose to his feet.

Time to go see his boss…and that thought made him grin.

He had only taken a few steps before Amber appeared at the door, Lola at her side. "Hi, Evan." He couldn't quite read her expression, but thought he saw a ghost of a smile, although it appeared forced.

In fact, if he had to describe what she looked like, his first guess would be…tormented.

He had an urge to hurry toward her, hold her against him, ask what was wrong. He wasn't sure where she had gone but wished he knew now.

"Hey, Amber, welcome back," he said. "Ready for more training demos this afternoon? Or a discussion about classes we can provide this week? Or—"

"Good guess that I want to command your presence now for a meeting with me." She laughed—sort of. "But you didn't guess the reason yet."

"Let me guess, then. You want me to participate in a guessing game?" If she wanted to attempt to keep this discussion light, he'd try to oblige her despite seeing pain in her lovely brown eyes.

"Nope. But I do want to give you a direction for the rest of the day, as your boss."

Uh-oh. He'd been attempting to look her straight in the eye but gave that up. "What's that?" He tried not to sound unhappy. He'd known what he was getting into by taking this job.

"You mentioned yesterday that you'd be willing to come with me to the area where my father was killed and bring Bear along, in case there's something he can sniff out about the location or murder weapon or whatever. I'd like you to do that now."

Really? He liked the idea, had thought of it himself. But not now, while she seemed to be in pain.

"I'm not sure this is the right time," he said.

"Sure it is. We'll make it a training session for Lola, too. My dad really loved her, as we do. He trained her, but not as an official K-9, just encouraging some of her best skills, like scenting and some tracking, that kind of thing. She won't do as well as Bear, but maybe she can help. If not, it'll be a good exercise for her." She paused. "We'll come with you to your house to get Bear, since the area is… It's that direction on the ranch property."

"All right, but, as we discussed, the chances of the dogs sensing anything are remote." Like, almost impossible after all this time. But what if the killer had dropped something that the cops, or their K-9s, had missed?

What if the killer had returned to the scene of the crime and left a scent or more? That happened sometimes, didn't it?

In any event, even if nothing helpful came from this outing, maybe it would at least offer Amber one more step toward closure.

"I understand," she said. "But let's do it anyway."

"Yes, please," said a voice from behind Amber. "I'll stay here so I won't hold you back, but I'll be eager to hear what happens." So Sonya, too, wanted to learn if the dogs could find anything else.

The pressure was on, Evan thought, though he'd already warned them that nothing was likely to result.

But he and Bear would at least give it a try.

This was undoubtedly a mistake, Amber thought as she led Evan, Bear and Lola up into the hills beyond the house where Evan and Bear now lived.

But it was a nice, pleasant day for a strenuous walk with the dogs. Both were leashed now, but

Amber figured they would let them loose when it came time to see if the dogs could find anything.

She had put on hiking shoes along with the work shirt and jeans she still wore, and Evan's athletic shoes also appeared comfortable beneath his dark gray casual clothing.

It was warm out now, but not too hot. Neither Evan nor she wore a jacket, and the hiker most likely to feel uncomfortable was Lola since her Lab coat was thicker than Bear's short German shepherd fur.

"How far is it?" Evan asked as they began climbing the rolling green lawn toward the top of the hills, which were covered by a small but thick forest.

"Right up there." Amber pointed. "Kind of on the edge of the trees." She hesitated. "It seemed strange to me, and to the cops, too, from what I heard, that whoever did it left my dad's b— Er, my dad outside instead of inside the cover of the trees, where it would have been harder to find him."

"Whoever it was apparently didn't want to hide that your father was dead," Evan said. "Only who killed him."

She couldn't say anything in response. On some level, that gave her the thought that whoever did it hadn't wanted to be entirely cruel to anyone but her dad. If he'd simply disappeared—been buried somewhere in the woods, perhaps, or somewhere no dogs would have discovered him easily, either— then she and her mother could still be wondering whether her father had simply decided to run away.

Not that something like that sounded like him, but they wouldn't have known.

"I guess that's a good thing," she responded.

Evan seemed to be holding back his stride to match hers. Of course, since he was taller and undoubtedly in better condition, this kind of trek was probably simple for him.

On the other hand, though it had been some time ago, Amber had learned from Evan's references when he applied for this job that he had suffered some injuries thanks to an IED explosion overseas...

"Would you like to slow down?" she asked.

"I'm fine," Evan responded immediately. "Are you okay?"

"Definitely."

He began a discussion about his anticipated work week. She confirmed that, as things progressed in starting new classes, he'd get a couple of days off each week that weren't necessarily Saturday or Sunday.

"I figured," he said. "Fine with me."

She heard the breathiness of her voice and realized the exercise was taking a toll on her, but she didn't slow down.

Eventually they reached the edge of the forest. She looked down the hillside. The ranch appeared like a line of homes, the largest in the center. A distance beyond, in the opposite direction from the way they'd walked, were the larger, more posh buildings of Nathan's hotel and resort.

The narrow road passing below both developments looked like a small, winding string. No vehicles went by as she watched.

"This is some view." Evan stood beside her, looking essentially in the same direction she did. The dogs sat on the ground beside them, both panting a little from exertion.

"That's for sure," she agreed. "It's right over there." She turned and pointed a distance away, toward the farthest edge of the forest from where they stood.

"Do you want to wait here?" Evan asked.

She felt grateful that he seemed ready to protect her. This was, in fact, an extremely difficult thing for her to do.

But she had to do it in case they had an unexpected result. Maybe the dogs would find some evidence that would ultimately lead them to identify her father's murderer.

"No," she said with no hesitation. "Come on, all of you. Let's see what these two amazing canine noses can do."

"It's right here." Amber's voice was soft and hoarse, and Evan almost couldn't hear it in the slight breeze that blew through the leaves of the trees to their right.

He had stopped walking when Amber did and now stood several feet away from her. He held Bear's leash carefully and looked toward Lola, who sat on the ground beside Amber with an anxious expression on her usually happy Lab face, her tail unusually still.

Did Lola have a sense about where she was, or

was she just reacting to how her handler and human, Amber, was behaving?

They were maybe a third of the way along where the trees began growing, then thickened and formed the forest covering the top of the mountain. Near them were bushes that soon gave way to a few oak trees with branches resembling people casting their arms out at distorted angles to beg. Beyond them, tall fir trees reached toward the sky.

The lawn, so rich and verdant nearer the homes, was dry and sparse here, and the ground was mostly covered with dirt and leaves.

A better place for the dogs to inhale scents of plant life and animals, mostly rodents, Evan figured. And birds that had landed here to seek insects in the underbrush.

And…any residual odor of a cadaver?

That was undoubtedly what Amber had meant when she mentioned those two amazing canine noses.

As neutrally as he could, he softly asked, "This is where your father was found?"

She gave two quick nods, her eyes facing the ground. "At least I think so. I wasn't living here then. By the time I came back, he'd been…he had been released from the medical examiner's office to the mortuary my mom chose, and his funeral was a few days later. I asked questions and Assistant Police Chief Kara was kind enough to walk me up here, though not too close since there was crime-scene tape everywhere and they were still investigating. I made as much of a mental note about where it was as I could, though at the time I doubted I'd ever be able to bring myself to come up here again."

Evan noticed that Bear continued to stand where they'd stopped, nose in the air. That could mean he smelled the normal stuff that Evan had thought about briefly on their arrival here.

Or it could mean he smelled something not so normal.

He wasn't alerting, so that could just be wishful thinking on Evan's part.

"But you did come back up here," he said to Amber.

"Several times. Not that I figured I'd see something official police investigators hadn't discovered or anything like that. It was more…well, stupid on my part. A ridiculous hope that, if my dad ever found a way to get through to me from—from beyond, it would be here and he could help set me on a path toward whoever had done this to him."

As she spoke, Amber's voice became more agitated. Evan had to try hard to understand her through her increasing raspiness, and he couldn't miss the tears flowing down her smooth cheeks.

"I can identify with that, at least a little. While I was overseas, and some of my fellow soldiers were—were killed—" He had to stop for a minute since the sights and sounds he had left so far behind were returning suddenly to attack his mind. "There were times I hoped they would talk to me, too. Tell me what awaited me, if things went bad for me."

Somehow he managed to keep his tone level, as if he was just discussing a business venture or something with no emotional background. He owed himself a pat on the back for that.

Better yet, a drink.

But he continued to watch Amber.

She was watching him, too. Her brows raised slightly, she asked, "And did they ever talk to you?"

"Only in my imagination," he admitted. "And your dad. Has he ever seemed to communicate with you?"

And then he repeated his own words at the same time Amber said them. "Only in my imagination."

He wanted to hug her as she managed a laugh. He did draw closer to her, but she turned away.

Clearly a hug wasn't on her current agenda. "Anyway," she said in a more matter-of-fact tone, "this is where my father's body was found. He had been shot twice, but the cops apparently never found the weapon the killer used. One of the bullets was still inside him, and the other was partially buried beneath him, so they were able to identify the kind of gun, but that was all."

"I gather that the Chance PD has a small K-9 unit. Did they bring any of the dogs up here?"

"I believe so, but I'm really not sure."

"This was a couple of months ago?"

"That's right."

Evan sighed internally. He had already warned Amber how unlikely it was that the dogs would smell anything useful after all that time. But now that they were here, he had to try.

"I'll give a command to Bear in case there's something helpful he can smell here. Will Lola follow a command like that, too?"

"I'm still not sure what all her training was, and what verbal orders my dad taught her, but go ahead and try with both of them."

He hadn't told Amber to bring anything of her dad's to provide a scent for the dogs to search for. Even if they somehow caught Corbin's scent up here, Amber already knew he had been here.

But with Bear in particular, a highly trained dog in explosives and other weapons, he had a couple of options. He could have told him "track" or "retrieve" without telling him what he was after, but for now chose "search."

With his training, Bear would follow the scent of any ammunition with that instruction.

He removed Bear's leash and called, "Bear, search."

Despite not wearing a duty vest, Bear immediately stood at attention, still with his nose in the air, then placed it closer to the ground.

For the next ten minutes, he seemed to hunt, and Lola did the same. Did she know the command or was she simply following what another canine was doing?

Evan had no idea, but he watched them take different paths, smelling everything around them, going into the underbrush toward the woods, then back again.

Eventually, they both returned, Bear to Evan and Lola to Amber. They sat and looked up.

"Good dog," Evan said, patting Bear. Amber followed his example with Lola.

And Amber, after praising her dog, just looked at Evan. "That's it, then? Nothing."

"For now," he said. "But I'll try to learn more about what the police know, like the kind of weapon used. Getting a sample of ammo to let Bear smell it would be best for the possibility of his locating something, but it's not absolutely necessary—although because of the timing, the chances are remote." He wanted to make Amber happy, but to get her too psyched up that something good could happen wasn't right, either.

It could lead her to another avenue of disappointment.

"Well...thanks," she said, but her tone was dejected. "I appreciate your trying. And you did say it was a long shot."

"Right."

She looked at him then, her eyes searching his face as if the answers she sought could be hidden there. "Do you have any other ideas?"

He stared straight into her eyes as if that posed no problems for him—and in fact it didn't. Not now.

"I've got a few but don't want to share them until I get a better sense of how to follow up."

"Thank you." Her tone sounded genuine, not just polite, and he wanted to thank her back.

Instead, he found himself right in front of her on the underbrush and dirt, the breeze blowing the branches and leaves nearby, the dogs sitting at their feet.

Maybe this was too impulsive, but he didn't care. He took Amber into his arms, and she didn't resist. In fact, her arms went around him, too, and suddenly her body was against him in a way he had barely imagined before. He felt her soft, sexy curves, especially those above, her firm breasts and more... and he bent his head down and met her warm, sensuous lips with his.

Chapter 13

Whatever Amber had been expecting, it wasn't this.

Hoped for it. But expected? No.

And yet, as she enjoyed the touch of his searching lips on hers, it felt as if she had been awaiting this heated, stimulating, sexually arousing kiss forever.

His body was strong and stiff against her, and she was fully aware of the hardness of his most sensuous area. That made her body ache for more. A lot more.

She pushed closer against him. Let her mouth, her tongue, question him, seeking answers—like, were they really turned on by one another?

She certainly enjoyed the feel of him.

And, yes, she was definitely turned on. Was he? It certainly seemed that way. She moved to deepen the kiss.

Except…

This wasn't right. Not here.

Not with Evan, no matter how attracted she was to him. He was her employee.

Not her lover.

Though the idea was a lot more appealing than it should be.

She heard rustling in the undergrowth near them. At least one of the dogs was on the move.

Did they have any opinions on their owners' actions? No, that was silly.

They certainly hadn't been trained to do anything in situations where humans touched one another in a nonthreatening way.

Amber pulled her mouth away just a little, but that apparently was enough to get Evan's attention. His grip on her loosened, and she immediately regretted her action, even as she stepped back and watched his face to see if he would look anywhere near her, let alone at her.

He stared her straight in the face and smiled, which made her smile in return. "Good thing we're out here, in the open," he said. "Even though it's unlikely anyone would come up here, there's no privacy. Otherwise, I'd expect you to seduce me."

She found herself laughing. "I think you're already trying to seduce me." Then she grew more serious. "More likely, you're trying to distract me from what's on my mind. I can't help thinking about my father, but I appreciate the effort."

"Anytime." His voice was soft and sympathetic.

He reached out for her hand, holding it firmly in his warm grasp in a way that made her once more think of touching one another in inappropriate ways. But she didn't pull back.

Holding hands wasn't a bad idea when a person possibly needed sympathy and more.

She might not need sympathy, though it felt good. And up here, where her father had died, she had hoped for more. A more that consisted of at least a hint at answers.

Evan must have somehow read her raw emotions in her expression. Or maybe it was just logical enough that he jumped on the idea. "I'm sorry the dogs didn't find anything, despite how remote the possibility was."

"Me, too," she said simply. "And…well, I appreciate your attempt to distract me to make it even a little easier to live with the disappointment."

"Yeah, that's what I was doing." He'd moved farther away and now faced to her right, where the dogs sat watching them. "Distracting you. To make things easier. And if you ever feel the need for distraction again, just let me know." He turned back toward her, again looking her straight in the face, which made her nearly shiver in anticipation of…well, needing distraction again sometime.

But if she did, it wouldn't—couldn't—be like this.

"Right." She squared her shoulders, preparing to return to reality. "Anyway, we're done here. Let's go back down the hill."

Which made sense. This visit to the crime scene had upset her in more ways than one.

Partly because she realized how much she had enjoyed that inappropriate and highly sexy kiss.

"Sure, let's go." Evan turned toward Bear, who sat on the ground looking at him with eyes that appeared quizzical. Or maybe just anticipatory. He was waiting for Evan's next command. "Hey, Bear," he said. "This is one of those many times I wish you could convey to me what you're thinking—what you smell around here. I know when you do smell something useful or dangerous from your reactions, though, so maybe this is enough."

He turned back toward Amber, whose smile seemed sad. "He's definitely a good dog," she said. "A smart dog. Lola, too, but I doubt her senses are a fraction as good as Bear's, or at least as useful after his training."

The Lab was now at Amber's side, nuzzling her hand as if demanding to be petted in payment for what she had attempted to accomplish here.

And what Lola had wanted was to please her mistress, even if she didn't understand what Amber had truly wanted: an answer to what had happened to her dad.

Well, these dogs had tried, even if they were unsuccessful.

"Bear, come," Evan said, and, after leashing his dog, began slowly walking down along the way they had come up the hill. He looked back at Amber, who had also attached a leash to Lola's collar. "I agree it's time to go back."

To the houses and reality and a place far from this crime scene that perhaps had yielded something helpful to the cops, but was now useless to a trained K-9, and one not so trained.

They still needed answers.

He needed answers, to help his employer reach some kind of closure over her father's death. But how could he do that?

Amber caught up with him, and they began walking side by side, unlike the way they had climbed the hill with her in front.

The leashed dogs were slightly ahead now but neither pulled as if they sensed anything needing their attention, not even wildlife smells.

Evan pondered what should come next. He had gone through a lot in the last years, had managed to come through it all and survive, and help his wonderful, brave, lifesaving Bear survive it, too.

Amber had also gone through a lot, though in a different way. The loss of her father in such horrible circumstances had changed her life, though. Had brought her here, changed her career and more.

He knew what had injured him: an IED blast, while he was at war. He knew what—who—had saved him: Bear. He also knew that he'd had to consequently save Bear, too. And he recognized that Bear still helped him deal with his remaining, though fortunately receding, psychological issues.

But Amber needed better answers about the causes of her pain to help her deal with it.

She had hired him, which was helping him get on with his life in a way he liked. He had to find a way to help her.

As he accompanied her down the hill, they talked about the forest and the temperature and the smells here that humans sensed.

They laughed at the dogs who'd accompanied them, not complaining that this trip had accomplished nothing except getting something out of the way in trying to learn what had happened to Corbin Belott.

Well, Evan would learn more. He had to. That would mean talking to people in town, like the cops. Learning what they'd found, or hadn't found, in their official crime-scene investigation.

And maybe there were other residents of Chance who could provide some insight into Corbin…and his killer.

Evan had a real job to do, which had to come first if he wanted to make Amber happy. He'd be a damn good trainer of dogs and their handlers.

But he was determined now to also delve into what had happened to Corbin—and help to find answers for Amber, too.

With Bear mostly sniffing in front of him, Evan soon reached the main house with Amber and Lola. It was late afternoon.

"This has been an interesting day," Amber said

as they neared her front porch. She walked slowly, which he believed was more a sign of sadness than exhaustion. He'd had no trouble staying at her side.

Trouble? Heck, he was damn happy to be there.

"*Interesting* is a good word for it," he agreed, then had to ask, "You okay?"

"Sure. The dogs might not have found anything helpful, but at least we eliminated another possibility, kind of as you said. No interesting scents left around there, at least not this long afterward. And...well, now you've seen the area. If you get any more ideas about what happened, how it happened—"

"I'll be sure to tell you so you can follow up with the cops."

He realized his mind would persist in concentrating on that very question—what really happened? If he came up with good ways to investigate further, he'd have to decide whether to mention them to Amber or not.

If that answer was *not*, he'd still continue on his own—with Bear's help.

Get the cops involved? Maybe, although he wondered about their competency since they hadn't solved the crime, even after the passage of months. Would they eventually?

That was their job, not his. But he wanted a solution fast. For Amber.

Meanwhile, he had to get through the rest of this difficult day—more difficult for Amber, of course, than for him. But how?

He would be leaving her presence soon, for now,

which would give him the opportunity to think and plan. But first, he had to do his job.

As it turned out, he thought of a way to do both together.

"I've been thinking about where we are, and I now really agree it's time to begin publicizing the classes to come," he said. "No matter what I said before, I'm ready now. First thing I'd like to do is to show some of the skills I'll teach later on, to let the police departments who might want to acquire trained K-9s, or to get ones they already have trained or retrained, know that this is the place to do it. I'd like to give a sort of public demo with Bear tomorrow. You said that Orrin acted as an agitator during your dad's training sessions, right?"

"That's right. But—"

"Good. And I assume you have a protective suit. If Percy's available tomorrow, this is the time for him to film a session, like he suggested, and put the whole thing up on your website as fast as possible as a teaser about what we're starting to do. Some of my training sessions with your young shepherds, too, within the next week. In fact, I want to run downtown now and recruit Percy, give him the parameters of what I'm thinking and get his thoughts about the best way to handle this. It's nothing you haven't thought about, but I'm ready to jump on it."

"Well, sure," Amber said, her eyes large, as if she was surprised at the direction of his thinking.

In a way, he was surprised, too. But encouraged

that he was allowing himself to be put on film, on the internet, in the public eye.

He would be casting aside his reluctance to even talk to strangers, let alone be stared at by them. He needed to get to the point that he no longer had any residual PTSD.

Hard? Hell yes.

But it was important to the job he'd been hired to do, and he knew he had to get there eventually. And it would help Amber even more.

Now was as good a time as any.

It also gave him a good excuse to go downtown, as Amber had done before.

"Just let me put Lola inside, and we can go." Amber started up the porch steps with her dog.

But Evan stopped her with his next words. "Thanks, but I'll give Percy a call and head down there myself—or just Bear and me." His mind quickly sought a good reason for her not to join them. Mostly, he initially just wanted to check things out with Percy on his own. "I'll only brainstorm with him now, then when he comes here, hopefully tomorrow, you can give him more detailed instructions."

"All right." She spoke slowly, not sounding happy. Her slight scowl underscored her displeasure. "I've got things I need to do around here anyway. But be sure to give me a rundown when you get back about what the plans are for tomorrow. Meantime, I'll check with Orrin about his availability." Her stare then made it clear she wouldn't accept anything less.

"Of course," he said. "We'll see you later."

* * *

Ending their outing this way made Amber feel even worse. No answers, or even additional thoughts on how to learn what had happened to her dad.

And now Evan had decided he was ready for something she'd already intended, though she hadn't pushed him on it: publicizing his training skills in a way they could really promote to the world.

Why now?

Well, why not now?

She raised one hand to wave goodbye to him though he'd already walked away, then led Lola into the house, feeling strangely bereft in many ways.

She was in charge, yet Evan had taken charge of something that should be her decision.

Her thoughts about her father were at the front of her mind, as they often were, and the little bit of effort Evan and she had made that should have helped her had only made things worse.

Now she was leaving Evan's presence for the rest of the day and evening. It hadn't even felt appropriate to invite him to dinner or even for a drink. Whatever he and Percy concluded, he'd probably just call to tell her about it.

He had something he wanted to do right away. Something that should benefit them both. But she'd feel a lot better if she had been able to remain in his company a little longer.

Bad idea. She didn't want to start relying on Evan for anything but dog training, especially not to help her sorry state of mind.

She opened the front door and scooted Lola in. "Hi, Mom," she called in as perky a voice as she could manage.

"Hi, dear," her mom called back from somewhere near the kitchen.

Good. Her mother was home. She'd at least have some company for the evening.

Although, she hoped she could avoid talking much about their visit to the murder site.

Despite what Amber had said, Evan knocked on Orrin's door. The ranch hand was there and, standing just inside with Bear, Evan gave him a quick rundown of tomorrow's possible plans. "Amber will be in touch with you later to make sure you're on board," Evan told the young guy, figuring that letting him know their employer expected it of him would get his cooperation, although he expected a scowl.

Instead, Orrin's smile moved the edges of his light brown beard and mustache upward. "Yeah. Sure. I've kind of missed that," he said.

Being attacked by dogs? Interesting. But Evan just said, "Great."

Then Evan hurried to his house. In the small living room, Bear lying on the floor beside him, Evan called Percy. Fortunately, the guy would be around his store for another hour or two. He sounded happy that Evan wanted to stop in and talk about possibilities for the K-9 Ranch website that he'd hopefully be able to help with.

Because he wanted the money, or because he'd

impress Amber? The latter made Evan frown, but he shook it off.

Then Evan got out his laptop and returned to a couple of sites that described the murder of Corbin Belott.

He concentrated on media interviews of authorities who'd investigated the crime, including Kara Province.

That information fed into the other reason he intended to head downtown. And finally, it was time to get on his way.

Four o'clock in the afternoon might not be the best time to catch the people he wanted to talk to at the police station, but he could at least initiate conversations he hoped to have.

"So what do you think?" he asked Bear, who rode in the back seat as usual. "I'll bet you can help with what I hope to do with the cops."

Reaching the first of the downtown Chance streets, he stopped at a traffic light and glanced into his rearview mirror. Bear, lying down, lifted his head and stared back, mouth open as if he had something to say, like "Can't wait."

Sure, he was putting words into his dog's mouth, but Evan couldn't help smiling at how much Bear wanted to please him, as usual.

He found a metered spot first near Cords and Clouds on Mercer Street, parked and got Bear out. He fed the meter, noted that there weren't many pedestrians or cars around, then went inside.

"Hi, Evan," Percy called right away. He stood up

from behind the table where he'd been sitting—unsurprisingly—behind a computer. The geeky guy's hair was all over the place, and he wore a white T-shirt with a logo in the middle depicting a memory stick. "Good to see you."

That was probably a lie. Or maybe it was true since he might be bringing Percy some business.

Keeping his gaze on Bear so he didn't have to look the geek straight in the face, he told the guy he'd been working with the young dogs at the ranch on their early K-9 training. "I'm with you now about those online videos we said we'd let you know about. It's time to start. It'll still be a while before the young K-9s learn what they'll need to be taken into police departments, but I want to demonstrate what we're doing here. It might even be good to record different stages on video, so we can put together a show of how we'll be training at the ranch. But there's something even more potentially exciting for getting the ranch's name out there that I want to start tomorrow."

"And Amber wants me to put all of it on the website to attract students for new classes?" The guy both looked and sounded excited.

"That's it," Evan agreed.

"Great. I'll be happy to come out and film whatever you're doing tomorrow, and other days, too. You can let Amber know. What time tomorrow?"

"I'll talk to her and we'll figure that out."

Evan thanked the guy and said goodbye. And sighed deeply as Bear and he left the shop. He'd be recorded for history tomorrow. Put himself out there, no matter how hard it still was. But all the reasons to do it were more important than his feelings.

"Come on, boy." He started leading Bear, on his leash, toward the police station.

He would start asking questions in the right, non-critical way to ensure, hopefully, that he'd get answers.

Especially from the town's K-9 cops.

Chapter 14

The walk with Bear to the police station in Chance's civic center didn't take long on sidewalks that were fairly empty except for a few strolling and chatting people who fortunately barely looked at him. Evan had been thinking about the best way to handle this initial conversation for a while and knew he had it covered.

Besides, since he had moved to Chance—had it really been only days ago?—he had been meeting a lot of new people, sometimes several at a time, and had been fine with it. He'd conversed with them fairly well, and given dog-training lessons, and he had felt even more comfortable when he spoke with Amber.

She was different from the other people he dealt

with, and he was glad he got along so well with her. Very glad.

He was proud of how he'd been doing. In fact, maybe he was making progress on finally getting past the last of his PTSD, or so he hoped, although he realized he was likely to always have at least a trace within him. After all, it had only been a couple of years since the explosion, but he had done well enough that the last counselor he had spoken with in LA had said he could do without more therapy unless he started getting worse again.

And the people he was about to speak with were cops.

He soon reached the station and entered the building. A few people milled around in groups in the lobby, none in uniform so he assumed they were civilians. He approached the reception desk, ready to ask the questions he had already decided on to try to get to see the K-9 officers.

But as he reached the tall enclosure, Assistant Police Chief Kara got there, too, from a doorway at the side of the room. "Well, hello," she said cheerily, glancing first into Evan's face, which made him uncomfortable, but he didn't look away. Then she looked down at Bear. "Is your dog on duty, or is it okay to pet him?"

"Sure, go ahead and say hi." It occurred to Evan that running into her first might be helpful. "Are your K-9 officers on duty? I didn't call first, but I was in town and thought I'd stop in to meet them."

"I think they're here, but I'll check. Why, do you think you can teach them something new? Or do you want them to teach *you* something new?" She smiled sardonically at Evan.

The assistant chief was a pretty woman, slender in her black, long-sleeved uniform and somewhat young, Evan thought, to have such an important job. Was it because she was particularly skilled, or because Chance was a small enough town that they hired whoever they could in official positions?

"Maybe a little of both." He managed a brief smile back at her. He wasn't about to tell her why he was really here: to ask the K-9 cops whether they'd visited the murder site when scents would still be fresh, and how their dogs reacted.

"Let me go check," she said. "Be right back." Kara walked toward a hall to Evan's right. She returned in a few minutes. "Yes, they're in the main K-9 room, at the back of the station. Come with me."

"Thanks. Bear, heel."

Kara had started walking back toward the hallway but stopped and looked down again. Unsurprisingly, the leashed Bear was following Evan's instruction.

"What a good boy," Kara said. That was potentially helpful, Evan thought. Whatever kind of cop this woman was, she apparently was a dog lover.

"Yes," he responded warmly, "he is." He paused. "Are you interested in observing a K-9 training session tomorrow? That's the main reason I came this afternoon. I'm doing a demo to be filmed for the ranch's website and thought I'd invite your K-9 officers to observe. It might be good for all of us." Especially if they described their own training. Had it all been by Corbin?

How well had they known Corbin?

And how hard had they attempted to investigate his death?

"Sure, I'd like that. I do watch our unit's internal training sessions sometimes."

The hallway was long, with doors in the white plaster walls that sometimes had names posted near them and other times led into additional halls. At the end, Kara opened a door with glass at the top. "Here we are." She pushed it open and motioned for Evan to enter, which he did with Bear preceding him.

The office was fairly large, with two desks facing each other at the end. A German shepherd sat in front of the one occupied by a guy in a black cop uniform similar to Kara's, and a golden retriever was in front of the other, whose occupant was a female uniformed officer. Both people rose, and the dogs moved only enough to look at their respective apparent handlers.

Well trained, Evan thought.

"Hi." He approached as if it was completely easy for him—and he was surprised that he didn't, in fact, feel uncomfortable. "I'd imagine Assistant Chief Province told you, but I'm Evan Colluro, the new trainer at the Chance K-9 Ranch."

That assistant chief stood beside one of the desks and nodded toward Evan. Apparently, he'd phrased that in a way she approved of. Good.

"Yes," said the woman. "I'm Officer Maisie Murran, and this is Officer Doug Murran. And in case you're wondering about the similarity of our names, we're not only the department's K-9 handlers, but we're also brother and sister."

"Good to meet you." Evan approached her with his hand out for a shake, then did the same with her brother. Good. He was, in fact, making progress.

They both appeared in their midthirties, older than Evan. Maisie looked a year or two older than her brother, with short hair a shade of light blond that Evan figured needed help to get to that color. Doug's hair was a light brown, shorter than his sister's—a professional law-enforcement-type cut.

"This is Bear." Evan gestured to his dog, who now sat obediently beside him. "And yours?"

"Hooper and Griffin," Doug said. Both dogs stood alertly as their names were spoken. "Hooper, go shake." The shepherd skirted around Bear as he approached Evan, sat and held out his paw. It was Griffin's turn next.

Once more, Evan was impressed with their training. Plus, he thought this an appropriate time to bring up the questions he'd come here to ask.

"I can give Bear a similar command," he said, "but I figure you know he'd do well at it. He's former military and I've given him additional training, too. He's now my example of a well-trained police K-9 in my classes."

"I'll bet he is," Doug said, "and we're glad you're there—assuming you're good at what you do."

"You're assuming right," Evan said. He jumped right in. "You're clearly familiar with the K-9 Ranch. Did you train at all with Corbin Belott?"

"Yes," Maisie replied, her tone soft and sad. "He was a good man. A good trainer."

"We've taken classes elsewhere, too," Doug said,

"but he was our first instructor, and though the department acquired Griffin from somewhere else, Hooper was one of the dogs Corbin selected as a young pup and trained to become a police K-9."

Evan thought about glancing toward Kara to see her reaction but decided against it. Instead, continuing to stand with just Bear near him, he got to the crux of why he'd actually come. "I heard what happened to him. It was a damn shame. And I gather that the crime hasn't been solved yet?" He let the last sentence become a question.

"No," Kara said from beside him. "It hasn't." Her tone was firm, as if instructing him not to go further with his inquiry.

He nevertheless inhaled deeply, steeling himself to go on.

"From what I heard, Corbin's body was found near the woodlands at the top of the ranch property." He decided not to say anything yet about having seen the area, but looked first toward Maisie, then toward Doug, who'd resumed sitting behind the desks, their dogs still in the middle of the room. "I'm not sure what your dogs' skills are—" although he assumed that, as K-9s, they were at least tracking dogs and most likely had other abilities, too, probably involving additional kinds of scenting "—but did you bring them to that area to see what they could find?"

"Yes," Maisie said. "They seemed to react at first, searched the entire area, but didn't locate anything we could use to track or identify the suspect." She kept her voice even but Evan sensed emotion behind it anyway. She probably wasn't happy that not more had been determined by their K-9s.

Neither was Evan, since when these dogs would have been brought to the site all scents would have been fairly fresh.

"That's a shame," he said nevertheless. He wanted to establish as good a relationship as possible with this local unit. Maybe he could even help them train their K-9s better, for next time. Although he hoped there wouldn't be a next time.

But since Corbin's killer was still out there, who knew what awaited this town?

"How about the murder weapon?" Evan asked. "Are they skilled at scenting something like that?"

"Yes, but they came up with nothing," Maisie said.

"Do you know the type of weapon?" Evan persisted, making himself look from one officer's face to the other's.

"Yes, although we haven't made it public," Doug said.

"Can you tell me the make?"

Both K-9 officers looked toward Kara, who was to Evan's left, and she shrugged. "He's not a suspect, so go ahead. Evan, this is to go no further. But if your dog happens to locate a weapon somewhere on the ranch, it won't hurt for you to know."

"Of course I'll keep it confidential," Evan assured them, and was told it was a Smith & Wesson—but they chose not to tell him the model, though they'd have been able to ID it from the bullets found.

"Is there anything else you can tell me that's not public? I mean, if the K-9s were there soon after the homicide, did they alert onto any kind of scent?" Evan knew he was treading on thin ice, but it didn't hurt to ask.

"Cadaver location only," Kara said, and the firmness in her voice made him back off. She continued, though. "But be assured that there are other things about the case we can't reveal that involve progress in solving it."

Evan saw the three cops exchange glances, as if confirming what she said. He wondered if that part was their standard spiel to tell civilians who asked about this case that had already grown cold, or if it actually was true.

He hoped it was the latter…but suspected the former.

"That's great," he said anyway. "You'll be seeing some publicity soon for classes I'll be giving at the ranch. Amber Belott has a lot of new ideas in mind." So did he, some on Amber's behalf—and a few had to do with possibly helping the cops increase their success. "Plus, I'm training the pups Corbin had started on initial K-9 skills. They won't be ready for a while, but you're more than welcome to watch my training and even make suggestions. I can let you know my routine once I get into one. And the main reason I came here today—" or at least the one he'd reveal to them "—is that I'm doing a police K-9 training session with Bear tomorrow to be filmed and put onto the ranch's website. I'll have an agitator work with us, too. It's to show some skills I'll teach in future lessons. Would you like to come watch?"

"That sounds great," Maisie said. "We'd love to,

as long as there are no call-outs we're involved in then. Right, Doug?"

Her brother agreed.

"I'd better get back to the ranch now," Evan said. "But if there's anything I can do to help you out, especially in your investigation of Corbin's homicide, just let me know."

As he left the office after saying goodbye, he realized that their asking for his help was as likely as their offering to hire him as one of their K-9 cops.

Amber kept an eye out for the return of Evan's car.

She'd watched him drive down the driveway and along the road toward town a while ago.

Why hadn't he wanted her along when he talked to Percy about filming tomorrow's demonstration and future lessons for her ranch's website? Well, no matter. Percy was her consultant, not Evan's. He wouldn't do anything without her okay. Not if he wanted the ranch to pay him.

Amber had just walked past the front of the house, as she'd done several times while the chicken she had begun cooking for dinner baked in the oven. Lola remained at her side, as if this was some kind of training exercise, and Amber appreciated the dog's loyalty and company.

The aroma of roasting chicken permeated the air and Amber assumed Lola enjoyed it. She'd heard a lot of stirrings and whines from the den where the puppies were enclosed and figured she'd put them in the fenced area of the yard soon for their early evening outing.

Her mother was in the living room watching TV news. Amber would join her in a while, but for now she headed back to the kitchen to start slicing veggies for a salad.

As she placed a head of lettuce on the cutting block and got a sharp knife out to cut it, her phone rang. She put everything onto the counter carefully and reached into her pocket. Was Evan calling about whatever he'd discussed with Percy? She smiled at the idea, but only for an instant. It was just as likely that Percy was calling about his meeting with Evan.

But when she lifted her phone she saw the caller was neither of them. Instead, it was Kara.

Was something wrong?

Or was something right? Had the cops figured out at last who had killed her father? That would be one heck of a coincidence after her visit to the crime scene that day with Evan and the dogs, but so what?

"Hi, Kara," she said after pressing the button to answer. "How are you doing?"

"I'd be better if your new employee concentrated on his job instead of coming to the department to question the competence of our K-9 officers and their dogs."

"What?" Amber's mind suddenly swirled around what Evan was even doing at the police station. He'd said he was going to town to run some ideas by Percy—or was that just a ruse?

"He came here and said he wanted to meet the members of our unit. That was fine. I even brought him in to see them. But then he started asking questions, including whether they'd even attempted to visit the crime scene after your father…well, you know. I got the sense he was criticizing them because the dogs hadn't immediately caught the scent and performed an immediate and successful search for the perpetrator."

"I… Sorry. I'll talk to him about that."

Had Evan mentioned they had visited the site that day?

That was most likely why he had decided to confront the police about what they'd found—or hadn't found.

A good idea? Maybe not. But Amber had wondered about that, too. She hadn't felt comfortable asking.

She was surprised—and glad—that Evan had.

"Did your officers mention that my father had given some lessons to them and their dogs?" she asked.

"Yes, and Evan invited them—and me—to watch, and even participate in, some of his upcoming classes, including tomorrow."

Wise, Amber thought. Realizing she was staring at the knife, she looked away and said, "That was probably the reason he dropped in there. We're still talking about all the possibilities for his classes. The rest…well, if your K-9s or others learned anything about what happened to my dad, you must know I'm eager to hear it."

"I understand. But you must also understand that the investigation remains ongoing."

In other words, as she was well aware, there were no answers yet. Maybe still no real suspects, though they wouldn't necessarily reveal that other than to ask questions that could help lead them to evidence.

"Of course. Anyway, sorry for any problems Evan caused. I'll talk to him about it." And maybe even cheer him on. "We should meet for coffee one of these days." Amber issued that invitation hoping to change the subject a bit, and calm Kara's ill will against Evan.

"Good idea. I'll call you."

"Great." But Amber suspected that waiting for Kara's call would be like getting a new, untrained puppy to roll over with just a hand signal. It might happen, but she couldn't count on it.

Evan took his time leaving the police station's reception area, partly because a few visitors gushed a bit over Bear. Since his dog wasn't on duty he encouraged it—and mentioned the upcoming dog-training classes at the K-9 ranch in case any of them had canine pets at home that could use some work.

He was really getting into this, he thought. Amber would be proud of him and what he was doing... right? It would hopefully lead to more classes at her ranch.

As soon as he and Bear exited the station and started down the sidewalk toward where he'd parked his car, Officer Maisie Murran hurried up to him. No dog was with her.

There were a few other people on the sidewalk near them, and Maisie motioned for Evan and Bear to move closer to the station's wall.

"If anyone asks," she said quietly as he complied

and stood there looking at her, "we're discussing my coming to one of your classes soon. But I wanted to let you know in private that things aren't exactly what they seem."

She appeared more bedraggled than when he'd seen her in the station, her blond hair messier, as if she'd either encountered a breeze or run her fingers through it. It wasn't particularly windy so he suspected the latter. She still looked official, though, in her uniform.

"Fine," he said. "And I hope you do come to our demonstration tomorrow, as well as future classes. But what isn't what it seems?"

"Our investigation. Not the K-9 unit's, since we did go to the crime scene with our dogs and seek evidence that way, scent or otherwise, but nothing materialized, as we said. And really, the rest of the department has worked hard but not very successfully at trying to find other kinds of evidence that would lead to the murderer." She stopped and looked away. "I probably shouldn't be talking about this at all, but I know you're now associated with the victim's family."

Associated with them? Yeah. He worked for them.

And right or wrong, he had begun to care about Amber. A lot.

"And you want them to know what you're telling me?"

"Yeah, I guess. I don't want them holding out a huge amount of hope that we'll have answers soon. Or maybe…well, this department is really good at solving a lot of kinds of crime, but there aren't many murders here in Chance."

He'd heard that before. "I assume that's a good thing," he said.

She nodded. "Of course, but that may just be an excuse. Right now, our detectives and superior officers have some ideas about who might have done it and why, but nothing definitive. Persons of interest, yes. Suspects they're ready to bring in for questioning, no."

"Then you may never figure out who killed Corbin Belott?"

She looked into his eyes, and he didn't flinch. Then she looked down, biting her lower lip and shaking her head.

"We will," she replied. "We're definitely working on it. And I gathered you're interested and maybe snooping around, too."

He hadn't mentioned their visit to the crime scene, but had she guessed? He didn't ask.

"I'm definitely interested," he said without addressing the other part of what she'd said.

"Well… I gather you're a good K-9 trainer, which might not help with this. But if you happen to get a lead on some evidence or anything else related to the case, be sure to inform one of us."

"You?" he asked.

"That'll work," she said.

Chapter 15

This was foolish, Amber thought as she followed Rex down the steps from her house and onto the driveway, holding the end of his leash tightly in her hand. "Heel," she told the rambunctious young shepherd who'd been pulling ahead of her, and this time he actually obeyed. They began walking slowly down the paving toward the street, where she planned to turn once more and head up the slope again.

Maybe Evan's training was really beginning to work this fast—a very good thing for this pup who, like the others, had been among the last selected by her father to eventually become a skilled police K-9. Amber had no doubt that the others would succeed, but as much as she loved Rex and his personality she had become concerned that they wouldn't succeed in getting him trained, even with more time, and they'd eventually have to find him a different, civilian kind of home. But now Evan had begun working with him and he had already started to learn. He might yet become one of those skilled police K-9s her father anticipated.

Evan. He seemed always to be on her mind. Right now, it was nearly seven o'clock. Evan had left hours ago. He had neglected to mention that he wasn't simply going to drop in at Percy's and give him some ideas for the website, like shooting footage of his practice classes tomorrow to post.

No, he had gone to the police station after their fruitless attempt earlier that day to get the dogs to find some hidden bit of evidence beyond the skills of career cops.

He'd even challenged them and questioned their skills, at least those of the K-9 unit, according to Kara. Amber knew she should wait until she'd cooled down a bit, but she wanted to confront him.

Tonight.

And so she'd been walking one dog after the other waiting for his return.

Although, if she really thought about it, she also wanted just to see him. Today's visit to her father's murder site had been grueling and Evan's presence and attitude had helped her deal with it.

And his apparent desire to help solve that mystery? She appreciated it. A lot.

But if he was pushing any of the local cops' buttons, angering them, accusing them of ineptitude—

well, she might wonder about the latter, but it wasn't a good idea for many reasons to engage in the first two actions.

Especially not if she really wanted the Chance K-9 Ranch to redevelop a good reputation with police departments interested in acquiring new K-9s or continuing their dogs' training. Criticism from the locals would not help with that.

She'd eaten a quick dinner with her mom in between walking Hal and Lucy. She had walked Lola earlier and probably would do so again later that evening.

Now she inhaled the brisk evening air as the sun was setting.

She hadn't told her mother her motivation for longer individual walks than usual, but the look in Sonya's eyes suggested that she suspected something was on her daughter's mind—and it wasn't necessarily a good thing.

Amber also hadn't told her mom much about the visit to where her dad had been killed, and neither had her mom asked any details.

It was better that way.

Amber reached the bottom of the driveway with Rex and glanced up and down the narrow road.

No cars at all. That wasn't too surprising at this hour.

But where was Evan? Kara had indicated he'd stuck his nose into the police station over an hour ago.

She could have called and told him to get his butt

back here—his tight, sexy butt, and she shouldn't have noticed that. He would have to listen to her. She was his boss.

But confronting him wasn't the way she wanted to begin the conversation she intended to have with him…at least not at first.

There. She heard a car and though Rex was pulling at the leash again to head up the driveway she called, "Stay," and looked.

That could be Evan's car.

"Good dog," she said to Rex, bending to pat the dog's head as she continued to watch the approaching vehicle.

Yes. It was Evan's black sedan.

She waited for him to pull into the driveway—slowly and carefully.

He rolled down the driver side window. "Hi," he said. "Good timing. I brought us some dessert. You and Rex get in and I'll drive us to my house."

Evan was a little surprised that Amber accepted his invitation. She directed Rex into the back seat, then got into the passenger seat of his car for a ride of maybe two minutes.

What had she really been doing out there? Walking Rex? Sure, but the scowling expression directed toward him on her otherwise lovely face suggested she had something else on her mind.

Most likely something he wouldn't want to hear. Except…well, the fact she was out here possibly waiting for him piqued his curiosity. He needed to learn what it was about.

"Nice evening," he said after she'd shut the door. He turned his car toward the back driveway behind his house.

It actually was fairly nice, cool but not too chilly, only starting to get dark, probably not a bad time for her to walk a dog. She still wore the work shirt and jeans she'd had on earlier, and they looked comfortable enough for this temperature.

"Sure," she murmured. He glanced toward her. She was staring through the windshield as if that part of her property behind the employee houses fascinated her. But she hadn't stopped scowling.

"So is Rex the first youngster you've walked this evening? Maybe I should put Bear inside, then join you with one of the others, and—"

"I thought you brought dessert." Her tone was almost accusatory, and he let out a bark of a laugh.

"Okay, I know what's important." He parked his car.

"Do you?" Uh-oh. She sounded even more than accusatory, and he looked straight at her—but only for a moment. Even expecting it, he wasn't ready to face her harsh expression, though it did nothing to make her look anything but beautiful.

He turned to pull his door handle, glad that exiting the vehicle was a logical thing to do. They could take this disagreement, whatever it was about, inside.

First, he opened the back door and grabbed the handle of Bear's leash, glad to see Amber do the same with Rex. "I'll get the dessert out of the trunk," he said and proceeded to do just that, choosing not to be gentlemanly by opening car doors. He'd hear what this was about soon enough.

He picked up the handles of the plastic bag holding the apple pie's container and slammed the trunk closed, then, without looking at Amber, preceded her toward the back door to the house. He unlocked the door, Bear behind him, and motioned for Amber to enter along with the young dog whose leash she held. "I assume Rex is okay since you were walking him, but I want to take Bear out for a minute." He handed her the bag, which she accepted, eyebrows raised in what appeared to be a hint of amusement. Good. Her scowl had eased a bit. "Be right back."

As always, Bear knew what was expected of him and didn't take long to accomplish it. Evan had taken him to some grass near the driveway, and they soon entered once more through the back door, going inside the same way Amber and Rex had. He locked things behind them.

He found his visitors in the kitchen, where Rex was drinking from Bear's bowl on the floor beside the refrigerator, and Amber had found plates and flatware. She was cutting the pie, which she'd placed on the small table in the center of the room, and didn't look up when he entered.

"This pie is good," she said. "I took a tiny bite as I started cutting." She looked up from it toward him. "I'll be fine with water, but do you want to make some coffee?"

"No coffee for me, either. I'll get us some water." Evan didn't think caffeine would be good for them at this hour—especially with the pending discussion, although he wasn't sure yet what it was about. She already knew his plans for tomorrow, plans that should ultimately help the ranch.

And even if she happened to have found out that he had also gone to the police station—

"I can guess why you consider our police department incompetent," she said, pushing a white plate toward him with a piece of pie and a fork on it, "but I think it's a really bad idea to tell them so. I'm sure they're doing their best to investigate what happened to my father."

He stood still, with Bear now lying down at his feet. He didn't look at the pie, or toward the cupboards containing the glasses. "I think so, too," he said. "What makes you think I told the cops they're incompetent?"

She described a brief phone conversation she'd had not long ago with Assistant Police Chief Kara, who'd made it clear she wasn't happy. She'd indicated that to him, as well.

"Look," he said, going to the cupboard for the water glasses, "I went there mostly to learn, after— after this afternoon, whether the Chance PD had sent their K-9 unit to investigate the site we'd visited closer to the time of the crime that occurred there." No use specifying her father's murder. She knew what he was talking about, and he knew how badly it hurt her. "They had. I invited them to watch our

K-9 demo tomorrow—and Percy is coming here to film it, by the way." He got ice from the freezer and a bottle of water from the fridge, filling both glasses before turning back to her. "Oh, and Orrin—"

"Yes, he told me you'd already asked him to participate even though I told you I was going to contact him."

"I happened to see him as I passed his house on the way back to mine earlier," he lied, putting the glasses on the table and sitting down.

"Well, all that's fine, and I hope at least the officers in the K-9 unit you talked to decide to come. They'll be able to compare your methods with what my dad did since they took some lessons from him."

"That's what they said." Evan ate a bite of pie and smiled. Good stuff. He glanced toward Amber. She, too, was eating. "And look. All I did was ask questions. I guess they could have read criticism into how I phrased things, but that wasn't my intent." Exactly. He'd wanted to keep them doing whatever they were still doing to solve the case.

Which Maisie had said was definitely ongoing— but far from successful. At least to date.

He considered telling Amber about his brief conversation with the female officer who was part of the K-9 team, but for now decided against it. Amber knew the gist of what Maisie had admitted to him anyway.

"I'll apologize to whoever comes here tomorrow," he said. "Just let them know it was my concern and curiosity talking, and that I wish them all the best in getting that crime solved as quickly as possible."

That wouldn't keep him from reminding them when he could, perhaps in a more subtle way. Or continuing to do what small amount of investigating he could on his own, with or without Bear's skills to help him.

Or, most likely, keeping Officer Maisie informed, as she'd asked, as long as that appeared to be in the best interests of getting the case solved.

He wasn't a cop or investigator or anything like that, except as a K-9 trainer for police units. This wasn't his work, or his business.

But nevertheless, and despite Amber's apparent irritation with him and what he was doing, he wanted to find out and prove who'd killed her father.

For her sake.

Because, never mind that she was his boss, he was coming to care for her too much.

Amber swallowed her last bite of the sweet pie and looked toward Evan directly across the table. "Okay." She leaned on her elbows toward him. "I've done what I promised Kara I'd do—tell you to back down on criticizing the Chance PD. But know what?"

He had just brought his own final pie piece up to his mouth—his sexy, broad mouth—and stopped.

"What?" he asked.

The more she'd thought about the situation, she realized what irked her most was that Evan hadn't kept her in the loop. Hadn't invited her to go with him to talk with Percy—or confront the cops, since he'd obviously planned that, too.

In some ways, maybe, it was best, since Kara and the others wouldn't blame her for pushing them now to do more on her dad's case, or at least couldn't blame her for what Evan had been saying. She could continue to be a sad, nonpushy family member of the victim and hopefully get their attention by sorrowful looks and comments without threatening to outsmart them at their own job, the way Evan could—and hopefully would—do.

"I'm concerned that pushing and criticizing them will make them reluctant to keep the investigation in the forefront of what they're doing," she said. "But if you continue to act that way, and I pretend to be irritated with you for doing so—well, it'll be a possible poke at them to keep emphasizing it, without their having a reason to get mad at me or my mom."

"Except that you hired me."

She couldn't help smiling at him. "Yes, there is that. So you also had better do a damn good job at what you do here."

"Yes," he said. "I'd better."

They were looking straight into each other's faces now, and he wasn't turning away. She wished she could stare through those gorgeous blue eyes of his into his mind, to see what he was thinking.

Although, she thought she knew. The way he looked at her was smoldering, sexy, hot. Which made her flush, but she couldn't look away.

This was bad, wasn't it? They were alone in his

house, except for the two dogs who now slept by their feet. She was his boss, and she was supposed to be angry with him, thanks to what Kara had told her. But she wasn't.

She tried to chill herself out by continuing their conversation. "I assume you can keep things confidential if *your employer* tells you to, right?" She emphasized *your employer* on purpose, reminding both of them. As if they needed it.

"Of course." His tone was soft, though, and sounded as sexy as he looked.

What she was about to say wouldn't fix anything. But it had to be said after what she'd told him earlier. "The thing is," she said, trying to sound gruff and in charge, and failing badly, "I don't entirely mind if you get on the cops' case and chew them out for not having answers yet. Like I said, I can't do it, since I have to maintain a good relationship with them for the sake of the ranch. And also, if I criticize them, they might use that as an unspoken excuse to let this cold case turn to ice. But if you remind them, and I act sympathetic to them and let them know I've told you to behave, and—"

"So we'll be working together in ways besides dog training," Evan said. "And at the risk of making you think I can't keep things confidential when I tell you I will—well, let's just say that one of the police hinted they're still on the case and intend to continue, but they wouldn't mind a little help if I happen to learn something they haven't."

"Really?"

"Yeah," he said. "But if you say anything like that to any of the cops, I'll have to deny it."

Wow. He really was making headway with the police department, or at least some members, despite his way of doing things. Maybe because of his way of doing things.

Amber realized she was smiling at him. Warmly. Maybe too warmly.

He rose from his chair, his eyes remaining on hers despite how difficult he'd apparently found that so recently. Was she somehow helping him, as he was helping her in other highly important ways?

She glanced down, stepping carefully around Rex, who lifted his head from the floor but didn't rise. "Yes." She attempted to sound stern as they approached each other. "We'll work together—"

She suddenly found herself in his arms. Again.

This kiss was as incredibly hot as the last one they'd shared. Maybe even more so. They'd been outside then—alone, yes. But now they were even more alone, inside his house.

Her arms were around his back, pulling him even closer than before. She felt his hands stroke her, first near the back of her neck, then downward until they touched her butt through her jeans. She felt his hardness against her even more than last time.

At the same time his lips searched hers, his tongue probed her mouth until it opened and she allowed her own tongue to play darting, sexual games with his.

He pulled back then, and she forced her mind to accept that this small amount of heated contact was more than enough…until she felt one of his hands move between them, then down, grasping the outside of her jeans and pressing harder.

"Evan," she gasped, and took the cue from him. In moments, she was grasping his hard erection from outside his clothing.

No. This shouldn't happen. But she wanted it. Craved it. She prepared to let him lead her down the hallway to the bedroom.

But he stepped back, releasing her. She wanted to throw herself back into his arms but didn't. Instead, she looked into his face once more.

His craggy features were more pronounced as he breathed hard. His expression was regretful.

"Sorry," he rasped. "I know when to keep things quiet—and should know not to try to seduce my boss, no matter how appealing that idea is. You're one sexy woman, Amber Belott. But—"

"Yes, *but.*" She managed to keep her tone light, though she doubted she truly hid her frustration.

"So…" he said. "Glad you came over for a piece of pie. Would you like me to help walk the other dogs for their last outing tonight?"

"No thanks," she said. "The others are pretty much done, except for Lola." And if he realized what she'd been doing, that she'd been hanging outside watching for him, well, so what? "Come on, Rex." She bent to snap the leash back onto his collar. "Time for bed."

She purposely phrased it that way, and glanced

into Evan's face before heading toward the door at the front of the house.

If she read his expression correctly—and she believed she knew him well enough to do so—she was glad to see a hint of surprise and frustration along with his amusement.

She'd intended to walk Rex back to her house by herself, but Evan insisted on accompanying them, Bear by his side. He seemed to scrutinize Orrin's house as they passed, but she saw no lights inside and neither dog seemed to sense any other people around.

"Good night," he said as she opened her front door. "See you tomorrow for our demo."

Chapter 16

Okay, he didn't have to back away before, Evan told himself while lying in bed later trying to get to sleep.

The same thought had pierced his mind from the time he'd walked Amber and Rex back to her house, strode around it with Bear without seeing Orrin and returned here. Now, though, he didn't have any distractions, like enjoying the chill of the outside air. Or the few sounds in this remote area, like hoots of owls and skitterings of whatever rodents lived nearby to grab Bear's attention. Not even the news on TV before heading to the bedroom…

Well, despite all that, there was little else he thought of except being with Amber that way. Especially now.

Could he have followed through and made love with her? Maybe. She'd seemed as interested as he.

Yet that could have been more because she'd needed to find a way to deal with the experiences of that day—their visit to where her father had been shot to death not long ago—than because she wanted to hop into bed with him.

He wanted her. No doubt about that. And maybe, eventually, he would feel it was the right time for her, too.

Anytime would be the right time for him…

Sighing, he pulled the covers down from around him—again—glad he'd thrown on fairly light pajamas over his scarred body. His mind was heating him as he focused so much on Amber…

"Damn it!" he said, then heard Bear stir on the floor near him. "Good dog," he called and forced himself to concentrate on planning tomorrow morning's demonstration. It was far from boring but was familiar enough to allow him to relax…and soon he felt himself starting to fall asleep.

He woke early on Saturday morning, way ahead of the time he'd promised to start his demonstration.

His mind was working, not particularly on the performance he would give later, but on Amber, then on the crime scene, and the cops, and— Well, too many things he could do nothing about.

He needed to find a way to relax.

It wouldn't hurt to do something that also could wind up helping with the new purpose he had taken on: learning more about Corbin Belott's death.

As he rose from bed, he called, "Hey, Bear, ready to take a hike with me?"

His smart shepherd undoubtedly heard something welcoming in Evan's words or tone. He'd already stood up from his blanket on the floor, and now his ears were up and his tail wagged.

It was as if he said, "Yes, Dad, let's do it."

Evan dressed in hiking gear, including a long-sleeved T-shirt, sweatpants and athletic shoes. He didn't intend to stay out long and figured Bear and he would eat when they returned.

He picked up Bear's leash from the counter where he kept it, but didn't snap it on. At this point, and maybe through the entire hike, both of them would be wild and free.

"Come," he told his dog.

When they exited his home, he stood on the stoop for a second and Bear sat down beside him. The morning light was still dim, as dawn had just broken. Evan looked left, toward the other houses, including, beyond the closest ones, the main residence.

He saw no one else outside, not Orrin or Amber or any dogs.

Good. He loved the sense of privacy, of being alone with his own dog under the blue sky on this cool May morning.

He also loved that no one would know what he was doing.

He turned right and started up the hill—in the general direction they'd gone to see the crime scene.

When they reached the area where Corbin had

been found, near where the forest began, he led Bear a distance beyond it at the same elevation.

For the heck of it, he called, "Search," and gave his dog the hand signal to move forward. It was a general command, one that allowed Bear to alert to whatever, or whoever, he found that he had been trained to look for or find by scent.

That included IEDs overseas…and weapons here, as well as people. Bear wouldn't always know if a person was a bad guy, but he did particularly alert to fear scents.

Not that Evan figured they were likely to see anyone out here at this hour, let alone a bad guy who'd be afraid of being hunted by his dog. Nor did he anticipate that Bear would find anything, or anyone, to alert to. But in case there was some evidence that hadn't been found, even by the Chance PD's K-9s…

Okay, he was reaching. He wasn't going to identify the killer today. But it didn't hurt to imagine an ulterior motive for this outing.

They hiked for an hour, up slopes, into a small portion of the forest, then down again. Evan saw in the distance part of the long wooden fence that surrounded the ranch property but didn't approach.

Instead, he gave Bear the command "Come" along with the appropriate gesture. It was time to get breakfast.

And Evan was just about ready to start his day and prepare for the demonstration he'd agreed to give.

Although he had enjoyed this hike enough to promise himself he'd do it again. Soon.

* * *

Amber awoke that morning with no alarm. "Morning, girl," she said softly, petting Lola, who'd risen when she moved.

Getting out of bed, Amber pulled a robe on over her pj's and headed toward the bathroom, eagerly anticipating what would go on that day.

As she showered, she thought about—what else?—Evan. In his interview and earliest demonstrations of his skills, he had shown, with Bear, how well he could work with a trained K-9 as well as beginner pups. And people, including small groups. She truly believed he had the proficiency needed to be the main handler at this ranch.

She had seen her dad sometimes perform amazing demos with the wonderful dogs he'd trained, to show how they would perform in a real police K-9 situation, where they had to subdue a bad guy.

Now it was Evan's turn to show his stuff. She was so glad he'd decided to have Percy film it for the ranch's website. She had been concerned before whether Evan would feel comfortable having his skills preserved in video form and displayed to the world to promote the K-9 Ranch. But she felt certain he'd never make a suggestion like that unless he really was ready.

Although...well, last night she recognized that in some ways she didn't know him as well as she'd thought. She'd been ready to jump into bed with him, to follow through with what their kisses and caresses had begun, no matter how foolish or inappropriate that was.

He'd stopped them, and she didn't think it was because of his PTSD. No, it was more because he was a smart, thoughtful man, a caring man who hadn't wanted to do something they both might regret later.

Even so…well, she wouldn't try to predict how things would be as time went on, at least not regarding how well Evan and she would remain at arm's length—or not.

But she did predict, in her mind, how much she would enjoy the rest of this day.

Amber was surprised at the small crowd gathering to watch the demonstration—although she realized she shouldn't have been. She could understand why each person near her, behind this part of the ranch's vast fence, was there.

Amber saw Orrin in the crowd, wearing the big, thick full-body suit to protect him, as the demo's agitator, from the planned dog attack he was in for. Her dad had stocked other protective training equipment, too, depending on what the lesson or demonstration was to be, including large padded sleeves.

Her mom was there, and standing beside her was their neighbor Nathan. She and her mother had eaten a quick breakfast together, and Sonya had told Amber that she'd invited Nathan.

A good thing? Probably not. After all, Nathan had suggested that Evan wasn't skilled enough, particularly with people, to be the ranch's trainer—although today's demo would focus on one dog.

"I just hope he does a good job today." Her mother had echoed her thoughts then, staring inquisitively at Amber before taking a sip of coffee.

"For more reasons than one," Amber had responded. Sure, it would be a good thing if Nathan saw a special enough event to make him retract his criticism. But his opinion was a minor factor.

The opinion of the cops who were coming mattered a lot more.

The cops, in their familiar black uniforms, had already arrived. K-9 officers Maisie and Doug Murran stood along the fence beyond her mom and Nathan. Surprisingly, Kara was there, too, along with her boss, Police Chief Andrew Shermovski. Although they had been friendly enough in their greetings when they'd arrived around ten minutes ago, the officers remained by themselves and were now engaged in conversation. They hadn't brought either of the Chance PD's K-9s, which was a good thing.

And Percy was there, setting up his filming equipment. The regular dog-obedience students, Grady, Aaron, Stewart and Julie, were present, too, without their dogs.

Now, if only this demonstration resulted in what Amber hoped: word spreading, perhaps virally after the video was posted on the website and social media, about how skilled their new head trainer was.

There he was. Evan had remained in the main house with Bear until now. Would more observers arrive? Amber didn't know, but Evan strode from the house as if he owned the world.

Excellent. No matter what he might feel inside, he clearly was ready. Leashed and walking beside him, Bear, too, appeared ready to go. Behind them lumbered Orrin, dressed to be an agitator.

Evan made his way through the crowd near the gate, and he and Bear entered the area of the rolling lawn. The other dogs remained inside the house.

This was Bear's show as well as Evan's.

Evan held the official dog vest that would tell Bear he was on duty when it was placed around him. He turned to scan the onlookers, not staring into anyone's face, but not appearing uncomfortable, either.

His gaze caught hers and he sent her a small smile and nodded slightly, suggesting confidence.

He then looked toward Percy and Orrin, who were close by. "Ready?" Both responded affirmatively.

Evan took a few steps farther into the field. "Agitator, please take your place," he called, and Orrin passed him. Evan kneeled and fastened the vest around Bear.

When he stood, it was clear the two of them were a team. As Evan walked, Bear remained close by his legs. He almost seemed to be a part of his handler.

For maybe five minutes, Evan walked, then stopped or turned abruptly, sometimes giving hand signals, and Bear followed each movement, looking up often toward his handler's face for approval and clues to what came next.

At the same time, Percy, holding a large digital

camera, scurried around filming them, changing locations and angles often. Amber hoped he was doing a good job. She'd be excited to see the results.

Soon Evan stopped, glanced toward where Orrin stood, then, in a voice loud enough for the crowd, who nearly all appeared as enthralled as Amber felt, shouted, "Hold and bark." He motioned firmly toward Orrin, the agitator, who prepared himself for what was to come by pulling his arms up in front of him.

In seconds, Bear was beside Orrin, loping around him and barking as if he would attack if the man dared to move. Which he didn't. Not at first.

But then, as he and Evan must have discussed before, Orrin lunged forward, away from Bear, as if about to run the way a real bad guy would.

Immediately, Bear leaped on him and began barking, then grabbed his covered arms, biting and worrying the outside of the hopefully sufficiently protective padding.

Evan joined them immediately, then gave another hand signal and called, "Down." Bear let go and stared up at his handler as if waiting for the next signal or command. This time, Evan threw an elongated toy, the dog's reward for behaving so well. Bear chased it and brought it back for Evan to hold in a tug-of-war.

That was the beginning. Evan had Bear engage in a few more attacks on Orrin, sometimes knocking him to the ground and biting his covered sides.

The show went on for about twenty minutes.

Amber remained thrilled, especially as she listened to the cheers and excited remarks of everyone around them—including, to some extent, the cops.

Then it was over. Evan rewarded Bear with the toy for the last time. Everyone else poured through the gate to congratulate them and check to make sure Orrin, who appeared tired but otherwise unharmed, truly was okay.

Amber hurried toward Percy. "Did you record it all?"

"Yeah," he said proudly. "We've got some good stuff here, and I'll sure have fun putting it together for your website."

Evan couldn't keep himself from grinning proudly as the people who'd watched came over to tell him what a great job Bear and he had done.

He knew they had, but it still felt good to hear it.

It also felt good to take it in without wanting to run into the house to get away from all these folks who kept talking to him. Well, not wanting to very much, at least.

"Hey, everyone," Sonya called. She'd been yelling and cheering and seeming to have as good a time as anyone, and even that critical neighbor beside her had seemed impressed enough to smile and cheer a bit. "Come into the house. I've got some coffee, tea and cake. We can celebrate in there—and hear what Evan has planned for more classes to teach other handlers what he's so good at."

Evan glanced in embarrassment toward the

ground, then made himself look up. He had done a good job. He had continued, since his hiring, to show how he would fix things around here.

He had earned their kudos.

"Hey, I'd love some cake and celebration," he yelled back at Sonya, then glanced toward Amber, who was approaching her mother. Was she okay with it?

"Me, too," she called out. "Everyone inside."

Evan removed Bear's vest and reached into a pocket for a dog treat for his wonderful K-9. He'd earned it.

Then, Evan checked on Orrin, who'd removed his protective jacket and carried it while following the others into the house.

As Bear and Evan entered the kitchen, where everyone was congregating, Amber approached. "My mom's got everything started. But I wanted to talk to you. To thank you. That was spectacular!"

"Thanks, but not really. It was just a regular K-9 demo. Your dad probably did that kind of thing and better."

"He did something similar, sure, but not exactly the same. I just wish…"

Her lovely eyes teared up then. Evan quashed an urge to take her into his arms. Instead, he said, "I wish your dad was here, too, giving the demonstrations with or without me."

"Oh, yes. Yes," she said loudly enough that everyone milling around the table, some with pieces of cake in napkins, others holding coffee cups or water glasses, turned to look at her. "Sorry, everyone," she said, "but everything here, like what Evan now does with Bear, and the website, and all the classes to come—they're all a tribute to my father. My dead, murdered father." She aimed her gaze in the direction of the police officers, who stood together in a corner. "My murdered father, whose killer hasn't been found. But he—or she—will be, right, officers?"

Kara didn't look pleased at the near accusation, again, of their possible incompetence, Evan thought. "You know we're working on it, Amber," she said.

"And I know you haven't solved it yet. But I'm not giving up. Not this K-9 Ranch and what my father started here. And not the search for who killed him. Right, Evan?"

This time he felt uncomfortable as the crowd turned their attention to him. Giving dog-training demonstrations was what he did now.

Admitting to sticking his nose into police business, not so much.

"I'm with you about not giving up." It was all he felt comfortable saying to this crowd. "Now, if you all have your beverages in hand—coffee, tea or water—we'll toast the K-9 Ranch and the classes to come, and our thanks to Corbin Belott."

Chapter 17

Amber appreciated Evan's toast to her father in many ways. He wasn't just addressing one person, or a couple, but this entire—though admiring—group, and that probably wasn't easy for him.

And the tribute to her dad? Appropriate, of course, and also very special.

"Hear, hear," called some voices, and others yelled, "To Corbin," as everyone in the crowded kitchen lifted a glass, cup or water bottle or even just their hands to participate in the toast. That made Amber feel all warm inside.

Especially when she caught Evan's glance and smiled her thanks toward him. He just nodded and looked down at his own cup of coffee.

She realized that he had proposed the toast not

only to honor her father—and to move the crowd's attention further away from himself—but also to ease the sting of her outburst at the cops. To protect her from their wrath, perhaps.

If she really wanted them to continue—or resume—their investigation, insulting them wasn't the way to do it.

She understood that.

She also understood that she had allowed her emotions to dominate her good sense. She may have expressed things too strongly. But now, she needed to have a nice, friendly, nonaccusatory chat with the cops.

Making sure her mother remained chatting with Nathan and a couple of students, and therefore not paying attention to her, she edged through the crowd toward the police.

Unsurprisingly, no friendly smiles were aimed toward her. She considered talking with Kara first but decided to start at the top and approached Police Chief Andrew Shermovski, whom Amber had learned was nicknamed "Sherm" when she was introduced to him.

Unlike his young immediate subordinate, Sherm had apparently been around for a while. Amber guessed he was in his sixties, with lots of wrinkles around dark brown eyes that looked astute and wary, as if he'd seen everything. Maybe he had. He was slightly taller than the other three cops, including Doug, and his build was solid. His salt-and-pepper hair was cut short.

Did he look like a police chief? Amber didn't

care, as long as he did his job right. And at the moment, she believed he needed to work a little harder.

Still, she realized she would get further acting humble than accusatory, as she had somewhat before. "Thank you so much for coming." She stopped in front of Sherm. "All of you." She glanced around until her gaze landed again on the chief. "I'm sorry if I seemed out of line before, but I'm sure you can understand how hard it's been on my mother and me to lose my father that way." Especially with no answers. "I really do appreciate what you've been doing to investigate. And I'm hoping to be able to contribute something to your K-9 unit—" she looked quickly at those two officers, then back again "—now that I have such a skilled trainer on staff."

And now's the time for you to tell me what you're still doing, she thought.

But Chief Shermovski just said, "Of course we understand. And we hope you understand that a lot of what we are doing can't be revealed until we have enough proof to arrest a suspect, and we're not quite there yet."

"Then you do have someone you're focusing on?" Amber couldn't help the eagerness in her voice, but felt her shoulders sag again at the way Sherm's expression hardened.

"That isn't something we can talk about," he said. "Now, please excuse us. It's time for us to return to the station."

No, Amber didn't excuse them…but she said goodbye as cordially as she could. At least they thanked her for the demonstration.

Kara held back a little from the others. "I wish we could at least tell you what we're up to," she said. "Sorry, Amber. But like I said, please be sure we're not giving up."

As Amber watched the assistant chief hurry to catch up with her colleagues, she wondered if she should be the one to give up.

But as she felt someone touch her arm, she turned to find Evan beside her, and Bear, too, and realized that, as long as she had someone like him on her side, she couldn't—wouldn't—ever give up.

"Are you all right?" Evan had kept an eye on Amber during his toast and afterward, when she had headed toward those in uniform. Had she been okay with his distraction from her clearly emotional dig at the cops?

He understood it. Agreed with it. But knew it wasn't the way to stay on their good side.

"I am now," she said softly. "And I appreciate your getting me to shut up in such a nice way."

He looked into her pretty yet sad face. She managed a smile, at least, and he had to smile back. "You're very welcome," he said. "I'd like to propose another toast, this time to you and your mother for putting up with all this ineptitude, but I can't figure out a way to phrase it that won't make things worse…again. Although the cops are apparently leaving."

They had paused at the kitchen door as they talked with the four people with pets in training here. He wondered what the conversation was about but wasn't close enough to hear.

"That's okay," Amber said. "Let's not do anything to cause them to stay—though I doubt they're dashing back to the station newly inspired to dig deeper into my dad's case. I appreciate the thought, though."

"Anytime."

"And thanks again for your impressive demonstration. I'll be eager to see what responses we get after the videos are up on the website. I bet we'll be flooded with inquiries from police departments everywhere looking for K-9s and handler training."

"I hope so," Evan said, and really meant it—as long as he could control how many were in a class.

"I'll be back in a few minutes," she said. "But for now…" She stood on her tiptoes and, to his surprise, kissed him on the cheek.

It felt good. Friendly. Sweet.

It shouldn't have gotten his juices flowing…but it did.

"Like I said," she continued, "thanks."

She followed the cops out the door.

All right, maybe that was dumb, Amber thought. No one appeared to pay attention to Evan or her, and she'd wanted to do something a tiny bit special to acknowledge his kindness.

She hadn't intended it to be sexy, and it wasn't.

But it reminded her of being closer to him. Pressing against him.

Trading much more heated kisses with him.

Oh, yeah. It hadn't been a good idea.

Now she headed down the empty hall to the den where the young dogs were housed. With people coming in and out of the house, she hadn't wanted to let them loose for fear they'd run out the door. It had been long enough, though, that they probably needed to go out.

But as she reached the closed door, she heard voices from inside. Male voices. She realized then that she hadn't noticed Orrin and Percy in the kitchen as she'd walked out, only the rest of the crowd less the cops. They must be in there playing with the dogs.

She considered knocking in case they needed a moment to calm the three future K-9s—but then she thought she heard someone say *Corbin*, most likely Orrin, but the sound was muffled by the door. She paused, smiling as she waited for her father's employee to sing his praises as Evan had done.

Instead, Orrin said, "He was a jerk of a boss. Always telling me what to do and not listening when I told him his ideas weren't working."

What? Why was he saying that now? Amber almost did burst in, but hesitated when Percy said, "Well, at least he wasn't my boss. But he was always telling me what to do with this ranch's damn website. I'm the one who knows tech stuff and what works and what doesn't online. But to get paid, I had to listen to him."

"Yeah, to get paid. That's the important thing, isn't it?"

"Hell yes. But at least with these women in charge not knowing what they're doing, I'm less worried about that—and charging more."

"Hey, good idea. I'm due for a raise," Orrin said. "Especially since I have to work now with that damn guy with PTSD and his dog."

"Anyway, I'm ready to leave. You?"

Not wanting to get caught, Amber scurried back down the hall in the direction from which she'd come.

Even as her mind swirled in puzzlement—and agony.

She had assumed these men, who had sometimes assisted her dad in various ways, had liked him—even Orrin, who'd mentioned their occasional arguments but still had seemed to respect him.

She had pondered the possibility that one of them could have killed her father, but pretty much written both of them off as not having had any real motive.

But now, these two men were near the top of her suspect list.

"Oh, there you are." Evan approached Amber along the hallway. Bear wasn't with him. "Visiting the pups?"

She looked both uncomfortable and defiant, and he wondered what she was thinking. But she just said, "Yes, I think they might need a short walk." Her voice was raised.

He realized why when the den door opened and Orrin and Percy came into the hall. They must have heard her from inside. Orrin had Rex and Lucy on a leash, and Percy had Hal. "These guys are acting like they want out," Orrin said. There was something off about his expression as he looked straight at Amber, then at him.

Evan didn't look away but couldn't read what was going on in Orrin's staring eyes.

"I'll take them." Amber held out her hands for the leashes.

"We'll take them," Evan insisted as he reached for a leash. First, it would be better for Amber and him, more used to handling dogs, to take care of them rather than these men.

Second, he wanted to talk to Amber alone, except for canine ears around. Something was clearly on her mind. Something else that was apparently difficult.

After grabbing Rex's and Lucy's leashes, she turned quickly and led the dogs down the hall. Evan aimed a shrug at the two men near the door and followed her with Hal.

He said nothing until they reached the front door. As she opened it, he asked, "Is everything okay?" He knew the answer.

"No." She didn't respond further, and he hurried outside behind her.

She headed down the driveway and around the cars parked there, toward the lawn. She opened the gate and sped through behind the two young shepherds, who both cavorted in front of her. Hal yanked on his leash to catch up.

In a minute, Amber had let her two charges loose behind the area surrounded by the chain-link fence, and Evan did the same with Hal. She continued to stare at the dogs but he suspected she wasn't seeing anything.

Then she pivoted toward him. Her face was pale, her brown eyes wide and damp. "Yes," she said, "something is wrong. I overheard Orrin and Percy talking about my father and now—now I'm wondering even more if one of them had something to do with his death."

She related the conversation she'd heard, and he could understand why she was upset...and why she now had placed those guys near the top of her suspect list. He did, too.

"I loved my father," she spluttered with a soft wail. "He was sometimes critical but always fair with his employees and those he did business with, so I don't know what they were talking about."

"Maybe they were playing some kind of game with one another," Evan said. "Who could bad-mouth their former boss the worst, or something like that."

"But why?"

"No idea." But Evan did think again about seeing Orrin walk around the ranch late at night—supposedly to make sure all was well. Was there more to it than that?

The three young dogs had run around the enclosure several times and were now panting in the cool May air. Time to take them back in, Evan figured.

And maybe start a friendly but inquisitive conversation with Orrin and Percy.

He had a feeling that, if he didn't do it, Amber would.

Chapter 18

Amber hurried back to the kitchen, the dogs she'd taken charge of now behind her. So were Evan and Hal.

She needed answers, damn it, not more questions.

Should she confront the two men who'd been criticizing her poor, dead father? Fire Orrin and let Percy know she would look for different tech help?

But as she reached the door, she stopped and sighed.

Both men were useful at what they did around here.

And Evan was right. They could have had a hidden agenda for that conversation—to impress one another, or a different reason they'd never reveal. After all, they'd thought they were alone, that no one could hear them.

She wished she hadn't—maybe. Was it better to know their attitudes?

To believe one of them could have killed her dad?

Well, she didn't know that. And in earlier conversations with them, they'd both seemed somewhat sad and sympathetic, in their own way. So, she'd just keep things as they were.

For now.

But she would try somehow to bring out anything either of them knew about what had happened to her father.

She entered the kitchen with Rex and Lucy still leashed. Bear and Lola maneuvered around a bunch of human legs to greet them, and Hal joined the other dogs from behind her.

"Hi, guys," said one of the students, Grady, who looked a little lost without his Dobie, Mambo. The young guy kneeled and began playing with one dog after another, teasing them as if he had treats, then gently pushing them away.

Amber was interested to see that both Orrin and Percy were with her mother. The guests remaining at this impromptu party—the other pet trainees and Nathan—were near the sink chattering and drinking.

Since those two men were closest to her mom, she suspected they were trying to make sure they were on her good side, in case Amber had heard what she actually had heard.

Or was she just imagining it all?

She glanced around and saw Evan supervising Grady's doggy games. She had an urge to join them. To silently take in Evan's support. But she decided instead that this was a good time for another cup of coffee.

She maneuvered around Stewart, Julie and Aaron until she was closer to Nathan, who was pouring the coffee.

"Would you like some?" He picked up the pot from its brewer on the counter.

"Please." Amber didn't like the hint of desperation in her voice, but maybe no one else would notice.

She had an idea then, not a good one but at least it would potentially confirm to Percy and Orrin that they'd better behave.

If either had killed her dad, it surely hadn't been both of them.

When Nathan handed her the cup of coffee she lifted it and raised her voice as she said to the group, "I really liked Evan's toast to my dad before, when the cops were still here. I annoyed them when I suggested they'd done a poor job trying to learn what happened to my dad, but I apologized. They, of course, made it clear they wanted me to stay out of it. Well, don't tell them, but until they succeed I'll keep trying to figure things out. How about the rest of you—anything new you can tell me, or the police, about who hurt my father?"

She purposely looked sympathetically toward her clearly shocked mom and not toward Percy or Orrin, but from the corner of her eye she saw at least one of them move.

If nothing else, she had probably made them uneasy. Good.

"Hey." Evan stepped up beside her. "We're all together here to celebrate your dad. And we all feel bad about what happened to him. But we know what a good trainer he was, so let's celebrate dogs, too." He made a motion and Bear, beside him, stood and started circling the feet of everyone close by.

"That's so cute," Sonya said.

"I agree," Amber responded. And smart. Without telling her off, Evan nevertheless had gotten her attention and everyone else's, as well. He'd reminded them of why they'd come: the resumption and demonstration of the Chance K-9 Ranch's dog-training expertise.

Thanks, Evan, she thought and looked straight at him, half wishing it was appropriate, with these other people around, for her to hug him.

As if he understood, he nodded slightly and sent her a brief but sexy grin. "Now," he said, looking down toward the dogs, "let's all go outside for one final demo today. Those pups—" he gestured toward the young shepherds "—will look great on a video for the ranch website, too, even though they're not far along in their training. Percy, would you do the honor of filming that, too?"

"Sure," the tech guy said. "As long as you do as good a job of getting them to show off what they do know."

Percy aimed a glance toward Amber that she couldn't quite interpret. A request for her approval? An apology?

"Sounds great," she said. "Let's all go back outside."

* * *

Despite the pleasant way he'd reacted outwardly to Amber's latest comments, Evan was peeved inside. She knew better. But the best thing he could do for her at this moment was move everyone's attention away from her words…again.

Without looking at Amber, he grabbed the leashes of all three young dogs and headed for the kitchen door, then out of the house, careful not to choke them despite his need to hurry. At least they didn't have any control collars on since he hadn't intended to work with them now.

He made sure Bear was following. So was Lola.

Good. He would spend a little time working with the dogs. They listened to him or they didn't get rewarded. It was as simple—and sometimes as challenging—as that.

Then there was Amber…who didn't appear to be listening to him.

Evan didn't check to see if she or any other people followed as he herded his canine pack into the fenced area, where he felt comfortable letting the younger ones loose with the older ones.

Instead of working with the dogs, at this moment Evan's preference would have been to shake some sense into Amber. But despite his irritation, he had already reacted in the way most likely to stay on her good side.

For now.

He understood her reaction to overhearing Percy and Orrin that way, ramping up yet again her need to learn who'd killed her dad. But to deal with Corbin's murder, reach a resolution and some kind of closure, she kept putting herself in potential danger. Didn't she understand that?

Or maybe she did—and figured that somehow, since she anticipated something, from someone, she'd be able to protect herself.

He organized the three young dogs in a row on the lawn. As he turned, he saw that Amber and the others had followed him and now stood behind the fence. Good.

He had an idea.

He beckoned toward her. "Hey, boss," he called. "Everyone has already seen me in action with Bear today. It's your turn to give it a try with the ranch's puppies. No agitator, though. Just a training session."

Would it be a good thing if she tried and the dogs didn't obey her? Embarrassed her?

No, but at least it would hopefully do as Evan wanted and get the subject changed.

The look Amber leveled on him was both quizzical and defiant. "You're right," she called, and eased herself through the gate.

Heading toward him, she patted Lola and Bear as they trotted at her side. It appeared like one determined canine pack approaching another, and the idea almost amused Evan.

He glanced toward the rest of the people remaining behind the fence—Sonya, Nathan and the four students. It was the same audience as his demonstration this morning, minus the cops.

A good thing?

Well, it might at least provide the distraction he wanted.

"Choose one of our student dogs to be first," he instructed Amber as she and the adult dogs reached him.

He wasn't surprised she chose Lucy. Most police K-9s were males because they tended to be easiest to train, but that wasn't so with Rex. Hal? Sure, she could have picked him, but she might identify more with the female puppy.

"Now," he said, keeping the leashes of the two males in his hands, "let her loose and see how many of the exercises I demonstrated earlier that you can accomplish with her." He spoke loud so the other people could hear. "Understand, though, that these young dogs have had only a small fraction of the training and experience Bear's had."

"Of course." Amber grinned ironically at him as if he was a teacher who hadn't yet figured out how smart his student was.

Her, not the dog.

"Ready?" he asked.

She nodded, then called, "Lucy, come." She made the gesture Evan had taught her and, of course, Lucy came.

For the next ten minutes, Amber put Lucy through the initial training paces that Evan had demonstrated and worked with her on during her prior lessons.

She did great with it. Even their observers must have thought so, since they all seemed to watch intently and clapped when Amber had Lucy do something particularly challenging, like heeling while she walked in strange configurations, almost as if this young dog was a fully trained K-9.

What she did, how she performed with the dogs, shouldn't seem sexy—but it did. Evan wanted to hug her, as much in admiration as because watching her turned him on. But he stayed still, cheering her.

His mood had changed, and it appeared hers had, too.

She performed similarly with Hal, then Rex, and all of them did a credibly good job, even the most energetic of the male puppies.

When her demonstration was over, he walked with her and the dogs back toward the gate.

He'd noticed from the first that Percy had his camera out filming Amber's demonstration.

"How'd it look, Percy?" Amber said as she neared the crowd.

"Really good." The guy looked pretty proud of himself as he waved his camera toward her. "It'll be great on the website."

"Thanks so much!" Amber sounded happy.

Maybe some of that happiness resulted from the fact she wasn't accusing anyone—now—of murdering her father. He knew she hadn't forgotten her worries.

Had these people?

Not if either guy was guilty, or *any* onlooker, since the cops considered at least some of Corbin's students as suspects.

"This has been a fantastic day," Julie said, bending to pat Lucy's head. "Such wonderful demonstrations. And you can be sure I'll be back with Squeegie."

"When you do, I'll have a new command for you to use," Evan said, recalling their earlier discussion.

"This has been so much fun," said Aaron. Was he, with his attitude, on the cops' list? "I really appreciate watching Amber go through the paces the way we should be. I'm learning a lot here at the K-9 Ranch."

Evan hoped so—for his dog's sake. "That's great," Evan said. "We'll soon post more information about upcoming classes on the website, so be sure to keep in touch." There. He sounded like a dedicated teacher— and was pleased to see Amber smile at him in recognition. He smiled back.

"Gotta go now." Aaron motioned to the others he'd come with. They said goodbye and headed toward their cars.

"Hey, come over here," called Nathan, who still stood beside Sonya near the fence. With the dogs following, Evan strode at Amber's side in their direction.

He noted that Orrin had headed back toward his house, while Percy stood at the edge of the driveway apparently reviewing the videos he had shot that day.

Evan was glad to see Sonya also smiling when Amber and he joined Nathan and her. "I didn't imagine how great the demonstrations would be here today," she said. "Thanks to both of you."

"You're very welcome," he replied, and realized he should thank them and all the other people who'd shown up. Any discomfort he'd felt that day was more involved with concern over Amber rather than being the center of attention of a whole group of people.

"I've had more fun today watching dog demonstrations than I've had for a long time," Nathan added. "I've invited Sonya for dinner at my hotel and would love to have you two join us."

That would mean more crowds.

He could do it.

But first he waited for Amber's response. "That would be very nice," she said a few seconds later, and Evan realized she had glanced at her mother to make sure it was okay with her.

"What time would you like us there?" Sonya asked.

"Six o'clock would be fine," Nathan responded.

"I'll drive us all there," Amber said, then aimed a glance at Evan as if daring him to say no.

"Sounds fine to me." And it did. Another good opportunity to hang out with Amber, even with her mother and Nathan along.

He wouldn't be able to scold her then for her ongoing rants and reminders that she wasn't resting until she found her father's killer.

His job here was training dogs, but his avocation was turning into protecting Amber.

Fine with him—as long as she actually did stay safe.

Chapter 19

Amber enjoyed their dinner though she continued to worry about her mother's relationship with Nathan.

He was an okay-looking guy, with his silvery head of hair and expensive-looking suit while on a date—and Amber had no doubt both he and her mother considered this a date. Sonya had dressed up, too, in a pale yellow dress and heels, and insisted that Amber wear a nice outfit, as well.

She'd chosen a white blouse and black skirt, hoping to look more like this was business than pleasure. But it was pleasure, as well—since she couldn't help admiring how well Evan cleaned up. He, too, wore a suit—a black one with a dark gray shirt and deep green tie.

The Resort Restaurant, as it was called, was fairly crowded, especially considering how far from civilization this was. Or maybe that was the reason, since hotel patrons didn't have much choice where to go unless they wanted to journey into town. It was a fairly formal place, complete with waitstaff wearing dark suits and white tablecloths on all the tables.

The prices reflected its elegance, and Amber was glad the resort's owner had invited them—presumably intending to pay for their dinner.

They had already ordered, and, after Nathan had tested and tasted it, wine had been poured into their long-stemmed glasses, an expensive merlot. Amber had considered asking for one of the pricier meals on the menu, but had decided to be more prudent, so she had ordered chicken escalope, not the cheapest item but not at the top, either. Her mother and Evan chose in that price range, as well. Only Nathan had ordered the works, including steak.

"Now it's my turn for a toast," Nathan said. "To the K-9 Ranch." He lifted his glass, and after everyone did the same he took a sip from it. "I'm not much of a dog person, but I admire what you've been doing there under such difficult circumstances."

"Thanks." Sonya looked happy, more or less, but there was a strain around her eyes. The toast, as nice as it had been, clearly reminded her of her lost husband.

It had caused Amber to think of him, too—not that she needed a reminder.

"Could I come and observe more demonstrations?" Nathan asked Evan, who looked him straight in the face yet appeared relieved to glance away as the server brought their meals.

When their food was in front of them Nathan again aimed his gaze at Evan, clearly wanting a response.

"I'm sure it'll be fine with Evan if you'd like to come watch some of his classes," Amber said. "But please coordinate with him first since some will require more privacy than others. Right, Evan?"

He appeared more amused at her taking over than upset by it. "Right."

If Nathan wasn't much of a dog person Amber wondered why he'd want to come watch. To criticize Evan's performance again? Most likely it would be an excuse to visit her mother—which made her uneasy.

They all began eating, and after a few minutes of silence, except for the surrounding restaurant noise, Amber was a little surprised that Evan was the one to break it. "Did you ever watch any of Corbin's classes?" he asked Nathan.

Amber glanced at her mother. Her eyes were wide, and she held a bite of pasta on her fork that hadn't quite reached her mouth. "Oh, Evan, you probably aren't aware of it but my husband didn't like to have people who weren't students watch his classes. Not any more than he wanted to have other trainers here as his employees."

Amber figured Evan felt the same way, but a warmth gushed through her as he said, "No, I didn't know that, but just like dogs are pack animals, I think it helps in their training to have other dogs, and people, around."

Even though that could be taken as a criticism of her dad, Amber could have hugged Evan right now. Whatever his own internal issues, he was holding them at bay to do what she wanted her head trainer to do.

"Great," Nathan said and continued eating.

So did the rest of them, and their conversation morphed into a discussion of the town of Chance, and why Nathan had chosen to open his resort here, and its clear success. He admitted that the rooms were nearly always filled, and there was a waiting list for certain busy times of the year.

When they were done eating, Nathan did insist on paying their bill. That part pleased Amber.

The fact that he said he'd drive her mother home in a little while, after they had a drink together in the bar, didn't please her at all.

But her mom was a big girl, and though it hadn't been long since she'd lost her husband, she did need to go on with her life—in the way she chose, not the way Amber did.

Amber restrained herself from glaring back toward the ornate doorway into the posh resort lobby after Evan and she walked through it to the parking lot. Dinner had ended, and she was still with her amazing dog trainer. He was a man who brought out so many emotions in her, even if she had to keep them under control.

"This was a pleasant evening," she said as they reached her car. She'd pulled her key out of her small purse and pushed the button to unlock the doors.

Evan again opened the driver's door for her. "Definitely." He grinned down at her after she was settled in the seat before he closed the door. "If you'd like to give me a raise, I'd be happy to bring you here often for dinner."

She laughed along with him, then he got into the passenger's seat.

On the short drive, they recapped once more how the demonstrations had gone that day, and Amber was pleased when Evan said he figured that would become an important part of the ongoing classes. "Not every session should be videoed, and I'll keep some stuff I teach private to make sure people will want to come for lessons and not just rely on trying to follow what I demonstrate on the website."

"Agreed," Amber said. They then got into a discussion of what should be kept private and what should be shown to the world.

It didn't take long on the empty road to reach the nearby ranch, and Amber soon parked in the garage behind her house.

"You can have tomorrow officially off," she said. "It's Sunday."

"Depends on what you mean by 'off,'" he responded. "I'll be working with all the dogs at the ranch, but I assume no one's coming here to watch, or for lessons, right?"

"Right, though some weeks you might wind up working both weekend days and getting other days as your version of 'off.'"

His laugh was short…but sexy. "Would you like to

come and say good-night to Bear?" he asked. There was a smoldering look in his eyes under the dim light of the garage that suggested he wanted her to do more than say good-night.

Her entire body, inside and out, grew warm, and she considered saying yes. Strongly considered it.

But her mother would be home soon, and she didn't want to have to explain to her how long it might take to say good-night to Bear.

And maybe she was reading this all wrong. Last time, she'd thrown herself into Evan's arms, kissed him, shared in such touching and stroking that it made her weak just thinking about it.

Then he'd pulled away.

Did she want to take a chance on that happening again?

"Thanks," she said, "but I'll stay here at my house. I've got some dogs of my own to say good-night to."

"Would you like me to help with their last walks of the night?" He wasn't giving up. Nor was he looking away.

He was tempting her. Strongly.

But she was strong, too. "No, we'll be fine. See you tomorrow, Evan." She opened the car door and got out.

As he walked from the garage toward the driveway, though, she felt a surge of regret.

Evan couldn't help looking—as always—toward Amber's house as he took Bear for his last walk of the night. He saw car lights approach up the driveway and figured Sonya must be home. The outside lights stayed on for a short while—an indication of Amber's final dog walks of the night. He also kept his eyes open for Orrin but didn't see him.

He'd enjoyed dinner that night as well as checking out the resort next door. Busy place. Too many people for his comfort, but he'd handled it. He'd especially liked seeing the obvious security guys patrolling the place in their suits. Too bad they, or their equivalent, hadn't also patrolled the nearby ranch when Corbin Belott was in danger.

"Just you and me, guy," he'd said to Bear after giving the dog a quick hug before settling into bed.

Evan slept well that night, despite a fleeting— well, not so fleeting—wish he'd been able to talk Amber into joining him in his house. Who knew where that would have led? He'd certainly not have backed away this time if she had shown interest in getting closer…in any respect.

When he woke up, he had no plans to meet with Amber today—though he'd see her anyway. He had a quick breakfast in his kitchen after walking Bear again. He saw Orrin leave his house while he was outside but didn't make a point of getting any closer.

Could the guy have killed his employer? His personality wasn't exactly friendly and he'd apparently argued with Corbin, but that didn't mean he'd murdered him—did it?

Or Percy. The geek was a bit…well, geeky. Evan thought that, of the two of them, Orrin was more likely to be the killer.

"What do you think, Bear?" he asked his companion, and got a tongue-filled smile and tail wag from his companion.

He had an urge to do something more to settle his nerves and relax a bit. Time to take his expertly trained dog on another long hike around the ranch.

Which he did. This one was similar to the last, in the same direction but not getting so close to the murder scene.

He again told Bear, "Search," and his dog trotted off as if accepting and enjoying his mission.

But no alerting this time, either. Just an enjoyable, mind-cleansing outing.

One enjoyable enough to convince Evan it wouldn't be the last time.

Amber was glad when, after breakfast the next morning, her mother settled in front of the television set to binge-watch one of her favorite shows.

That gave Amber a chance to walk Lola and the pups, then sit down at the computer.

Not to check things on the ranch website, although she took a peek, but so far Percy had made no changes. Nor to search more information about Evan, despite that idea appealing to her. A lot.

No, it was time to do some planning. She'd have to run everything by Evan, of course, but she started figuring out a potential schedule to incorporate all the kinds of dog training he would start with, including instructing and refreshing K-9 police officers with their own dogs, as well as teaching pet owners how to train their dogs. She also wanted to introduce their own three young shepherds to potential future purchasers for existing K-9 units when they were ready.

After spending an hour creating online notes and a tentative schedule, she needed a break. Or so she told herself.

There was actually something she wanted to look up on the internet. Someone. As she did frequently these days…her dad.

Not that she'd ever found anything useful.

Before she got started, though, the doorbell rang, and four sets of barks—three young and shrill, and the other a bit older—sounded throughout the house. All four dogs joined her at the front door, since she hadn't locked the youngsters in their den.

It was Evan. Not surprising. He'd indicated he wanted to give lessons to the shepherds despite it being Sunday.

"Hi," he said, then gestured toward the dogs. "Mind if I take those three out for a while?"

"I don't mind at all—especially if I can come later and watch."

"You're more than welcome." His tone, and the sexy look he shot her way, indicated his words were true.

"Great." She invited him inside, got the pups' leashes, then watched as he took all three with him. Lola, beside her at the door, looked sad, but her mom joined them.

"I think someone needs attention," she said. "I'll take Lola for a short walk—the other way."

She soon left Amber in the house alone. Amber took that time to do a Google search of Corbin Belott.

His obituary came up first, as always, then his dog training and the ranch's website.

Nothing new.

Amber had an urge to do something on social media to remind people about him, and that his murder remained unsolved. But Evan's chastisement of her for even mentioning that to their visitors after his demo popped into her head, and she knew he was right.

Sure, she hated loose ends, and this one had so much emotion attached that she'd never get over it.

But she appreciated that Evan cared enough to try to tamp down her rash impulses.

She only wish he cared more about… No. Things were fine between them.

She had to let that alone.

But maybe it was a mistake to even look up her dad. Her state of mind was ruined. She couldn't just sit at the computer now.

Or maybe she had simply been hoping for an excuse to go watch Evan work with the young dogs.

She popped her head into the living room—her mom had returned and was watching television. Amber let her know she'd be outside observing Evan's lessons.

And then she went out to do exactly that.

The day was progressing quickly, Evan thought. He hadn't been surprised when he first saw

Amber striding toward the chain-link fence as he and the young dogs were working on their obedience lessons, with Bear staying back, good dog that he always was.

Amber didn't say anything at first, just watched him. Once, it would have made him uncomfortable, but now just gave him the incentive to do the best job possible—which he would have anyway.

When he finished working with each youngster he gave Amber the option to conduct her own lessons, which she did. By the time both completed their instruction, it was lunchtime, and Amber invited him, with Bear, to join her mother and her at their place. No reason not to accept the invitation, so he did.

After they ate, Amber asked him to join her by her computer to go over some initial class scheduling—including for the upcoming week.

Another reason to spend time with this dedicated woman who attracted him so much.

More lessons that afternoon, again in Amber's presence. More discussions, and games with all the dogs, and Evan felt himself smiling from the inside out. What a wonderful supposed day off even if— especially because—it was spent with his boss.

"Tomorrow," Amber began when she said goodbye at her front door, "as I mentioned before, I've a few other local students lined up to begin pet classes here—some people my dad had taught and I'd contacted to let them know we're resuming lessons. We should get more of those, plus additional students, as time goes on. Then we can start looking for some help for you." Her grin showed she was pleased, but he had managed not to punctuate it with a kiss.

For dinner and the rest of the evening he and Bear were alone. He took his dog out again later for a walk, though, circling the ranch right after he'd eaten.

He hung out for a short while around the main house, but though he saw some lights come on he didn't see Amber, or even her mother. Then he headed back to his place, again not running into Orrin.

Just an ordinary day, he thought as he entered his house with Bear.

But he wished he'd simply knocked on the main house's door and said good-night to Amber.

Chapter 20

Amber had gotten into a discussion with her mom after dinner about a reality TV show with contestants competing over their singing, and they'd watched a two-hour episode that night.

She was therefore running late when she got ready to take the dogs out for the last time that day—too late to just give them an outing in their fenced-in area. That wasn't as much fun anyway.

First, she leashed up Rex and Hal. She took them out through the front door, locking it behind her. She'd already checked the other doors, from the kitchen and into the garage.

She'd started doing that yesterday, when her suspicions about Orrin had ramped up, at least a little. She had promised herself to stay more alert, especially on walks, plus she didn't want to worry about their handyman popping into their house and jeopardizing her mother's safety. Too much anxiety on her part?

Maybe so, but better safe, or at least safer, than sorry—even though she didn't want to think that Orrin had been her father's killer.

Now, outside, she kept this walk short. It was dark but the standard lights around the driveway and houses were on.

While she was out there, she realized she hadn't talked to Mirri for a while and placed a call to her friend while following the leashed dogs.

"How've you been?" Mirri asked right away. "And how are you and that gorgeous dog trainer of yours getting along?"

"He's not mine—though I have to admit he is gorgeous. And he's definitely a fine employee." As well as overly protective at times…but that wasn't a bad thing.

"Well, we need to get together one of these days to talk."

"Fine with me. I need to drop by Pets and Products soon for some stuff for the dogs, so I'll call first and we can set up a time to go out for coffee."

"You're on," Mirri replied. They said their good-nights and Amber hung up.

Meantime, she had circled the house a couple of times with her current charges. Fortunately, Hal and Rex had been cooperative, so it was time to accompany them inside.

Next, she took only Lucy out, since she tended

to walk Lola by herself. The slightly older dog, who wasn't destined for more serious training and being taken in by a police K-9 unit, was entitled to separate attention from her family, after all. And like the male pups, Lucy did what she needed to do fairly quickly.

Then it was Lola's turn. Though it was only around ten o'clock, Amber no longer heard the TV and popped into the living room to check on her mom. Since Sonya wasn't there, Amber assumed she'd already headed to bed. When she reached the hall she heard water running in the bathroom, so she figured she was right.

As she passed by, the bathroom door opened. Her mother, in pajamas, looked at her groggily. "Good night, dear," she said.

"Good night, Mom," she responded. Her mother entered her bedroom and shut the door behind her without asking the status of dog walking for the night. That was fine. Amber had usually completed it by now, so Sonya probably assumed that was the case tonight.

With the three younger dogs shut in their den, Amber leashed up Lola, who'd been following her, and once more locked the front door behind her.

For fun, she decided to make this walk a little longer, with a short venture down the narrow road toward the employee houses.

And if she happened to see Evan there, out with Bear? Well, that would be an extra benefit of the walk.

She saw no indication of Orrin outside, but as she passed his house her cell phone chirped, the sound indicating she had received a text. Odd. She did exchange texts sometimes with friends, but this was a bit late for one. She figured it was probably Mirri with some kind of follow-up thought.

But when she pulled her phone from her pocket this time she didn't recognize the displayed phone number.

She pressed the button to look at the text—and gasped.

It said, I have heard you are asking too many questions, pushing too many people. Back off now or what happened to your father will happen to you.

Evan was on his laptop when he heard heavy and quick knocking on his front door. Bear immediately started barking, and they both hurried down the hall.

Evan pulled the door open, concerned why someone was knocking on his door at this hour. He wasn't surprised that it was Amber. But he was surprised at the look of panic on her face as she pushed past him into his entry, pulling leashed Lola behind her.

"What's wrong?" he demanded, closing the door, then taking Amber into his arms. For comfort only, he told himself. And because he was damn worried about her.

"This." Her voice was shaking, and so were her hands, as she handed him her cell phone.

He read the text and nearly smashed the phone on the floor. But that wouldn't help to find out who dared to make this threat. And he *was* going to find whoever had done it and ensure the person was locked up—with maybe a few bruises first to take to prison.

"Okay," he said. "Just stay calm, and we'll discuss what to do now." Like, remain here, in his presence, so he could protect her tonight. And tomorrow?

He already had several ideas.

"I can't believe it," she said, pacing the floor of his small entry. "I didn't do anything today to look for my dad's killer. And yes, I was a bit foolish with the things I said yesterday, and this seems to indicate that the person who sent it heard about that. Should I approach everyone who watched the demonstrations yesterday and ask who they talked to about what I said?"

"Of course not," Evan said. She should leave that to him. Better yet, to the cops—if they actually jumped in to follow up on this. It could even have been one of them who spoke out of turn, although if so they'd never admit it.

But then, who would?

"Look, here's what we'll do," he continued. "First, come in and have a beer so you can relax a little. Although..."

"Although what?"

He'd thought about Sonya. The text seemed to threaten only Amber, but if the killer wanted to hurt her in more ways than one, he—she?—could go after her mom. "Is your mother okay?"

"I made sure the doors were locked and saw her close the door to her room before I left," she said.

That didn't mean she'd be fine all night, but he

would check on her later. "Okay. Let's discuss what to do next, then I'll walk you back there."

"Fine."

He led her into the kitchen, where he got from the refrigerator bottles of his favorite dark beer for each of them. He watched until Amber took a swig, figuring if nothing else the brew might relax her a bit.

He also made sure Lola knew where Bear's water bowl was and gave each of the dogs a treat.

When he joined Amber at the table, her hands were clenched around the bottle, and she was trembling. He moved his chair beside hers and gently pulled one cold hand away and held it.

"First thing we should do," he said, "is call the cops—your buddy Assistant Chief Kara if it's possible to get hold of her at this hour. Tell her what happened and have their techies on staff trace the phone number—though I'll bet it's an untraceable burner phone."

She nodded, and her reddish hair bobbed slightly as it framed her pale and sad face. "That's what I figure, too."

"We'll visit the station tomorrow and show them the text. We'll schedule it around the class you planned."

"Fine." She looked at him as if she wanted to say something, but it took a moment before she began. "I shouldn't be so upset about this. I wanted to out whoever killed my dad, and that person is apparently upset enough to start making threats. Maybe this is a prelude to learning, at last, who it is."

"Maybe, but it would be a good thing if you stayed alive long enough to find out."

"Yeah, there is that little angle, isn't there?" She took another swig of beer, but at least now she seemed to be calming a bit. She appeared more determined, and that worried Evan. What if she started blabbing all around town her intention to find out and reveal who the killer was, just to see what occurred next?

What if she put herself in more danger?

Damn, but this gorgeous—and foolish—woman exasperated him.

And that wasn't all she did to him...

He moved his chair even closer to put an arm around her, draw her nearer. "Look, Amber. I don't know what you're thinking, but you need to be especially careful now. I don't want anything to happen to you."

She turned and looked him straight in the eye.

Not long ago, he'd have been highly uncomfortable with that. Looked away immediately, maybe gotten up to retrieve another bottle of beer.

Not now, though.

He started to reach over to pull her into his arms, but she beat him to it. They were suddenly both standing. Amber pressed herself against him—and raised her mouth to his.

Bad idea, Amber thought as she reveled in the feel of Evan's lips against hers, his tongue inside her mouth teasing hers. She felt every hard plane of his body as he held her close—and that wasn't all she felt against her.

His erection below was like an agitator—not a person wrapped in a big, protective balloon of a suit, but a taut, hard shaft that agitated, triggered, all her sexual needs.

Don't pull away this time, she begged him silently. And at this moment, at least, that possibility seemed unlikely. His hands explored her back, then downward, gently squeezing her butt. One of them kept going, along the top of her jeans-clad thigh and to her front, staying below, grasping her most sensitive parts from outside.

"Evan," she breathed, making sure her own hands were equally engaged in touching his buttocks, then moving forward until his hardness was beneath her grasp outside his jeans.

"Come with me," he whispered against her, and without ending their kiss began walking slowly with her.

She knew where they must be going: his bedroom. She knew the layout of this house, and it wasn't far down the hall from this kitchen.

In moments, they reached that room. He didn't turn on the lights, though there was slight illumination from the hall behind them.

She listened and heard doggy paws on the wooden floor, but figured that kind of audience would be just fine.

But...was this a mistake? An unconscious—or conscious—way to deal with the threat she had received?

So what if it was? This man had attracted her from the moment they had met, no matter how inappropriate that might be. Maybe this would satisfy her enough to get any further idea of sex with him out of her mind forever.

Or not, she thought as he began pulling off her T-shirt. And then her jeans.

Before he could reach for her undergarments she returned the favor, stripping him of his outer clothes.

Oh, my. He had always been dressed in clothing that hid what was beneath: his gorgeous physique... and the scars all over it that were a better explanation than anything he'd said about the origins of his fortunately dwindling PTSD.

Maybe that was why he had backed away last time...

"Oh, Evan," she breathed.

He looked at her then and must have seen where her gaze was focusing. "That was a couple of years ago," he said. "It hurts some now and then, but mostly I'm fine."

Except for his state of mind, sometimes. And Amber wanted to bend and kiss every one of those horrendously painful-looking scars.

Instead, he removed her remaining clothes, then his own shorts. She was definitely distracted.

He took her hand and led her to the bed, pulling down the coverlet as if they were old hands at this, experienced in going to bed together. He kissed her again—they kissed each other—and suddenly they were lying on the sheets and his hands were touching her breasts, and he was kissing them, even as his fingers found her most sensitive area below and began stroking her.

"Evan," she gasped, a plea for him to continue, but he pulled away. Was it like last time, an ending to a hot, sexy fairy tale barely begun?

But no, this time he reached into the top drawer of the bedside table and extracted a condom.

He was not only sexy, but also smart and responsible.

"Me." She held out her hand, and with a little help from him she didn't just get to grasp and feel his erection, but she sheathed it, too.

Then he was inside her, gently pumping and moaning softly, even as she did the same.

She reached her climax much too soon, but she could hardly complain. He seemed to reach completion, too, judging by the way his body tautened, then relaxed.

She just lay there for a moment, wondering what to say or do next. But he beat her to it. "Doesn't seem like either of us needs lessons for this kind of exercise."

She laughed as he rolled back onto her and kissed her again.

He'd have liked to have done it again. And again. But for the moment, he actually was sated.

And not terribly uncomfortable or embarrassed that she had seen the ugly, scarred state of his body. It hadn't kept her from engaging in what felt like the best sexual act in his entire life, either before or after his injuries.

Right now, he needed to get up and get dressed and be there when Amber called the cops about that damn text message. At least alert them, see if there was anything they could do that night—before he accompanied Amber to the station to show them the message and learn what they would to do to protect her.

That was his assignment for tonight.

In a few minutes, he would walk Amber and Lola back to her house. He would sleep on the sofa with Bear at his feet, for tonight and maybe longer. Until they got the cops to take over whatever they could do to make sure the SOB who sent that text couldn't make good on the threat it contained.

Or at least get some backup here, like the obvious security guys he had seen patrolling the resort when they'd had dinner there.

One way or another, he was going to make sure whoever it was got what was coming to them.

Chapter 21

The delay had been delightful. No, a whole lot more than delightful.

But Amber wanted—needed—to make that phone call to the cops. Not before she'd checked on her mother, though.

Even so, she felt reluctant to get out of bed. Was this the one and only time she would have sex with this incredibly hot and desirable man?

It should be, considering their situation. In fact, considering their situation, it shouldn't have happened at all.

But she was glad it had.

She tossed Evan a smile and slid out of bed, fully conscious of his eyes on her, which made her begin warming once more, especially in her most vulnerable areas. "I've got to get back to the house," she said unnecessarily as she began getting dressed. To chill herself as much as possible, she turned her back on him.

"We both do." She heard a rustle behind her and figured that he, too, had risen and was putting his clothes back on.

A shame—but it needed to be done, especially since he had confirmed he was accompanying her to her home, which she highly appreciated.

Soon they both were clad once more in what they'd previously worn. Amber couldn't help pulling her phone from her pocket again. No more texts, but she looked again at the one she had received earlier, the threatening message that had turned her life upside down, at least for now.

Would she have made love with Evan if she hadn't received it? Would he have made love with her?

And now, what was going to happen? Could the police figure out who'd sent it—and do what was necessary to arrest that person and keep her safe?

She wished.

"Ready?" Evan asked from beside her. On the floor nearby, both dogs skittered, tails wagging, as if they knew it was time for another outing.

And since dogs were always insightful, reading clues as well as human minds did at times, Amber had no doubt they knew that the people with them were taking them for another walk.

Perhaps the dogs were also on duty to protect them. Their dear friends were programmed, after all, to alert them to any dangers outside. But Amber had no reason to believe anything would happen to them on the way back to the house.

Although maybe her father hadn't believed anything would happen to him on his own property... and as far as she knew he hadn't been warned.

"Are you okay?" Evan asked, and Amber realized she was staring at the floor rather than putting her shoes on.

"Better than okay," she said firmly, attempting, at least, to cast all those negative, frightening thoughts aside.

But he must have read her mind, or at least recognized what she was likely thinking. "It'll be all right, Amber. I promise."

How could he make such a promise? Although she trusted him, wanted to rely on him...

"Now, let's go to your place, check on your mother and make that call."

Evan couldn't help it. He was concerned, too—mostly for Amber's safety. Once they were out his front door, he locked it, then bent down to the ear of the dog at his feet and whispered, "Bear, protect."

He looked up to see Amber staring at him. Had she heard him? Understood him? Her slight smile suggested she knew what he had done and approved of it.

Bear stood straight then, despite not having a vest on telling him he was on duty. He knew.

Now Bear leaped ahead, ears up, nose in the air—

clearly ready to protect them from whatever happened to appear.

Nothing did, though. Lights were on inside Orrin's house but the guy didn't come out, not surprising at this hour unless he actually was the bad guy and planned to harm them this night.

In a few minutes they reached Amber's door, which she opened with a key. Only then, with humans and dogs all inside, did Evan allow himself to take a deep breath.

He was too worried over a stupid text—maybe. He'd have been less concerned if he'd been the one to receive it instead of Amber.

But once they were locked inside he said, "Let's go check on your mom."

"I'll bet she's asleep," Amber said. "She was heading for bed when I left with Lola."

Hopefully, that was the case. And in fact, when they reached Sonya's bedroom door, Evan swallowed his concern and allowed Amber to open it quietly and peer inside.

If anything had been wrong, he'd rather be the one to discover it.

There was no light on in the bedroom. "Can you see?" he whispered to Amber.

She nodded, watched for a minute, then closed the door. "The light from behind us was enough for me to see she was lying in bed, breathing," she said, also quiet as they turned and walked back down the hall. "She's fine."

"Good."

They went downstairs to the kitchen and Evan said, "You need to be the one to call the cops so they'll capture your cell phone number and, hopefully, know it's you. But put it on the speaker so I can participate."

"It's too late and too calm right now for me to call 911," Amber said. "But I have the general number for the police station programmed in."

Her tone was sad and ironic, and Evan felt bad for her, even as he understood why she might have that number so readily available: to call and check on the status of their investigation into her dad's murder.

He doubted she ever did that, though.

They sat at the kitchen table. Amber pushed a couple of buttons on her phone, and he heard it ring. "Chance Police Department," said a female voice. "Is this an emergency?"

In a way, Evan thought, but was glad Amber said, "No, but it is important. I'd imagine the answer is no this late, but is Assistant Chief Province there?"

"No, ma'am," said the operator. "Can someone else help you?"

"I hope so, though I'm not sure who to ask for." She gave a brief description of who she was and the text message she'd received.

"Let me connect you to Sergeant Guyan," the operator said. "He's in charge here tonight."

"Fine," Amber said.

After a wait of a minute or two, a male voice said, "Hello. This is Sergeant Guyan. I understand you're the daughter of Corbin Belott, and you've received a threatening text message."

"That's right."

"Tell me about it."

Amber repeated what she had told the person who answered the phone. When she was done, Evan said, "This is Evan Colluro. I'm Ms. Belott's employee at the K-9 Ranch and live in one of the homes here. She was walking a dog outside my house when she got the message so she knocked on my door, and I've been with her since then."

Of course he didn't mention what they'd been doing for part of that time, although the brief recollection did cause a reaction down below that he ignored—or at least tried to.

"I'm concerned about Ms. Belott and her mother," he continued, "so I'm going to stay with them at least until tomorrow. You may not know it, but Chief Shermovski and Assistant Chief Province, along with your two K-9 officers, were here yesterday for a demonstration of some of the dog training the ranch will be providing. Ms. Belott has been talking with Assistant Chief Province in particular about what happened to her father, and we'd like to see the assistant chief as soon as she's available."

He felt Amber's stare as he talked, and now he glanced toward her. Her face was pale, her expression somber, but she nodded and mouthed the words *thank you*.

"I can schedule an appointment for eight thirty tomorrow morning, if that works for you. Meantime, I'll send a couple of officers to your place to touch base, and make sure patrols go by often for the rest of the night."

"Sounds good," Evan said, and again Amber nodded at him. "About how long will it take for the officers to get here?"

"I've set up a visit even as we speak. Someone should be there in ten minutes or less."

"Thank you, Sergeant," Amber said.

"You're welcome, and be sure to let us know if you get any more texts tonight—or if anything else happens."

"I will." Amber's voice rasped, and she closed her eyes before looking back toward Evan. "I certainly hope not."

"Me, too, ma'am." They said goodbye, and Amber pushed the button to end the call.

"Do you want to wake your mother to let her know what's going on?" Evan asked. "She's bound to hear the cops arrive, especially because the dogs are likely to bark."

"You're right," she said. "I'll go get her."

Sending him a look he interpreted as both resigned and sad, she left the kitchen.

He bided his time by checking a few things on his cell phone—including searching for news stories originating around Chance. Nothing stood out.

A few minutes later Amber reentered the kitchen with her mother behind her. Sonya was dressed in a robe, and her reddish hair was askew.

"Amber told me about that text she received, and

that the police are coming," Sonya began. The timing was perfect, since the doorbell rang then.

All dogs in the house, including Bear, began to bark. Evan easily shushed him, and Amber did the same with Lola, but the young dogs in the den kept it up.

Evan watched, poised to protect her, as Amber looked out the peephole, then opened the door. Two uniformed officers, one male and one female, stood there. "We understand you received a threat," said the female officer. "May we come in?"

Amber stood aside, then shut the door again after the cops entered. She showed them into the living room.

The conversation was short and to the point. They asked Amber to show them the text, which she did. They said that a tech expert would be at the station tomorrow morning when she came to see Kara Province and would check out the phone and source of the text. Meantime, as the dispatcher had said, patrols would go past this area more frequently than usual tonight. And if there was anything else Amber, or anyone else in the household, could tell them now, she should do so.

But everything had already been related. Amber thanked them, and so did Sonya and Evan. Evan noted that both gave brief pats to the two dogs in the room, which raised them up a notch in his estimation.

Then they left.

"How can we get any sleep tonight?" Sonya asked when they were gone. "Will we be safe, even with the dogs?" At least the young ones had finally settled down, and Lola was lying at Sonya's feet on the living room floor.

"You'll be safe," Evan promised. "Bear and I will sleep right here." He gestured toward the couch, where all three of them were sitting. "And I'll go with Amber and you to the police station in the morning."

"Oh, thank you, Evan." Sonya definitely sounded relieved.

Evan just hoped he could do as promised, and keep them all safe.

Despite the small size of the Chance Police Department, one of their crime-scene investigators also had skills in computer and technology forensics. Or that's what Amber heard from Kara the next morning when she, her mom and Evan arrived.

They were in Kara's office, and she'd been given the rundown on the situation that had been related by last night's phone call and the visit to the ranch by the cops.

Amber had been glad Evan had stayed the night in their house, though fortunately nothing happened. They both walked dogs in the morning and said hi to Orrin as he came outside to work, but everything seemed normal—except when she pulled her phone from her pocket to look at that terrible message again.

Now Kara stood behind her large desk, which now had a couple piles of paper on it. She held out her hand to Amber. "Give me your phone and we'll have it checked."

Amber wondered at how relaxed Kara looked this morning in her dark uniform. She also appeared sympathetic, and Amber hoped that this woman who'd become a friend of sorts, as well as a frequent skeptic, actually gave a damn about whether she and her mother were in danger. Kara's brown eyes almost appeared sad, especially when she looked toward Sonya.

"Thanks," Amber responded, handing her the phone.

Kara stepped out of the office for about five minutes. When she returned without the phone she asked, "Now tell me what you think the texter meant."

Amber aimed a glance at Evan, but he was staring over Kara's shoulder. He must have realized she had looked at him since he turned and met her eyes.

She half expected him to jump in and tell Kara she should know, but instead she responded. "I'm not sure, but I figure that whoever sent the message is probably the person who killed my dad. He or she heard about my rant after the demonstrations at our place on Saturday, and isn't happy that I'm not leaving it alone, that I actually want to find out who that person is and get him or her arrested."

"Who do you think the person heard it from?" Kara asked.

"That's a big question," Amber said. "If we can figure it out, maybe we can determine who the killer is."

"The person could have been there but decided to phrase it this way to make it sound like he or she wasn't," Evan said, jumping in.

"Of course." Amber knew that but figured she would let the authorities take over—and Kara was surely intelligent enough to think of that herself.

"Of course," Kara repeated.

The discussion continued, but Amber didn't derive much optimism from it.

Soon, Kara brought things to a close. "Now, I unfortunately have another meeting to prepare for. I want to reiterate—again—that we're still working on Corbin's case and won't stop until we figure it out. But for now—well, you've all got to be careful." She looked directly at Amber, then her mother. "Don't mention the situation to anyone else, not the text, or that you've been here. Since we don't know who's involved, any kind of discussion, if learned by the perpetrator, could lead to consequences none of us wants."

"Right," Amber agreed, also glancing at her mother. Sonya was looking down at her lap. "Are you okay, Mom?" she asked.

She looked up, and Amber saw her brown eyes bathed in tears. "No," she wailed softly. "I'm not okay with any of this. It's still so painful to have lost your father, and now to have you threatened this way. I just can't stand it."

"I understand, Sonya," Kara said. "We don't like it, either. Any unresolved case is a thorn in our side, and a murder is the worst. I know Amber doesn't believe it—" she looked toward Amber, who knew her pain, for her mother's sake as much as her own, was written on her face "—but we really are still making this investigation a top priority. I can only hope this text gives us additional information that leads to the killer's identity. Right now, though, we're somewhat at a loss, which is why I said to let us know if you happen to hear anything."

"But you don't want Amber to jump in and look on her own, right?" Evan said. "Or to ask questions or anything else to anger whoever did it." He stared straight at Kara's face, which surprised Amber.

"As I said, I don't want any of you to do anything to put yourselves in danger," Kara responded. "Now, please keep in close touch with me, especially you, Amber. But right now—"

There was a knock on her office door, and it opened. A young uniformed officer walked in holding Amber's phone. "I've got all the info I can for now from this," he said. "So far I haven't been able to find the source, and though I may not be able to I'll keep trying. But the text didn't just come from a burner phone, it's one that must somehow be routed from overseas. Sorry, but I can't tell you who made the threat."

Chapter 22

They left the police station and walked toward Amber's car in the slight chill of the late May morning. Evan wished he could keep both women downtown with him and not return to the ranch, or anyplace else the person who'd made the threat might be able to easily find Amber.

He even considered taking them someplace farther away, a nearby larger town, or even San Francisco.

But that wouldn't work.

First, they hadn't brought any of the dogs with them on this venture to the police station—and even if they had, the three youngsters weren't well behaved enough yet to handle traveling that far.

Also, Amber had said she'd scheduled a small

class that afternoon with a couple of people bringing their dogs for training. They had been students of Corbin's, although they hadn't been for long, so they weren't as well trained as the members of the other class Evan had already taught. She checked her email on her cell phone, which had been returned to her, as they walked, and said the students had confirmed they were on their way.

Plus, those same people were coming for two lessons, one this afternoon and one tomorrow. They were residents of San Luis Obispo, not far, but they apparently were staying overnight.

The class could be postponed—but Amber didn't seem inclined to do that.

"So what do we do now?" Sonya looked at Amber as they navigated the busy sidewalk toward the Chance main shopping area, where they'd parked.

"Go home and act normal." Amber walked between her mother and Evan, and her voice was soft as she first looked toward Sonya. But he wasn't surprised when she turned her head and shot him a glare he considered defiant—as if anticipating his objection.

"That's what we'll do." He apparently surprised her, judging by the arch in her reddish eyebrows. He had an urge to hug her because she was being her ornery and determined self. Not that he'd do it here in public, or anywhere near her mother. Or maybe ever again… Heck, he knew he would, given the chance. "But I've got a lot of questions, plus Bear and I will be—"

"Hanging out with us," Amber said, finishing his thought. There was a hint of a smile on her lovely face now, as though she approved.

A good thing, since he intended to stay as close as possible to them. He figured Amber would watch the class as he gave it, as well as his workouts later with the young shepherds. He nevertheless felt hopeful that if Amber and Sonya were inside the locked house after he'd checked around it, he might take the opportunity to chill out with another hike with Bear...if he found the right time.

They stopped in the grocery store to pick up enough supplies to allow them to stay home for several days. They also visited the town's deli and bought sandwiches for today's lunch. Then they went to Pets and Products, where Amber chatted with her friend Mirri, while Evan helped Sonya pick up more food for the dogs.

Finally, they headed back to the ranch. Amber pulled her SUV into the garage and Evan helped remove everything they'd bought. He carried most of it inside and wasn't surprised to be greeted by both Bear and Lola while the other dogs barked in their den.

He insisted on going outside again to look around, then allowed Amber to help him walk all the dogs.

He looked down the driveway as often as he could, hoping to see that the cops still patrolled the area. If so, they did it subtly since he didn't see their vehicles. He hoped that was the case and would call eventually to find out—especially when darkness approached later in the day.

Amber, Sonya and he indulged in small talk at the kitchen table while eating lunch, not discussing or even hinting at the reason they had gone to town that morning. But there was still tension in the air that Evan knew resulted from their unease.

The doorbell rang almost as soon as they'd finished eating, and the members of the small new class came in—a mother and her adult son, who both had medium-sized mixed breeds about a year old that appeared to have come from the same litter, probably part terrier and part who-knew-what. They were Debbie and Gene Halven, with Marley and Sudsy. Both had taken two days off from work to come here and hopefully pick up their lessons where Corbin had left off.

Evan liked the idea that there were just two of them plus their dogs. They seemed pleasant enough when Amber made the introductions, not pushy, not particularly staring at him, so he felt more or less comfortable. In a few minutes he, with Bear at his side and Amber following, led them outside with their leashed dogs, leaving Sonya inside with Lola. He showed them to the part of the driveway used for classes, excused himself for a minute, leaving Amber in their company, and took another walk around the area with Bear to check things out.

Orrin was in the backyard now, doing some weeding. Evan considered asking about his texting skills but didn't really think he was the culprit—or at least he hoped not. He merely said hi with a brief wave that Orrin imitated before turning back to his task.

Even if no police patrolled the area, Evan saw nothing to make him worry about security around the place and Bear acted normal without alerting to anything, so he joined the group and soon began his lesson.

Things became more difficult when both mother and son started criticizing Evan for some of his techniques since they were different from Corbin's— though they criticized Corbin's techniques, too. They glared at Evan, together and separately, and he did his best to glare right back before going on to the next instructions with their dogs.

Whatever their problems with Corbin had been, they must have liked him well enough to take follow-up classes here at the K-9 Ranch. And when Evan had Bear demonstrate how things were supposed to go with a well-trained dog, they both settled down and followed his lead.

But their young, mostly untrained dogs were rambunctious, and the lesson ran on for longer than Evan had anticipated.

When they were done, Debbie asked Amber about accommodations for that night. "I didn't think to call that place next door to see if they had a room available. Do you think they will?"

"Let's check."

As the two people strode ahead, pulling their leashed puppies in the direction they headed, Amber held back to walk with Evan and rolled her eyes without criticizing them aloud. He understood. They were paying customers.

But he appreciated when she asked in a low voice, "Are you okay?"

"Fine," he replied, equally softly. "It's just another kind of challenge for a dedicated dog trainer." He smiled at her and she smiled back, warming him inside.

Reaching the house, they all went into the kitchen, where Amber called the Chance Resort's reservations desk. She was given a bit of a runaround and, holding her hand over her phone, told the others she had the impression the place was full.

"Let me take care of this," Sonya said. She'd been standing near the sink away from the crowd but stepped forward. "I'll call Nathan. He'll figure something out."

She took her cell phone from her pocket as she walked out of the kitchen. And Nathan apparently came through, finding a room at his resort.

Evan was glad when his latest students and their dogs headed to the resort next door. He'd work with them again tomorrow but would know what to expect and be prepared.

It was too late, and he felt too wired after the class and the rest of the afternoon's events, to take a hike with Bear, but he did conduct quick but necessary individual classes with the ranch's young dogs.

Then, with Amber, he took them all for brief walks close to the house.

* * *

The day had been a strange one, Amber thought as she later helped her mother put together fixings for hamburgers for their dinner that night. But she was proud of the way Evan had handled those people who'd come for the classes.

She was surprised at the attitudes of the mother and son. But everything seemed to be turning out okay, partly thanks to her mom's friendship with Nathan, so at least the second class would be able to go forward as planned tomorrow.

Evan was out of the house now. He'd said he needed to stop by his own place for a change of clothes and more.

But when he'd left, Amber had looked out a couple of the house's windows and seen him walking around the place with Bear, obviously checking it to make sure no one was out there casing it…and ready to make good on the texted threat from yesterday.

Not that Amber was speaking out again to get people with suspicions or more to let her, and the cops, know who they thought had killed her dad.

Not now, at least. And maybe from now on she'd merely hint at it. People who knew who she was, and who her dad had been, and what had happened to him…well, they'd know what she was thinking.

"How about the onions?" her mom asked, patting the last of the burgers into shape. "Should we just slice them or fry them up to put on the burgers?"

"I prefer them cooked but I don't know about

Evan," Amber said. She continued to flake the lettuce to be used on the sandwiches. "Let's make some of both available."

She put the final bit of lettuce onto a plate since they each would choose the fixings for their burgers. Her mother had already mixed a salad, and they would also have mashed potatoes.

A reasonable dinner, Amber thought. There were enough burgers that she figured the dogs would all get at least a small taste, even if giving them people food wasn't the best thing for them. They'd like it anyway. And this place was all about dogs and, while training them, keeping them happy.

It was still light outside, and things were pretty much ready for their meal once the burgers were fully cooked.

Amber had gone outside with Evan after the Halvens left, and they both worked with the young shepherds. After the rowdy and disobedient dogs in the class before, it felt like a relief to give the ranch's pups commands that they pretty much followed, even Rex. Once they had run the pups through their paces and given them praise—and hugs from Amber—she and Evan had talked a bit about the text and the cops and how to handle it all.

Amber was utterly frustrated and—she'd admitted to Evan—even a bit scared. They didn't know who the killer was, and though the cops said they were still on the case, it had grown cold, and the authorities' interest might only be a bit warm because Amber kept goading them.

Evan, sweet man that he was, had told her—again—to back off.

Why did she consider that sweet? Because he promised to stay on it and look for her dad's killer even as he tried to limit her involvement for her safety.

Sweet? Yes. But that didn't mean she would obey him.

There. The burgers were ready. Her mother was about to put them on the table with the fixings Amber had already set down there.

Amber pulled her phone from her pocket, figuring it wouldn't hurt to call Evan and tell him to get that gorgeous male butt of his over here…not that she'd phrase it that way.

And now that she'd thought about it, she kept visualizing that wonderful, firm butt and what else had gone on when she happened to have seen it.

Maybe she should leave the kitchen to make this call. That would give her time to chill out.

"I'll let Evan know we're ready," she said to her mom. "Be right back."

But just as she exited the kitchen door, Lola right behind her, her phone made the sound that a text had arrived.

She froze, remembering the last time she had heard it—and what that message had said.

But this time, it had to be Evan asking what time he should get back there, or something equally bland and innocent.

Right?

Amber found herself inhaling deeply, steeling herself to read this text, even as she tried to laugh at herself for her silliness. Or what she at least hoped was her silliness.

Problem was, when she raised the phone and scrolled to the screen to read the text, she had been right to worry.

This time the text message read: Wasn't my last message enough? Now you're talking to cops. This is my last warning. Back off now or what happened to your father will happen to you and everyone else at your damn ranch, dogs included.

Chapter 23

No. No, no, no. Not again.

Amber couldn't help it. She slipped into the bathroom, leaving the door open but suddenly needing to be alone.

She held out her trembling hand once more, fiddling with her phone.

She looked at the earlier text. It was still there. There were now two threatening messages—the second even worse.

Amber was scared. She was also furious. How did the killer know she'd talked to the police again? Even if Orrin was the culprit and kept an eye on her comings and goings, he wouldn't have known she had gone to the police station…would he?

Was the killer a cop? One of the local students?

Did any of them work downtown? If so, were they watching the police station?

Was it Percy, tracking her whereabouts via her cell phone?

She doubted it was another trainer who'd been angry with her father, since they wouldn't harm dogs, yet hers had been threatened now, too—unless that was just a ploy.

Was it someone she hadn't even considered? Someone watching her. From where?

And right now…where was Evan? She needed him to protect her. No, to calm her.

As if she'd screamed his name, he seemed to magically appear at the bathroom doorway, Bear at his feet. Her mother was at his other side and had apparently let him in the front door. They both stared at her in apparent concern.

Only then did Amber notice the pups barking in the den. Presumably, Evan had knocked on the door—but she had been too preoccupied to hear it.

Lola remained on the floor looking up at her, clearly sensing the emotions hurtling through her.

"What's wrong?" Evan asked immediately.

"Honey, what is it?" her mother said.

Without replying, Amber stepped into the hall, then took the phone clenched in her hand and held it so they both could see.

She heard her mother's gasp and saw her raise one hand to her mouth. "Oh, no. Not again. And—and how did they know you talked to the police?"

"That's what I'd like to know," Evan growled.

"I want to tell Kara about this." Amber nearly choked as she spoke. "But what if whoever it is has tapped my phone?"

"I'll call." Evan motioned for the women to follow him into the living room, where he sat in the middle of the sofa. They took their places on either side of him. He pulled his phone from his pocket. "Number?" Amber looked at her log list and gave him the station's number. He pressed it into his phone, said, "I'll talk, you just listen," then put on the speaker.

He asked the person who answered for Assistant Chief Province. Apparently Kara was still there since he was asked who he was, then requested to hold.

In less than a minute, Kara said, "Hello, Evan. Is everything all right?"

"No," he said almost curtly, then read the latest text message off Amber's phone, which she held in front of him.

"Damn," Kara said. "Look, we'll want our tech guy to check this one, too, but he's gone for the day. And your bringing Amber here tonight is not a good idea since we don't know where the suspect got the information that she was in touch with us. Where are you now, and where is she?"

"I'm here, Kara," Amber said, hating the throatiness of her voice—and also pointedly not looking at Evan as she disobeyed his order. "We're at the ranch."

"That's not a good idea, either," Kara said. "I'll get more patrols in that direction but it's too remote a location. You and your mother need to spend the night somewhere else, with more people around. Maybe one of the hotels here in town."

"How about the Chance Resort?" Sonya suggested. "We can get there easily and I understand it's pretty full tonight. That means a lot of people around."

"That's probably okay," said Kara. "And it'll look fairly normal if I send some of our officers there to check on the place. They probably have some form of security, too."

"I thought it was completely full, Mom," Amber said.

"It is, but Nathan has been so nice... I imagine he'll be able to fit us in. At least we can go there to check and be around more people. If he can't find a room for us then maybe his reservations staff can find a place for us to go."

A good idea? Well, it certainly was better than staying here, at least for now.

"Okay," Kara said. "Check in with me later and let me know where you are. Call my cell." She gave them the number. Amber programmed it into her phone, then Evan did the same with his.

"Will this at least help you figure out who the killer is, once and for all?" Amber asked Kara.

"Let's hope so."

As Evan hung up his phone, Amber said, "But what about the dogs? Mom, will Nathan let us bring them?"

"Probably not the youngsters," her mother said sadly. "Maybe Lola and Bear, though."

"Don't worry about any of them," Evan said. "I'll go to the resort with you and make sure you've got a place to stay, then come back to check on the dogs— as long as you're safe and under security's observation."

"But you live here, too, so the threat includes you. You have to stay at the resort. But if the person is watching this place and we're not here, the dogs might be in danger, and I just can't—" Amber said, but Evan interrupted her.

"I hope they're watching and make it obvious. I'll ensure the dogs are okay, and maybe we can use those stupid threats to end this once and for all."

Amber appreciated his attitude—sort of. She wanted to throw herself into his arms so he could soothe her, to assure her everything would be all right. That *he* would be all right—and her, and her mother, too.

And the dogs.

But she was terrified about whether Evan, with his aggressive attitude, would survive that kind of "once and for all."

"Don't worry," he added, watching her as if reading her thoughts. "I'll come back to the resort and stay with you tonight once I make sure everything's okay here."

It made sense to do it his way, Amber thought. Maybe.

She wished now that, for Evan's safety, she had gotten Orrin to work with the dogs so he could be their sitter and protector. But Orrin lived here, too, so he'd also been threatened. Should they warn him? But he wasn't likely to be first on the threatener's list.

Plus, what if he had made the threat and included himself as a tactic?

What Evan said was probably best. What Amber didn't mention, though, was that once her mother was safe and settled at the resort, she would come back here with Evan to check on the dogs.

If Evan had considered keeping these women downtown and away from their ranch before, now it was one of the most critical intentions on his mind.

He would not let anything happen to them. Either of them.

He had come to care for Sonya like a surrogate mother. That was because she was the actual mother of the woman he had really fallen for. Heavily. Even if the only future in it was remaining her employee as long as he could.

That presupposed she remained healthy and alive.

And stopped getting those damn threats.

Where was the menace? Around here, watching Amber? Well, he would check the ranch—soon. But first he needed to get the women away from this place.

"Okay," he said. "Grab some overnight clothes. I'm going to drive you both to the resort right now. And, Sonya, you might want to call Nathan and give him a heads-up."

Evan considered calling the guy, too, to warn him that nothing had better happen to the women while they were there. After meeting him, he'd considered Nathan a possible suspect in Corbin's murder like everyone else he'd met, and hadn't taken him off the list despite there being no apparent motive—except, perhaps, his interest in Sonya. And that seemed recent, originating only after Corbin was gone, or at least that's the impression Evan got from Amber.

Well, even if the guy was guilty he wouldn't do anything while under the observation of Evan, the cops and even his own security guys—and Evan would make sure the staff knew to keep close watch over Amber and her mother.

He'd also let Nathan know.

"But, Evan, it's too dangerous for you to come back here," Sonya said. "Pack a bag and stay with us. We'll lock the dogs in the house. They'll—they'll be okay." But she choked on the last, evidencing her worry.

"Oh, I'll only return for a short while to check things out. I'll lock the dogs up then and head back to the resort." To make sure the women remained safe. "And I won't be here by myself." Evan patted the head of Bear, who, as nearly always, sat beside him. His dog looked up and gave his closest approximation of a smile, as if he understood and was proud to take care of his human.

"Let's get ready, Mom," Amber said, then followed her mother down the hall toward their bedrooms. Evan waited where he was.

Amber, first to exit her room with her bag, faced Evan, staring into his eyes. That should have made him uncomfortable. It did make him uncomfortable, but a lot less than such things used to. Because it was Amber.

"I appreciate your driving us to the resort and offering to come back to check on the dogs, but that's potentially dangerous."

He appreciated her concern. He appreciated *her*, and the warm and worried look she aimed toward him.

"I'll be careful," he responded.

"Well, so will I." Her expression changed into one of her bossiest, as if daring him to protest.

Evan felt his eyes widen as he started to demand what she meant. She wasn't coming back here tonight, that was for sure.

But now he saw Sonya approaching. He didn't want to argue with Amber in front of her mother. But he knew he'd have an ally in Sonya if Amber repeated her foolish suggestion. "Great. Looks like you two are ready. Let's go."

"I didn't reach Nathan yet but left a message," Sonya said.

Evan picked up the small bags they'd each packed and headed toward the front door. "Wait here, and I'll get my car. Lock the door behind me."

He and Bear left, hurrying toward his house. He drove back toward the main house as quickly as he could.

Soon, with Sonya beside him in the passenger seat and Amber and Bear in the back, they drove to the resort. He parked in the temporary lot in front since he didn't intend to stay long. But Amber would—as long as there was adequate protection available.

Carrying the bags once more, he accompanied the women inside. The lobby was filled with people. Good. He didn't see his students of that day, the Halvens, which was also good. And there were some guys in suits that he'd figured before weren't all reception but included security staff—another plus.

Almost as soon as they reached the front desk, Nathan appeared. Evan motioned for the resort owner to join him off to the side. "I don't know what Sonya told you," he said, "but they've received some strange communications so they've decided to stay here for the night. I expect you and your staff to take good care of them." In other words, you're under scrutiny.

"Of course." The guy sounded insulted and looked down at Bear as if the dog was a slimy rodent.

"Great," Evan said. "Thanks."

Evan watched Nathan approach the women and begin talking with them. He also studied the people in the lobby. Other than possibly the greeters and security guys, no one looked familiar. That didn't mean they were all wonderful visitors who'd never hurt Amber or her mother.

Without knowing the killer or motive, or the possibility of accomplices, Evan suspected everyone. But there should at least be safety in numbers, especially if the cops came through and sent patrols through here.

Soon, Nathan went to the front desk to talk to the reservations people, which allowed Evan, Bear at his side, to head for the concierge desk. He asked to be taken to the security office.

The guy in charge was tall and rotund, dressed, as most of the male staff, in a dark suit. His name tag identified him as Jack, the security chief. Without explaining details, Evan told the guy that the two women with Nathan Treggory were under police protection, and hotel security should also keep close watch on them to ensure their safety—even patrol the floor where the room they were staying a lot more frequently than normal.

Jack gave Evan an offended look but promised to take care of the women.

Then it was time. Evan could leave.

For now, but not for long.

As he returned to the lobby, Evan saw a couple of cops walk through it. Good. Kara was making good on her promise.

He also saw Amber and her mother with Nathan at the far end of the lobby. He quickly headed in that direction.

"Has Nathan found you a place to stay?" Evan asked.

"He says he has," Amber said. "I'll get my mother settled into the room, then you and I can go back to check on the ranch."

"No," Evan said firmly. "I don't want to wait—and you need to confirm your mom is okay. Just make sure he's found you a nice, safe, out-of-the-way room where you can lock yourselves in. Call me later and tell me where you are."

"But—"

"But you know I'm right. You have to take care of your mother." And stay here, where it should be a lot safer than what he was going to do. "But don't trust anyone."

A frisson of unease coursed through him—on her behalf, not his. He waved toward Jack, who stood by the wall near the hallway to his office, and gestured toward Amber to make sure the guy knew who the security staff needed to protect. Even so, Evan had second thoughts about leaving for any reason. Yet he needed not only to check on the dogs, but also to look, without Amber's presence, for any evidence at the ranch of who was threatening her since he figured that, even if she stayed here for the night, she'd insist on returning there tomorrow.

It was up to Evan to make sure the place was safe.

Amber still didn't like the way Nathan seemed so smitten with her mother.

And her mom, usually so withdrawn and quiet these days, also appeared more outgoing and friendly.

Amber hoped it was only friendship—though it really wasn't her business. At least not much.

But Evan had been right—sort of. She had to stay here for the moment to make sure her mother remained okay.

After Evan left, Nathan led them into an office behind the front desk, where two more reservations employees sat inside. "I know we're pretty full," he said to his staff members, "but surely you can find a place for these lovely women."

"Sorry, sir, there's still nothing," the older lady said.

Her younger counterpart nodded vigorously. "We've been nearly booked up tonight for a week, and the few rooms that were left filled up today, too." That explained how the Halvens had gotten a room, but there were apparently none left now.

"That's okay, Nathan," her mom told him. "I'd really appreciate it if your wonderful reservations people could find us something else, in downtown Chance."

That might be their only choice, Amber thought. She'd have to call Evan to drive them there. Which meant he'd stay safe, away from the ranch.

But the dogs…?

Well, sweet Evan was on his way to check on them. She would do nothing to change that. Maybe they could take a taxi.

"No, you're staying at the resort," Nathan said. "Come here, please." He motioned them away from the desk. Near the door, he continued, "You may not know that I have a separate house on the resort property, and though I almost never invite anyone to stay with me, you two are the exception. I'd have suggested it right away since I figured there'd be no room available, but was concerned you'd say no. Now you have good reason to join me. I'll show it to you first. The rooms at my place each have their own bathroom, and though it's not quite as plush as this hotel, it's a nice place. Is that okay with you?"

Amber felt a bit relieved. She didn't like the idea of staying with Nathan, of course, especially with her sad, vulnerable mother. But at least that meant no concerns about where they'd stay in town and how to get there.

"That's so kind, Nathan," Sonya said. There was a radiance on her face that Amber hated to see, but she, too, thought the guy was being kind—even if he had an underlying seductive motive. "We accept your invitation. Right, Amber?"

"Yes, thank you, Nathan," she said—and figured she wouldn't get much sleep. Not with all that was happening, with her concern about Evan, herself and the dogs…and she'd be listening to make sure neither Nathan nor her mother slipped into the other's room.

Chapter 24

They were in the lobby getting ready to head to Nathan's home when Amber felt her cell phone vibrate in her pocket.

She had turned off the sound because she didn't want to hear it if she received another text—or impose the noise on anyone else. She pulled it from her pocket and casually glanced at it after confirming that Nathan and her mother were nearby talking to a bellhop, most likely about the two small bags they had brought.

It was a phone call from Evan. Her heart rate sped up. Talking to him right now about anything, especially the dogs, would cheer her. As long as he, and they, were okay, at least. At the moment, she felt angry, concerned, sad, scared and even lonely despite the large number of people around that included her mother.

Being threatened with death apparently stirred up all sorts of emotions Amber hadn't imagined—and being threatened a second time, along with loved ones, only brought more.

Had her dad— No. She wouldn't think about that now.

Looking around, and seeing that the man in a dark suit who'd been staring at her mother and her since they'd exited the reservations office—probably a security guy, since he was so obvious—was still watching, she hurried toward the nearby ladies' room for privacy as she answered. "Hi, Evan," she said.

"You okay?" he asked.

"Sure. You? The dogs?" She was inside the restroom now and was glad to see it otherwise empty.

"We're all fine. Do you have a room for tonight yet?"

She had an urge to demand that he pick her up so she could sleep in her own bed—but she would be too worried about her mother even if he agreed. Instead, Amber explained that they'd be in Nathan's personal home on the resort property.

"I don't know about that…" Evan sounded concerned.

"We'll be fine," Amber said. "You just hang out with the dogs, make sure they—and you—remain okay." She'd really love to do the same. But she had to act rationally after receiving that threat and obey what Kara had told them, as much as she disliked it, since it made sense for her mother's sake. "Did you talk to the hotel security staff?"

"Yeah, or at least the guy in charge, who hangs out in the lobby and has a security name tag."

"Well, he may be the one keeping an eye on us. I'll tell him where we're going so he can check on us there, too."

"Great. Now, be careful and, like I said, don't trust anyone."

"I don't."

He didn't say much more, and Amber wished again that she was with the dogs.

And with Evan.

Evan was inside Amber's house as he spoke with her, providing attention to Lola and the young shepherds. He'd soon leave them again to head back to town.

It was critical that he do everything necessary so that Amber wouldn't be hurt. Sonya, too.

Even so, he had things to accomplish now at the ranch, to ensure as much as possible that the pups and Lola remained okay. And more important, in case he couldn't prevent her return tomorrow, that Amber would remain safe here.

At least Jack, the security honcho at the resort, appeared to be doing his duty as Evan had requested, keeping watch over Amber and her mother. Even so, he'd get back there as soon as possible. Maybe even faster than he'd initially planned.

But with the latest threat Amber had received,

Evan had needed to get her away from here. Now he wanted to do a sweep around the ranch, make sure no one was obviously hanging out watching… or worse. With Bear, of course, using his well-trained dog senses to search for anything, or anyone, who shouldn't be here.

The people living here, and dogs, too, could be vulnerable to all sorts of attacks, as threatened. And no matter what he said or did, Evan felt sure Amber would continue to insist on returning here soon.

Was he acting foolishly by not staying with her, glued to her side all evening? He kept wondering that, but he also had a gut feeling that some of the answers he sought were right here on the ranch. This might not be the best time to seek them, but maybe it was, considering the latest threat.

Though he didn't like the idea of Amber and her mom staying in Nathan's private quarters, at least they wouldn't be here. And Nathan, and the women, would all be under the scrutiny of Jack and his security guys, and hopefully more cops would be around, too. Evan didn't trust Nathan any more than he trusted anyone else, but figured the guy was smart enough not to do anything he didn't want the world to know about while being watched so closely.

Even so, concern for Amber and her mother made Evan want to run back there immediately.

Well, he'd do it soon. And the fact that sweet, smart Amber would also follow up with Jack to keep an eye on things…well, it gave him another reason to want to take her into his arms and kiss her. And more. As if he needed a reason…

"Okay, gang." He rose from where he'd been sitting on the kitchen floor petting the dogs. He'd already fed them, taken them outside to do what they needed while he stayed fully alert and brought them back in.

He now enclosed the youngsters in their den, promising to spend more time with them as soon as possible. Lola was left loose in the rest of the house. She might be an asset on this kind of walk someday, if he worked with her more. Not now.

Then he called Orrin with the excuse of letting him know that Amber and Sonya were spending the night elsewhere. Orrin said he was home and would keep an eye on the place. He sounded his usual grumpy, indifferent self, though his indifference could have been an act. Just in case, Evan mentioned that he happened to be there right now, and Bear and he were taking a walk around the ranch. He hinted that something was wrong without elaborating. If Orrin knew what he was talking about, he should feel disturbed.

Finally, Evan was ready to go.

He circled the houses and, with extreme caution, Evan decided to take Bear on a quick hike in an area of the ranch they hadn't yet covered—the side of the property closest to the Chance Resort, where Amber and her mother were at the moment. He and Bear would check for intruders in both places, including anyone visibly hanging out where no one should be on the resort grounds.

It was late enough in the chilly evening that he first hurried to his house and got his black hoodie, which he donned along with comfortable hiking boots. He also put the vest on Bear that told the K-9 he was officially on duty. Then Evan grabbed a flashlight, since he didn't know how long they'd be hiking, and they went out once more.

He knew Orrin wasn't outside since Bear didn't alert about him when Evan commanded, "Search."

Instead, Bear's nose went up in the air as he walked with Evan past the employee houses and back toward the main house, then beyond it.

Bear seemed to enjoy his work, sniffing and turning his pointed ears to listen for anything out of the ordinary. But Bear always enjoyed his work—and had found nothing so far.

Was this a mistake? No, because Evan at least felt confident that no one was hanging out here waiting to hurt Amber or her mother, or the dogs. Unless, of course, it actually was Orrin, who was inside his house. Still, he apparently wasn't sweating in fear after Evan's call or Bear would have smelled it and alerted as they passed that building.

Daylight was waning but it was still too early for a flashlight. They walked along the paved area connected to the driveway and beyond, onto the grounds that were mostly bare except for blown leaves and branches from the woods above.

Evan directed Bear up the hillside first, where

the roofs of the resort buildings were visible in the distance. Bear continued his search for all he'd been trained to find—bad guys, IEDs and weaponry while in the military, and since Evan had also worked with him to diversify his training after their return to the States, he would also alert on drugs.

Evan figured the only thing Bear was likely to find now, though, if anything, was whoever had been threatening Amber.

Was that person actually hanging around here, after murdering Corbin Belott? Unlikely. But whoever it was knew too much to be very far away, or so it appeared from the threats.

They walked back downward, then crossed to be closer to the open wooden fence between the two properties. Bear didn't alert to any people on the ranch side, and the few folks Evan saw at the front and side of the main resort building were too far for Bear to pay much attention to.

This outing was quickly drawing to a close. A good thing, because it was starting to get dark, and, more important, Evan was determined to hurry back to Amber.

The last part was at the top of the hillside. They reached the base of the wooded area, and Evan encouraged Bear to enter it. His smart, well-trained dog would behave as he should while scenting rodents and other wildlife in the area, but remaining on duty.

Evan was therefore highly surprised when his unleashed dog ran through the underbrush in the direction of the resort.

He was even more surprised when Bear sat down just up the hill, but right beside the fence—it was a signal that he had found something and was now alerting to it.

Evan looked around. They were beneath a couple of trees, and the ground cover of dead leaves looked the same as when they'd entered the forested area.

He looked in the direction Bear faced and then noticed that some of the ground cover on the far side of the fence appeared…well, different. As if it had been moved at some time and returned, or at least smoothed a bit beneath the dead leaves.

As if something had been buried there?

"Good boy," he said, praising his dog, then he carefully maneuvered over the low fence. If anyone was watching and didn't want whatever had happened to be discovered, he was probably toast. But he immediately squatted and used his hands to move the ground cover aside and discovered a metal box buried there.

Carefully, he pulled off the top.

And saw that it contained a Smith & Wesson plus some ammunition.

He knew the kind of firearm used to kill Corbin had been some model of a Smith & Wesson. He now felt certain it was this one.

Did the location point to the suspect? Did it mean the person whose property it had been buried on was the murderer?

Not necessarily.

But Evan was ready to find out. And he finally had something he could tell K-9 Officer Maisie.

Nathan's house was as posh and attractive as his main resort building, and Amber felt certain that the other structures—convention areas and a gym and such—were equally classy. She had no interest in seeing them, though. At least not now.

Nathan had already provided a tour, and the house seemed quite nice, with a couple of guest rooms at the end of a long hallway, complete with their own bathrooms.

Now they sat on some clearly expensive furniture in his living room, snacking on food items a couple of his employees had brought over. Amber figured this would be their dinner. She certainly wouldn't need any more.

"This is so kind of you, Nathan," her mother said again between sips of wine from a long-stemmed crystal glass she had lifted from the coffee table in front of them. She sat on the antique blue velvet sofa beside Amber. "And your home—it's gorgeous."

"Thank you." The silver-haired man sounded humble, and his gaze remained on Sonya. He had excused himself as soon as he'd given his tour, and now wore a plaid shirt and jeans, appearing more like a regular guy than a resort mogul. Amber and her mother had thrown on equally casual clothing before, so they all appeared to be on the same wavelength. Maybe.

But for a moment, Amber wondered where Jack,

the security guy, happened to be. She also wondered why she was so concerned. Everything seemed fine.

Except for those texts… And Evan's warnings.

"You know," Nathan said, still watching Sonya as he, too, sipped some wine, "I've been worried about you two on that ranch. I know you have some employees living there, but since your poor husband… well, it's not a good situation for a couple of wonderful women to be so far from town and all, especially under the circumstances."

"Oh, we're doing okay," Amber asserted. She was holding off on the wine for the moment, watching the others, but she did eat some sharp cheddar on a flaky cracker.

"I appreciated the demonstration of your employee's dog-training skills the other day." Nathan was now looking at her. "But…how many classes has he given? And how many more are planned? I don't know anything about dog lessons, but are you making enough money from them?"

"We will," Amber said, "once we've gotten more lined up. My father did fine with his dog training, especially the K-9s for the police, and we'll work our way back up to his success soon."

"Really?" Nathan leaned forward in his leather recliner chair. "Well…you may not know it, Sonya, but Corbin and I had a couple of conversations in which he hinted that things weren't working as well as he'd hoped. That's when I first suggested that I buy your ranch. And now…well, it seems like it would be a lot better for you not to have to worry about your dog lessons or what else might happen to you while you're there and all. I suggested it before, and now I'm asking again."

His tone sounded concerned and caring, as if he gave a damn about what happened to them. And maybe he did care that way about her mother. Yet… Amber couldn't believe he'd had the kind of conversation he had described with her father. Not without her mother knowing about it, at least.

But he might have an ulterior motive for lying about it.

Amber had learned over time to trust her instincts—and now they told her to get out of there. She'd briefly considered Nathan as a possible suspect in what had happened to her father, but he'd seemed so kind to her mother. Too kind. She'd been more concerned that Sonya was getting too emotionally involved too fast.

But there might be multiple reasons for Nathan to be encouraging that…

It could all be about his wanting to buy the ranch.

"You know," she said brightly as she stood, "this wonderful snack is whetting my appetite. Let's go back to the restaurant in the hotel for dinner, and—"

"Oh, I can feed you more here," Nathan said. His expression and tone had morphed from kindly to cold.

"That's okay. Mom, just you and I can go. That'll be fine." She stepped closer to her mother and put out her hand.

"I'm not hungry, dear," Sonya said, "but I could keep you company."

"No, you two are staying right here." Nathan's voice had turned to ice. "We're finally getting everything resolved. Period."

He was staring at Amber, and she knew her life was in danger. So was her mother's.

Where was that security guy now? Or the cops who'd promised to drop in at the resort?

And why hadn't she insisted on both her mother and her returning to the ranch with Evan?

"What do you mean, Nathan?" Sonya was standing now, puzzlement written in the wrinkles on her forehead and set of her mouth. "What are we resolving?"

"He wants to buy the ranch, Mom," Amber said, glaring at him. What could she do now to protect them? Was there a way to reach into her pocket and call Evan?

"That's right," Nathan said almost pleasantly. "If you two agree to sell me your ranch right now, sign some papers I've already had drawn up, you can stay here tonight and move out as soon as possible. If not—"

"If not, he'll kill us the way he killed Dad."

"What?" Her mother, now pale, stumbled and fell back onto the sofa. "Nathan, Amber didn't mean that."

"Oh, she did, and she's right," Nathan said. "Not that I left any evidence that the police can link to me. I know how to avoid fingerprints and to hide things well. If you claim I admitted the killing, of course I'll deny it. And you can be sure I've been keeping my eyes on you so I can make good on those texts if necessary." Amber nearly leaped to scratch those horrible eyes out as he continued, "But you can both stay nice and healthy if you just sell me the ranch. And the amount I'm willing to pay for it is actually fairly generous."

"It's time to leave," Amber said coldly.

"Oh, I don't think so." Nathan reached into a drawer of the coffee table and pulled out a gun, aiming it at Amber. "I'll be quite happy to kill you. Your return here nearly ruined everything."

"And that's why you sent those damn threatening texts," Amber growled, wanting to jump on him but knowing better.

"Exactly." He almost purred the word, making her even angrier. "I meant every word. You should have kept everything to yourself. Good thing I was watching you."

"But…but if you kill us," Sonya whispered, "they'll know you killed my poor Corbin, too. You can't get away with it."

"Your own security staff knows we're here and is looking out for us," Amber reminded him.

"Oh, they're my staff, like you said, and they know the rules around here, like staying out of my way. They'll soon hear from me that Amber brought the gun here, that she thought I'd killed your husband and intended to shoot me in retaliation. I fortunately got the gun away from her, which is why my prints are on this one. It's not the same gun or make that killed Corbin, by the way. No one will ever be able to prove I harmed him. Oh, and once you're dead I'll make sure your prints are on it, too." He now sounded so smug that Amber wanted to slug him with that damn gun, or something worse.

But, of course, she stayed still, her mind shrieking silently for something to do to save them.

Evan heard everything Nathan said. Although the doors to this place, fortunately the only single home on the property, were locked when Bear and he arrived, he'd managed to open a window into a back bedroom, then lifted his dog inside, too.

Too bad he hadn't brought the gun and ammo he had found buried so he could use it on Nathan.

Instead, he quietly walked Bear to the door to the living room and gave the appropriate command. "Attack!"

Bear leaped into the room, running toward Nathan.

"What the—" The guy jerked so the gun was pointing toward Bear. Fortunately, the dog was fast, but Evan still feared he would get shot.

That was when Amber catapulted over the coffee table and shoved Nathan, who crumpled to the floor even as Bear grabbed his wrist in his mouth and bit it ferociously.

Nathan dropped the gun.

Only then did Evan allow himself to breathe deeply again.

With Bear guarding, Evan called 911, and almost as soon as he'd related what had happened to the police dispatcher, there was a knock on the door to the house.

After a nod from him, Amber went to open it, and two cops and Jack burst in. It apparently hadn't hurt that Assistant Chief Kara had made good on her promise to make sure that officers showed up often at the resort that night, or that Jack must have figured he had to follow them around, even to his boss's house.

Evan commanded Bear to release Nathan but to guard him, and the killer was wise enough to remain on the ground so he'd suffer no more bites.

Amber explained what had happened, that a now-protesting Nathan had confessed to her father's murder. A tearful Sonya confirmed what she said.

But after being helped to his feet by the cops and getting his arms cuffed behind him, Nathan started a tirade about how Amber had done it all, brought the gun, aimed it at him, insisted that he confess to her father's murder until he got the weapon away and aimed it at her.

Those protests got nowhere. Not when Evan, smiling ironically, removed his phone from his pocket and began replaying the threats that Nathan made just before Bear and he jumped in.

"I'll also be able to show you where the murder weapon is buried, Officer," Evan told one of the cops. "Although from what Mr. Treggory indicated, there might not be prints on it. But based on what he said, and the fact it's buried on his property…well, it may not be conclusive evidence but it might help."

The taller cop with the deeper skin tone walked away and spoke on his radio while his colleague watched over Nathan, who was bleeding slightly from his neck. In a moment, he told everyone, "We've got EMTs on the way to see to this guy's wounds, and a crime-scene team'll also be here in a few minutes. Oh, and I gather that Assistant Chief Province is on her way, too, as well as our K-9 unit." Good. Evan's calling Officer Maisie on his way here had undoubtedly helped. The cop who was here looked down at Bear. "Do we need to restrain that dog?"

Evan made himself smile into the officer's face before he looked down again at Bear, who stood beside him. "Bear, sit," he said, and of course the good dog obeyed. "Now, shake."

Bear's front paw went up in the direction of the cop, who grinned. "Guess not," the officer said, kneeling to shake Bear's paw.

Amber, too, stooped to hug Bear. "Good dog," she said lovingly.

"He certainly is," Sonya said, still sounding hoarse. She looked at the dog, then at Nathan. "He's definitely a lot better than you, you terrible, terrible man."

She burst into tears, and Amber stood to embrace her mother. Evan wished she was hugging him instead of Bear or even Sonya—not in thanks, but because he wanted her in his arms.

This wasn't the best time. He knew that. But maybe soon…

Chapter 25

"Class dismissed," Evan called, and Amber watched under the warmth of the July sun as the five cops who had come with their own police units' K-9s, from different departments all over the western states, gave signals to their dogs. All five of the K-9s sat, but only for a minute. Evan and their handlers quickly threw a toy for each of them, and the various German shepherds and Belgian Malinois—including Bear, who'd helped Evan demonstrate the exercises—dashed after their rewards.

Amber grinned widely, wishing she could throw herself into Evan's arms and kiss him for another job really well done.

Standing at the side of the top of the driveway where the training session was held, she found it hard to believe that Evan had been here for six weeks. The number of students had increased, so he taught a couple of classes most days, often with multiple students and generally with pets rather than K-9s, and he handled them all well. He'd even given a couple of complementary classes to the Halvens, who hadn't received their second scheduled class after all that had happened while they were around.

This was the first training and review class he had given for K-9 officers and their dogs, but he'd performed this vital part of his role here brilliantly, and Amber knew that publicity, including word of mouth, would lead to a lot more to come.

Even Assistant Police Chief Kara had indicated again that she might be a candidate for basic K-9 lessons.

That all meant they'd have to hire at least one training assistant for Evan soon.

Hearing a noise, Amber turned to see her mother, Lola at her side, exit their house carrying a basket of dog treats they'd bought at Pets and Products as rewards for their canine students. Though Evan still frowned on food rewards at classes, he didn't mind as much when they came from people other than the dogs' handlers.

Amber had kept Mirri at Pets and Products fully informed about all that had happened around here. She'd also made sure that Percy kept the ranch's website up to date. There were additional things to add and change, like class descriptions and more training demo videos. And though the geeky guy had wanted to add something about the apparent solving of the murder of the ranch's owner, she had made it clear she didn't want it on the website.

"Okay to take this stuff off?" Orrin had waddled his way in his bulky suit from the sidelines up to Evan. As always, he had acted as agitator and did well with it—being the apparent bad guy and allowing the dogs to attack and bite him on command.

"Sure," Evan told him, turning away from the officers he was speaking with. "Good job, Orrin."

"Thanks." He sounded genuinely pleased about the praise rather than his old grumpy self. His parents had come for a visit recently, seen him in practice as an agitator and seemed quite happy with his progress. They were nice people and thanked Amber and her mother. Though his job was pretty much all physical and following instructions, and didn't require a lot of thinking or planning, at least he was working.

He'd also admitted his continued worry about being the man of the ranch after Corbin's death, which was why he sometimes wandered at night in the hopes of protecting the two women.

And his—and Percy's—criticism of Corbin? Amber had asked, and they'd been embarrassed that they'd bad-mouthed the dead man, who'd been in some ways their benefactor. Even if he had been critical sometimes, it may have been justified. But, they'd agreed, Corbin had been a good friend and boss, even if he hadn't been perfect.

"Evan, may I pass out these treats?" her mother asked, holding out her basket.

"Fine." Evan was now surrounded by the officers with whom he'd been working. Each thanked him and said how much they looked forward to the rest of the week. They'd all come distances and were staying in the area, a couple in the ranch guest houses and the rest in town.

Although the resort remained open, its future remained unclear with its owner incarcerated on a murder charge. Amber wasn't sure when Nathan's trial would be, but she and Evan and her mom would be required to testify.

Not that there was much question about his conviction. The guy had a collection of burner phones and hadn't discarded the ones used for the threatening text messages, though he'd hidden them. And he'd not been seen around his resort for a few days during the week after Corbin's death, so investigators were looking into whether he happened to have traveled to Las Vegas and used a credit card stolen from Corbin there, then destroyed it. The dates appeared to correspond, but apparently the police department's tech expert was still looking into how at least one of the texts appeared to come from overseas.

Kara had been grateful for what Evan and Amber had done. She never apologized for the cops not having solved the case, but Amber hadn't expected her to.

"Hey," said a uniformed cop, turning from Evan to Amber. "I've been here for classes before, when

Corbin gave them. I've seen they've got a suspect in custody and the stories indicated that you had something to do with catching him."

"The media sometimes exaggerates," Amber said noncommittally. She really didn't want to talk about it.

Not until Nathan was found guilty.

And never in front of her mother.

She glanced at Sonya now. Her mom appeared engaged in passing out dog treats, but she seemed to concentrate on it so much that Amber knew she had heard.

The whole Nathan thing had been hard on her. It had been horrible for her to lose her husband, and then to be courted for nefarious reasons by the man who'd murdered him...

Well, Amber had made it clear she was always there for her mom. So was Lola.

And so, as it turned out, was Evan. In fact, he was the one who came up with the idea that Sonya should be the one to at least start writing the book they'd talked about regarding Corbin's training methods. It was a goal, a distraction for her.

Plus, sweet guy that Evan was, he'd started a couple of weeks ago to have Amber and Sonya over occasionally for a pancake breakfast.

Right after the episode in Nathan's home, Evan had not only shown the cops where he had found what was apparently the murder weapon and done all he could to help them gather other evidence against the resort owner, but he had also made it a point to keep Amber and Sonya informed, and to be there for them—for planning dog-training lessons, for eating with them, for…well, anything they wanted.

Almost.

Amber had been delighted that, though it still sometimes appeared difficult for Evan to be around groups of people and interact with them, he did a good job of it, even if he didn't look most people in the eye. He had even begun teaching a new command at the end of each pet-training class, which particularly made his first students here happy. And after each class, he would glance toward Amber as if for her approval.

Which she always gave.

And more. In fact, it had become more than a habit for her to visit Evan in his house during the day…and often during the night.

It was more private there than in her own home. She figured her mother more than suspected what was going on, but it was too soon to make a big deal over it.

Although it felt like a big deal to Amber.

And now, once the dogs were all given treats and the officers got ready to drive them back to wherever they were staying that night, Evan joined Amber and her mother on a walk back to the main house.

"I need to do a few things at my place," he said, "but I want to give your shepherds another quick lesson today." As he'd done that morning after breakfast, before the K-9 officers arrived.

"I'll walk with you," Amber told him. "I want

to go over some ideas I have for scheduling next month's classes, okay?"

She glanced into his face and saw amusement—and more—in his eyes. "Okay," he said.

"We'll be back for the shepherds soon, Mom." The young dogs had made a lot of progress and soon could start their more vigorous K-9 training—and their new official handlers to acquire them for police units would be sought. Amber would miss them, and gave them lots of extra hugs now. Eventually, though, Evan and she would seek more puppies to train that way.

They'd all been walking in the same direction, and Amber watched as her mom and Lola walked to their house's front door and entered.

Orrin had gone to his place to change, so it was just the three of them, including Bear, who headed to Evan's house.

As they walked inside, Evan closed the door and grabbed Amber, just as she'd wanted.

Their kiss was way hotter than the air outside, and she felt Evan's hands begin their welcome, heated search beneath her T-shirt…then downward.

"Oh, yes," she said, but then forced herself to step away. She wanted him, really wanted him.

But there was something she had to do first, and not for the first time.

"Thank you, Evan, for everything you've done here to save the ranch and train our students and—"

"And get to the point," he said with a big smile.

"You first," she countered in her bossiest tone while letting her lower lip jut out in a pout.

"Okay. Amber Belott, I love you." His eyes danced in pleasure—and desire.

"And Evan Colluro, I love you."

He bent toward her and kissed that pout away.

Amber felt certain now that she had hired the absolute best trainer possible...and that their future together would involve a whole lot more than running the Chance K-9 Ranch.

* * * * *

Get 4 FREE REWARDS!

We'll send you 2 FREE Books plus 2 FREE Mystery Gifts.

FREE Value Over **$20**

Both the **Harlequin Intrigue®** and **Harlequin® Romantic Suspense** series feature compelling novels filled with heart-racing action-packed romance that will keep you on the edge of your seat.

Get 4 FREE REWARDS!

We'll send you 2 FREE Books plus 2 FREE Mystery Gifts.

FREE
Value Over
$20

Both the **Romance** and **Suspense** collections feature compelling novels written by many of today's bestselling authors.

YES! Please send me 2 FREE novels from the Essential Romance or Essential Suspense Collection and my 2 FREE gifts (gifts are worth about $10 retail). After receiving them, if I don't wish to receive any more books, I can return the shipping statement marked "cancel." If I don't cancel, I will receive 4 brand-new novels every month and be billed just $7.49 each in the U.S. or $7.74 each in Canada. That's a savings of at least 17% off the cover price. It's quite a bargain! Shipping and handling is just 50¢ per book in the U.S. and $1.25 per book in Canada.* I understand that accepting the 2 free books and gifts places me under no obligation to buy anything. I can always return a shipment and cancel at any time by calling the number below. The free books and gifts are mine to keep no matter what I decide.

Choose one: ☐ **Essential Romance**
(194/394 MDN GRHV)

☐ **Essential Suspense**
(191/391 MDN GRHV)

Name (please print)

Address   Apt. #

City   State/Province   Zip/Postal Code

Email: Please check this box ☐ if you would like to receive newsletters and promotional emails from Harlequin Enterprises ULC and its affiliates. You can unsubscribe anytime.

Mail to the Harlequin Reader Service:
IN U.S.A.: P.O. Box 1341, Buffalo, NY 14240-8531
IN CANADA: P.O. Box 603, Fort Erie, Ontario L2A 5X3

Want to try 2 free books from another series! Call 1-800-873-8635 or visit www.ReaderService.com.

*Terms and prices subject to change without notice. Prices do not include sales taxes, which will be charged (if applicable) based on your state or country of residence. Canadian residents will be charged applicable taxes. Offer not valid in Quebec. This offer is limited to one order per household. Books received may not be as shown. Not valid for current subscribers to the Essential Romance or Essential Suspense Collection. All orders subject to approval. Credit or debit balances in a customer's account(s) may be offset by any other outstanding balance owed by or to the customer. Please allow 4 to 6 weeks for delivery. Offer available while quantities last.

Your Privacy—Your information is being collected by Harlequin Enterprises ULC, operating as Harlequin Reader Service. For a complete summary of the information we collect, how we use this information and to whom it is disclosed, please visit our privacy notice located at corporate.harlequin.com/privacy-notice. From time to time we may also exchange your personal information with reputable third parties. If you wish to opt out of this sharing of your personal information, please visit readerservice.com/consumerschoice or call 1-800-873-8635. **Notice to California Residents**—Under California law, you have specific rights to control and access your data. For more information on these rights and how to exercise them, visit corporate.harlequin.com/california-privacy.

STRS22R3

Get 4 FREE REWARDS!

We'll send you 2 FREE Books plus 2 FREE Mystery Gifts.

FREE Value Over **$20**

Both the **Worldwide Library** and **Essential Suspense** series feature compelling novels filled with gripping mysteries, edge of your seat thrillers and heart-stopping romantic suspense stories.

YES! Please send me 2 FREE novels from the Worldwide Library or Essential Suspense Collection and my 2 FREE gifts (gifts are worth about $10 retail). After receiving them, if I don't wish to receive any more books, I can return the shipping statement marked "cancel." If I don't cancel, I will receive 4 brand-new Worldwide Library books every month and be billed just $6.49 each in the U.S. or $6.99 each in Canada, a savings of at least 30% off the cover price or 4 brand-new Essential Suspense books every month and be billed just $7.24 each in the U.S. or $7.49 each in Canada, a savings of at least 38% off the cover price. It's quite a bargain! Shipping and handling is just 50¢ per book in the U.S. and $1.25 per book in Canada.* I understand that accepting the 2 free books and gifts places me under no obligation to buy anything. I can always return a shipment and cancel at any time by calling the number below. The free books and gifts are mine to keep no matter what I decide.

Choose one: ☐ **Worldwide Library** ☐ **Essential Suspense**
(414/424 WDN GRFF) (191/391 MDN GRFF)

Name (please print)

Address   Apt. #

City   State/Province   Zip/Postal Code

Email: Please check this box ☐ if you would like to receive newsletters and promotional emails from Harlequin Enterprises ULC and its affiliates. You can unsubscribe anytime.

Mail to the Harlequin Reader Service:
IN U.S.A.: P.O. Box 1341, Buffalo, NY 14240-8531
IN CANADA: P.O. Box 603, Fort Erie, Ontario L2A 5X3

Want to try 2 free books from another series? Call 1-800-873-8635 or visit www.ReaderService.com.

*Terms and prices subject to change without notice. Prices do not include sales taxes, which will be charged (if applicable) based on your state or country of residence. Canadian residents will be charged applicable taxes. Offer not valid in Quebec. This offer is limited to one order per household. Books received may not be as shown. Not valid for current subscribers to the Worldwide Library or Essential Suspense Collection. All orders subject to approval. Credit or debit balances in a customer's account(s) may be offset by any other outstanding balance owed by or to the customer. Please allow 4 to 6 weeks for delivery. Offer available while quantities last.

Your Privacy—Your information is being collected by Harlequin Enterprises ULC, operating as Harlequin Reader Service. For a complete summary of the information we collect, how we use this information and to whom it is disclosed, please visit our privacy notice located at corporate.harlequin.com/privacy-notice. From time to time we may also exchange your personal information with reputable third parties. If you wish to opt out of this sharing of your personal information, please visit readerservice.com/consumerschoice or call 1-800-873-8635. **Notice to California Residents**—Under California law, you have specific rights to control and access your data. For more information on these rights and how to exercise them, visit corporate.harlequin.com/california-privacy

WWLSTSUS22R2

Get 4 FREE REWARDS!

We'll send you 2 FREE Books plus 2 FREE Mystery Gifts.

FREE
Value Over
$20

Both the **Love Inspired®** and **Love Inspired® Suspense** series feature compelling novels filled with inspirational romance, faith, forgiveness and hope.

HARLEQUIN
PLUS

Try the best multimedia subscription service for romance readers like you!

Read, Watch and Play.

Experience the easiest way to get the romance content you crave.

Start your **FREE TRIAL** at
www.harlequinplus.com/freetrial.